# CELIBATE SARAH • JAMES BLYTH

**Publisher's Note**

The book descriptions we ask booksellers to display prominently warn that this is an historic book with numerous typos, missing text or index and is not illustrated.

We scanned this book using character recognition software that includes an automated spell check. Our software is 99 percent accurate if the book is in good condition. However, we do understand that even one percent can be a very annoying number of typos! And sometimes all or part of a page is missing from our copy of a book. Or the paper may be so discolored from age that you can no longer read the type. Please accept our sincere apologies.

After we re-typeset and design a book, the page numbers change so the old index and table of contents no longer work. Therefore, we usually remove them.

Our books sell so few copies that you would have to pay hundreds of dollars to cover the cost of proof reading and fixing the typos, missing text and index. Therefore, whenever possible, we let our customers download a free copy of the original typo-free scanned book. Simply enter the barcode number from the back cover of the paperback in the Free Book form at www.general-books.net. You may also qualify for a free trial membership in our book club to download up to four books for free. Simply enter the barcode number from the back cover onto the membership form on the same page. The book club entitles you to select from more than a million books at no additional charge. Simply enter the title or subject onto the search form to find the books.

If you have any questions, could you please be so kind as to consult our Frequently Asked Questions page at www.general-books.net/faqs.cfm? You are also welcome to contact us there.

General Books LLC™, Memphis, USA, 2012. ISBN: 9781150951053.

CELIBATE SARAH PROLOGUE

I

THE APPROACH OF DEATH

ARAH! Sarah! Don't you hear me? If you won't

O get me my tea I must get it myself," roared the voice of the old man who had been inarticulate for half a year.

"Wake up, Laura! Wake up," said Celibate Sarah, shaking the woman in bed beside her. "Oh God! What is't. Surely ta can't be the guvnor!"

The third stroke, which had fallen six months previously, had left William Leicester Claybrooke a living, moving, intelligent entity, but cut off by aphasia from all means of communicating with his fellow-creatures. The deprivation was so complete that he could not even suggest his wants by means of a dictionary. He was unable to answer any question that demanded more than a simple negative or affirmative reply. His writing was like his speech—a quaint medley of gibberish and sense—and this he seemed aware of, though he was never able to understand why others could not grasp the meaning of his tumbling syllables. But he would shake his head and squinny at his writing, chuckling with infinite pathos.

The worry incident to failing means and expenditure of capital was undoubtedly the cause of the paralysis. Claybrooke had been a manufacturer of silk and woollen stuffs; and in the early seventies, when the French trade was practically non-existent, he had made eight or ten thousand a year, and spent the whole of it, and more. Then came the revival of Paris and Lyons after the peace, and new and cheap methods of weaving which the old man was too proud and too conservative to adopt. The large business retail houses swamped the little ones. The oldfashioned friendships between manufacturers and retailers became obsolete or useless. The system of bribing buyers for immense establishments obtained so generally, that those of the old school who refused to pander to the new tricks found their orders decrease alarmingly. Threefourths of Claybrooke's looms at Odinton, in Norfolk, stood idle.

Death joined his forces to financial calamity, and the loss of his wife shook the aging man terribly. His three eldest sons were scattered about the world—failures. His eldest daughter, a kind and brilliant woman, had married a very wealthy merchant, and, after a bitter disillusionment, died, not long before her father's first stroke. There remained to him Laura, his only surviving daughter, Rupert, his youngest son, and Sarah Chindaffy (nicknamed "Celibate Sarah "), Laura's companion.

When the dumb palsy struck the old man, Rupert was twenty-four years of age, serving his articles with Messrs. Chapman and Starling, a firm of solicitors in Lincoln's Inn Fields; and for years previously Cambridge and school had claimed more of his time than Andersham-by-Odinton, where his father lived. It thus befell that Laura and Sarah had the helpless man in their sole charge.

Laura was at this time a woman of nearly thirty. An attack of infantile paralysis, and an affection of her eyes in her childhood, had afforded an excuse for remitting all early education—a defect which she never attempted to remedy in after years. She was, as a girl, good-natured and kind-hearted; but both her character and her intellect were weak, and her unfortunate ignorance joined with her disposition in making it an easy matter for Celibate Sarah to obtain such influence over her as to succeed in effecting a change in her very thoughts. At the age of twenty-nine Laura was as ignorant as most children of eight. She believed that Sarah was her refuge and her strength. She saw with Sarah's eyes, spoke with her words, and was for the most part as subservient to her wishes as the most susceptible subject under the hands of a powerful hypnotist. There was still a little tenderness left in her heart for her old father, still a little love for Rupert. But apart from Sarah she felt lost, and love and tenderness were as nothing when weighed in the scales against her implicit reliance on her companion.

Sarah had first come to the Claybrookes' service partly as an object of charity, partly as a kind of nurse-companion to Laura, when the latter was thirteen years old, and she herself eleven years older. She was one of the old Norfolk family of Chindaffys, but was quite unaware that, her uncorrupted name was "Chien-de-feu." The Chindaffys had fallen on evil times. Their old estates were gone, and the proceeds thereof. Nothing now remained but the Norman character and Norman nose. These their descendant possessed in perfection. During Mrs. Claybrooke's lifetime Sarah had presented so demure, so grateful, and so considerate a demeanour, that her employers believed they had found a treasure. After the three eldest boys had come to disgrace, Sarah confessed to her mistress that her virtue had been attempted by each of them in turn, but had gloriously survived the ordeal. Mrs. Claybrooke was a shrewd woman, and the story of the maiden's prowess did not please her. She showed by her manner that her trust had been shaken. She determined to keep a sharper eye on her daughter's companion. When the story came to the ears of the third young Claybrooke he chuckled, after the manner of the wicked, and affixed the nickname to the possessor of virtue that was destined to stick.

Before Mrs. Claybrooke was able to make further investigations in the matter of Sarah's character she became seriously ill. She found Sarah an attentive nurse, but in spite of all the attentions lavished upon her by her *protegee,* death followed in a few weeks. The old family doctor shook his head doubtfully when he signed the certificate. "I suppose I ought to insist on an autopsy," he said to himself; "but Claybrooke wouldn't like it, and I've known him all my life." So the certificate was signed out of kindness, as many thousands of such things are.

Sarah said her mistress's last words were, "Sarah! I leave my dear daughter in your lovin' care. For I trusts ye, an' I'm certain the trust ain't misplaced. Dee yew watch over har, as a know ye will, an' don't yew never leave har. Promise as yew oan't." "An' I never will!" Sarah used to say with an expression of self-sacrifice. "An' I never will. "

Old Claybrooke accepted this version of his wife's last words, and did not attempt to terminate Sarah's association with his surviving daughter. He was an easy-going old gentleman, and knew that Laura really required someone to look after her and superintend the servants; and Sarah always seemed devoted to the interests of her charge.

But soon he found that Sarah was getting altogether too assiduous in her attentions to himself. And he had to smilingly remind her that her duties lay rather with the daughter than with the father.

"Lor' bless ye, sir," said she, "I can't abear to see ye so lonesome now that the pore missus ha' gone; an' I ha' got a plenty o' time to look arter both on ye. Now doan't say no! There's a dear."

"That's enough, Sarah," said the old man. "No doubt you mean well, but I wish you to confine your attentions solely to Miss Laura. Be good enough to remember that in the future. You'd better see if she wants you now."

"The old," muttered Sarah, as she left the room.

"I thought I might ha' come over him! But he know tew much, him. I can't do narthen with him. I wish I could pay the old somehow."

She had her chance sooner than she anticipated. When Claybrooke's great helplessness came upon him, and he could no longer complain, blame, or praise, the natural brutality of the woman showed itself. Not content with neglecting the details of diet and nursing prescribed, and which there was no one now to prevent her from taking upon herself, she seized every safe opportunity of insulting her master. She would repeat vile gibes at the poor old man till she forced comprehension upon him, and would laugh at the flushed face, the reddened eyes, the burst of inarticulate remonstrance, which showed his shame at the indignities he suffered. The doctor gave no hope of his recovery, and Sarah thought herself secure. It was natural that after six months' enjoyment of inflicting torture with impunity, the sound of her victim's voice thrilling the passages of the house, clear, articulate, and furious, should have brought pallor to her cheeks and tremor to her limbs.

It was half-past eight on a lovely August morning, and the patient's early cup of tea had been due an hour.

"Wake up, Laura! Wake up!" Sarah cried again.

And Laura woke, and the two women hurried on dressing-gowns and left the room.

Outside the door a few steps led down to the main passage of the sleeping-rooms. At the foot of these stairs William Claybrooke was standing, clad only in his nightshirt. His arms were thrust forward against the wall, and his whole body quivered. As he saw the two women his mouth opened, and the muscles of his throat and tongue swelled through his bare neck and throbbed with palpitating effort. "Laura," he gasped out, "send that woman —Go—God!"

The flash was over. He was inarticulate again.

Laura ran to him. "Father," she cried, "what is it? Oh, what is it you wish to say?" Tears rained down her cheeks, and for the moment she was free from Sarah's influence.

The old man turned his eyes to her, piteous in their animal helplessness. He struggled once more to warn her against Sarah; to beg for some other nurse—some kindly attendant for his last moments. A mere jumble of guttural sounds, blended with chopped syllables of words, issued; and the passion of agony at his inability to speak brought on an attack of the choking sobs that are so terrible in masculine age. He hid his face in his hands, and staggered as he lost the support of the wall. Then he shook his fist at Sarah tremulously, turned, and dragged himself slowly back to his room.

"Laura, me dear," said Sarah, greatly relieved, "he've gone clean crazy! That doan't fare safe. We'd best send for Mr. Begge."

"Yes. And wire for Rupert, too," said Laura, still crying.

When the family doctor came he watched his old friend sadly. "He won't live a couple of days now," he said. "That momentary power of articulation is absolutely diagnostic. It is the harbinger of death. I don't give him twenty-four hours' consciousness."

"Hadn't I better send for Rupert, Mr. Begge?" asked Laura.

"Certainly, if he can come, my dear," said the old doctor, taking her hand.

"Come? Of course he'll come if father's dying," she cried.

"Your father may be able to say good-bye to him," said the doctor. "He may speak a few words more before he becomes unconscious."

"Oh Lor'! I hope he oan't, then!" said Sarah to herself.

"But I don't expect that he'll be able to complete a sentence. Still, you may expect a little easier comprehension from him, and possibly an intelligible expression or two."

"Drat it!" mumbled Sarah. "Nobody's never safe! Yew can't never tell what's agoin' to happen."

"I'll wire to Rupert myself," continued the doctor, "and come again this afternoon. Good-bye, my dear." The kind old man's voice shook. "Try to bear up. I know that your father has no wish to live on as he is now. He often told me after he had his first stroke that he hoped he would never drag out a helpless existence. And we can do nothing for him."

With bent head and uncertain footsteps the old friend of the house went on his way to summon the absent boy.

Laura wept upon Sarah's breast, who made an admirable show of sympathy and of solicitously comforting her charge.

And the hours dragged on through the irritating everyday matters incident to a household. While over all the paltry details of diurnal existence hung the abnormal density of the shadow of approaching death.

II DEATH COMES THE telegram despatched by the doctor was taken up by a clerk in Chapman and Starling's office to the room in Judges' Chambers where Rupert was attending a summons before the great Binns-Jones. This functionary was just making his favourite joke, and informing a dirty little Jew clerk that those seeking the relief of the Court of Chancery must come into court with "clean hands." Rupert was shaping his lips to the conventional smile that the chief clerk expected when the tidings of his father's imminent death was placed in his hands.

Though he was the youngest of the family, a deep love and friendship (and these are by no means synonymous terms when parents and children are spoken of) existed between him and his father. He still thought it no shame to put his lips to the old man's forehead; and the father looked on the boy as the last of his sons in whom he could find a cause for pride. His eldest sons were failures. His eldest daughter dead. And Laura had too little intelligence to be able to afford any companionship to the old gentleman, who in his best days had associated with Dante Rossetti, Swinburne, William Morris, Burne-Jones, Fred Sandys, and the rest of the brilliant Pre-Raphaelite band that made the dingy little club off the Strand a veritable palace of art in the days when Bohemia could still be found by earnest explorers, before the tidal wave of respectability and the whirlwind of County Councils had swept the last remnant of those pleasant shores away.

Old Claybrooke had been a celebrated oar in his time, and Rupert had stroked his college boat. A simple fact enough, but one that strengthened the bond of sympathy between age and youth to a vast extent. There was nothing the old man liked better than to row his races over again in his son's company, or to compare the physique of rowing men forty years back (who thought nothing of racing the steam-packet from Yarmouth to Norwich by way of a training spin of thirty-two miles) with the degenerate users of sliding seats and outriggers.

Rupert paled to the lips as he read the message. He gave hurried instructions to the clerk to remain and see the order on the summons made, and (most important of all) to get the solicitors' attendance marked on the chief clerk's papers to be allowed as costs in the action. Then he walked quickly back through "the Fields" to the office.

He had just time to catch the 1.20 from Liverpool Street to Odinton.

As soon as the train started he settled himself back in his corner, and had time to think of his sorrow. God knows that his thoughts were sad enough during the journey. Yet through after years he bore in his memory the quaint converse of two fellow-passengers. It is a common trick of Destiny to destroy its own pathos with a touch of the grotesque.

Rupert paid little attention to the company till Bishop's Stortford was passed. He sat silently brooding over the great sorrow that was coming upon him. He knew that he was one of the executors of his father's will, but a feeling of delicacy had prevented him from settling it as the old man had wished. From this it may be seen that he was not likely to make any great success as a lawyer. Indeed, there was little of the law's chicanery about him. He was to learn in after years that delicacy and unselfishness are unappreciated vices.

Voices in crescendo, accelerando, drew his attention to the further side of the compartment.

"I'm sure it's 'Emstead. 'Emil 'Emstead!" said a small, colourless, spare man, dressed in decent black, with a turn-down collar and black ribbon tie.

"I tell y' there's an 'Ampstead 'Eath near London!" said the vis-a-vis, who looked a butcher going down to Odinton to buy fat stock. "Think I don't know? Why I goes there reg'lar wiv the old Dutch on Bangk-oldy."

"Yes! Yes!" simpered the first speaker. "But that's a different place. *I* mean 'Emil 'Emstead."

"Aoh! If it's a difrunt plice," retorted

the other, "why di'n't ye sye so at fust? On'y that's no good atryin' to make out as there ain't a 'Ampstead 'Eath near London."

The voices dropped, and Rupert resumed his sad imaginings as the train ran past Cavendish, and pulled up at the four hundred yards of dulness that Cambridge Station consists of in vacation time. He shook himself impatiently with a long breath of disgust at the impotence of his sorrow, at his inability to smile at his companions, at things in general. He went to the refreshment-room and swallowed as large a dose of whisky as the cautious caterers supply for a shilling, and felt a trifle better. He had had no lunch, but the idea of food was repellent to him.

The compartment was empty when he returned to it, but just as the train started the two disputants jumped hastily in. He in black bore a bag of buns. The other a flat pint bottle of whisky.

"They will serve the coffee so 'ot," said the former, "that I'm sure it's quite a struggle to drink it in the time."

"They don't want ye to," grinned the butcher. "Then that does again."

"Oh, why can't they hold their silly tongues?" groaned Rupert inwardly, wondering why speech should be given to man for such misuse. He tried to insulate his hearing, and partly succeeded; but not for long. Before Waterbeach was reached the man in black touched him on the knee. "I think, sir," he said, "that you have had the advantage of a university education. I observed that you were recognised at the station of the noble institution which we have just passed."

Rupert grunted out an assent. Ordinary civility was impossible to him in his state of nervous tension.

"Thank you, sir. Then, perhaps, you may be able to tell this gentleman whether Edinburgh is east or west of Glasgow. I am a schoolmaster—a certificated board-schoolmaster, but he won't believe me."

"I tell y' I've been there," said the butcher. "An' when we left Edinburgh we kep' edgin' to the heast along by the sea hall the time. That show as the maps is hall wrong. That's no good tryin' to make out as they ient."

Modern geography is not a subject in which a Cambridge undergraduate receives any special tuition, and Rupert knew more of the relative positions of Athens and I-acedaemon than of the two towns in question. But he had a vague recollection of seeing Glasgow on one side of the map and Edinburgh on the other.

"Hang it," he said, "I always thought Edinburgh was right on one side to the east, and Glasgow was right opposite on the west. There can't be any doubt about it."

"Thank you, sir," said the schoolmaster. "Now, perhaps, you'll admit you're wrong."

"Hev ye ever been there, mister?" asked the butcher.

"No," Rupert replied, heartily wishing to be left alone.

"Then you on'y knows from maps, an' I tell ye they're hall wrong. Hall the time from Hedinburgh to Glasgow the trine is mikin'to the heast. Garn! Hi hev been there! An' you're a nice beauty to be learnin' the kiddies hall wrong, an' School Board rate so 'igh! It's disgriceful. That's what it is!"

The schoolmaster sought for a glance of sympathy from Rupert. But he had succeeded in closing his ears again, and his eyes were peering out on the rich flat marshes with such a depth of weary pain in them that the little pedagogue was awed, and let him be till the end of the journey.

"How is father? Is he still alive?" were Rupert's first words on greeting his sister and Sarah. But for some few minutes no intelligible answer was forthcoming.

"Oh Rupe! Rupe!" sobbed Laura. "Poor old daddy. Mr. Begge says he can't live twenty-four hours."

Laura's faded forget-me-not-coloured eyes were swollen with weeping. Though still a young woman, she already gave promise of the grossness of figure that made her so unwieldy in after years. She was like an agitated jelly bag. She lay heavy on Rupert's shoulder, and it was no light task to support her. Sarah's hard features and little piglike eyes were puckered up in a quaint grimace. She had with effort pumped up a few drops of lachrymal secretion (tears they could not be called), and she imparted a fine quaver to her voice as she spoke. "He's still livin', pore dare," she said. "But I doubt his mind ha' gorn."

"I'll go up at once," said Rupert. "Who's with him?"

"I'll go up along o' ye," suggested Sarah. "Jane's watchin' on him."

"No," Rupert answered. "I must see my father by myself. Good-bye for the present, dear old girl," he added, as he kissed Laura again. "Try to bear up bravely."

The young fellow doubted his self-control in the presence of his dying father. He had the affection of habit for Sarah, but he felt that the meeting between father and son was too sacred for alien eyes to witness.

His heart beat in quick, irregular throbs, that half stifled his breathing as he went up. His father's bedroom on one side opened out on a little staircase leading from Rupert's own quarters. On the other it had a door through into the drawing-room. Rupert went to the foot of the little staircase and called the servant. She was crying, making little cooing noises of animal appeal and sympathy when she saw Rupert. After a kind word or two he went up and closed the door behind him.

"Laura," said Sarah, "p'rhaps that 'ud be as well if I went upsteers into the drorin'-rewm an' listened. 'Tis for yar sake, me dear."

Rupert stood by his father's bedside for a few minutes motionless. The old man was lying with his eyes closed. He was breathing heavily, his mouth partly opened. Moisture was glistening on his forehead. The window opened to the south on a verandah overlooking a sweep of lawn down to the River Thorwater, that rippled and guggled in the sunlight. All about the window were hanging huge clusters of amethyst blossom, like lovely fragile grapes. The magnificent wistaria was in full bloom. A pleasant wind stirred the leaves and flowers of the mighty creeper in the golden heat. The window was partly open, and the murmur of insects, the rustle of leaves and masses of bloom, the music of countless birds came in. The whole scene outside was instinct with the glorious life of a summer day. Within, the shadow of death hung with incongruous mystery.

The old man opened his eyes, and a pleased message of welcome passed from them to Rupert.

"Father!" was all the boy could say. He took his father's hand and, bending over the bed, kissed the dear forehead. A sob burst uncontrollably from his throat.

"Boy—dear—Yupe "The father's lips tried in vain to fashion a sentence. The look that had momentarily brightened all the worn features with hope, almost with promise of life, gave way to an expression of anxiety and dread.

"Do you understand me, father dear?" said Rupert, choking down the climbing sorrow with an effort, that he might not cause pain by a display of grief.

A nod of assent answered him.

"You want to say something?"

Another nod.

"About Laura?"

A dissenting movement of the head.

"About your will?"

"Yes, yes," the father managed to say.

"Oh, don't trouble about that now, father," pleaded the son. "Wait till you are better."

But the old man knew as well as Rupert that that would never be. With a mighty effort, and after many abortive attempts, terrible with the agonised consciousness of their failure, the father at last said anxiously, with a gesture indicating Rupert, "All right? You—all right?"

"Oh yes, yes!" sobbed the stricken boy, overcome by the evidence of his father's love and care at such a time. "Never mind me."

But a great excitement had come to his father. He raised himself in bed. His eyes grew bright with intelligent endeavour. His lips moved rapidly as if searching for the right words and practising their utterance. Then with a burst he said, "You'll have—pay—five million pounds."

Rupert recollected that there were legacies left to the elder brothers. Perhaps his father was referring to these. But the boy shook his head at the sum.

"Yes, yes!" eagerly insisted the father. "But you'll— all right? Boy—dear—yourself—all right?"

"Yes, father, yes. Pray don't worry about me. I shall be all right."

"You will!" urged his father, catching his son's hand and pressing it. His strength was failing fast, his power of partial articulation dying. With a last effort he gasped, "Look out—Sarah—a devil!"

He raised himself once more and then said as clearly as ever in his life, "Kiss me, my dear boy. God bless you."

His elbows bent, and he fell back upon the pillow. At once a restless, pitiful look came over his face. His eyes wandered from time to time and fixed pleadingly on his son's. A faint smile of love illumined his face once more as he once more took Rupert's hand feebly. Then the eyes lost the conscious look of intelligence and flickered to and fro meaninglessly, like the eyes of a blind man.

Rupert sank on his knees beside the bed, and held his father's hand and kissed it unrestrainedly. A movement became apparent under the bedclothes, and by horrible degrees the breath grew more stertorous. Suddenly the muscles of the limbs contracted and expanded in violent spasms. Convulsions had set in. The last struggle of a vigorous frame before it was stilled for ever.

Sarah had carried out her scheme of listening. But she ran down before the ultimate blessing and was saying, "Five million pound! Five million pound! Five million pound, he say! D'ye hear that, Laura? Whatever can a mean? Deary me! Five million pound!" when Rupert's voice was heard calling loudly and impatiently from above.

"Laura! Laura! Come up directly. Father's in convulsions. Tell Sarah to send for Mr. Begge at once."

And Laura went and joined her tears to Rupert's.

And Mr. Begge came and looked sadly at the twitching body of the dying man, and said that nothing could be done.

When the dusk fell, the movement grew less and less. "Is he conscious?" asked Rupert. The doctor lit a candle and passed it slowly before the c glazing eyes. The action seemed horribly cruel and coldblooded, but the eyes showed no knowledge of the flame.

"He will never be conscious again in this world, my dears," said Begge. "I can do nothing, and you will prefer to be left alone. Good-bye, old friend," he added, with more feeling than is usually shown by a medical man at a death-bed. "Good-bye. I shan't be long after you."

He had gone but a few minutes when the weary eyes closed for ever. No sign of life remained but the heavy stertorous breathing.

Rupert took his father's hand again. It was cold. The breathing grew fainter and fainter—and then ceased.

## Ill THE FUNERAL AND THE FARCE

AMINUTE or so later Sarah, who had again been at the post of observation, opened the door of the deathchamber and entered.

"So 'tis all over," she said, with a kind of hiccough. "Well, I s'pose 'twas to be, or else ta wouldn't ha' happened. Death come to all alike. That's no use cryin' over"

"' And common *is* the commonplace,
And vacant chaff well meant for grain,'" said Rupert. "Come, Laura. We can do nothing; and there is work for others."

"You'll find a bottle of champagne on the dinin' table," said Sarah, "an' a bottle of the old guvnor's brandy. I took the keys an' got 'em out o' the cellar. I thought you might be glad of a some'at. "

"You'd better give me all his keys," said Rupert. "I'm one of the executors. But we can go into that another day. The will's in the deed box."

"Laura'd better hev the keys, hadn't she?" said Sarah. "I s'pose she'll keep house till the home is broke up."

"Well, we're not likely to quarrel about that, are we, dear?" said Rupert.

"But old Howard is sure to ask about them. He's the other executor. But I'll get the will out to-morrow. I expect you and I can do as we like."

"You take them, Rupert," answered Laura. "I'd rather you did."

"Why didn't you keep the keys?" asked Sarah of Laura, when they had all gone wearily to bed. "I'd ha' had the will out afore mornin'. That might be the better for alterin'. An' look arter yourself you must, else you'll get done brown, an' that's a fact."

Rupert found the will the next morning, and read it to an admiring audience of Laura and Sarah. He was pleased at being able to air his professional knowledge. For the moment the stupidity of its provisions escaped his legal acumen.

The lives of all three were to be regulated and controlled by the dead man's hand. It was not the first time or the last that a sordid tragedy emanated from the office of a careless or short-sighted solicitor.

Briefly the will, after providing for certain legacies to the elder sons, with *£800* for Rupert, directed that a sum of 6,000 should be held by the executors as trustees upon trust to invest the same in certain specified securities, and to pay the income to Laura during her life. After her death, in the event of her having children, the fund was to be divisible amongst the children. Should she die without issue, she was to have the power to leave 3,000 as she liked. The other,£3,000 was to be divided among such of her brothers as should be living at her death. The residue was left equally between Laura and Rupert.

The futility of the will as a provision for a woman of weak intellect at once becomes apparent when it is seen that it would be to the interest of anyone having charge of her that she should remain single, and die as soon as she had made a will leaving,£3,000 to her companion or keeper, as the case might be. When, in addition, it is remembered that she was of a full-blooded constitution, and had a mania for fancying every man in love with her, the chances of her being sacrificed either to a petty fortunehunter (for she had the power to give a husband a life interest in the fund), or to a woman of the class that was all ready to hand, seemed desperately high. No doubt the testator had reckoned on the supervision which Rupert would be able to exercise; but he did not take into consideration Laura's ludicrous fits of dignity or Sarah's power. Neither did he remember that if Rupert was to carry on his profession in London, the supervision that would be possible for him would be of the most limited description.

The funeral was fixed for the following Saturday; and it was by no means a pleasant surprise for Rupert to learn that the wealthy brother-in-law, Marmaduke Redfern, intended to accept the invitation sent him out of courtesy, and to stay at Orford House from Friday to Monday, to pay a respect to the dead that he had been far from showing to the living. He was a little middle-aged man, who was only tolerated in even third-class society on account of his money. It sums up his character to say that he never hesitated to tell suggestive stories in the presence of his wife and children. He had a great idea of his own humour, which was Rabelaisian only in the grosser characteristics of the great satirist. If the definition of a gentleman as "one who never hurts the feelings of another intentionally" be correct, and for other reasons, Marmaduke was a cad.

For some time a coolness had existed between him and the Claybrookes. When misfortune fell upon the old manufacturer, Redfern had spoken of it with the obscene jocularity of a Yahoo; and this had come to Rupert's ears. But of old the two brothers-in-law had been much together. Rupert's love for his elder sister in her lifetime, and for her children after her death, made him submit to an intimacy which was distasteful to him in many ways. Redfern, for his part, had sought the society of the young fellow because his musical powers and his conversational charm had lent an attraction to the rich man's table of which it stood sorely in need. The two men dined alone on the night of Redfern's arrival. Laura did not wish to leave Sarah, and Sarah did not intend that she should.

"Is there any of the old governor's thirty-fours left, Rupe, my boy?" said Marmaduke during dinner. "I pay two hundred shillings a dozen for some of my port. But it don't beat the old governor's. Ho! ho!"

Satisfied as to this, and under its influence, he discoursed freely as to the situation.

"You know," he said pleasantly, "you'll have to buckle to, my boy. Now that poor Mary's gone, you can't expect me to keep your family, and I don't suppose the old governor's left much more than enough to bury him."

"Oh, it's not quite so bad as that," answered Rupert.

"Well, so long as you don't ask me to put my hand in my pocket, it's no business of mine. But you'll have to buckle to, my boy. You've only got yourself to depend on. / can't help you. There are reasons I'll tell you about. Ho! ho! You ain't out of your articles yet, and you'll have to pass your final, and pay your fees, and wait for a berth. Ho! ho! You'll have to buckle to, my boy! Have one of my cigars. I pay two shillings and sixpence each for them. They'll be a treat for you. I don't expect you've tasted one like 'em since you dined with me last. Two shillings and sixpence each! You won't get many like those."

In such encouraging converse the hours dragged on till bedtime. As Rupert escorted his guest upstairs past the room where the coffin lay ready for the morrow, Marmaduke jerked his head in that direction.

"Old boy nailed down? Hey? Quite right. Wonder if he can see us! Funny thing, death, ain't it? Ho! ho! Poor Mary'd have been quite upset. But she went first. You'll have your hands full looking after Laura. She's a damned fool. He! he! Good-night."

"Great God!" said Rupert to himself. "And I've got to put up with this sort of thing till Monday! And he's coming in the carriage with me. Poor old father! That man could have eased all your anxieties, and saved your life for another ten years. Mary was worn out with disgust at him before she died. She told me so. And she loved him once! Women will love anything!"

While the men were dining, Laura and Sarah were discussing the future. The coming of Redfern suggested to the former that he might be pleased to have her to look after his establishment; to chaperon his daughters, and to take the end of his table. She never realised her incapacity, and thought that she would be an attraction in any sphere. Her income would then be ample to provide her with personal necessities and to keep Sarah with her. For she could not imagine any life independent of the woman who had gained such ascendency over her. Sarah at first opposed the idea. She saw too many chances of matrimony in it, too many possibilities of events which might distract Laura's attention from what she owed her faithful Sarah. But Laura had occasional interludes of self-importance, amusing in their transparent futility, but very real for the time. And when she assumed her "Miss Claybrooke" air, it was useless to contend against it either by argument or persuasion.

"Nothing could be more proper, Sarah," she said, "than that I should look after Mary's children now that father is gone. I'm sure that Marmaduke will wish it."

"Drat the gal!" said Sarah under her breath. "She'll never do without me! She can't look arter herself, let alone anybody else. Redfern 'oan't hev her. That's one blessin'."

"I shall speak to him to-morrow night," continued Laura. And when the two went to bed she expatiated on what she would do when mistress of a home where the supply of money for housekeeping was unlimited.

"Did you ever, Sarah?" she said. "He's got thirty thousand a year."

At last Sarah got her off to sleep to dream of her coming splendour.

Besides Rupert and Redfern, only four mourners followed the hearse. These were Begge, Howard, and two old business acquaintances of the dead man. Sarah persuaded Laura to stop at home, intending to make another endeavour to dissuade her from the idea of attempting to join Redfern's establishment.

Rupert had no experience of funerals. When his sister Mary died he was just going up for his Tripos; and it was thought better that he should not leave Cambridge. What he knew of the dismal rites he had gathered from *ReadyMoney Mortibey* and *Evan Harrington;* and in both the funerals described in these admirable works of reference there had been mention of the port and sherry that afforded the light comedy of the scene. It was true that the social status of the mourners of the "Great Mel" was distinct from that of the friends who might be expected at Orford House. But there were bankers present at the Mortiboy funeral, and surely that might serve as a precedent. So poor Rupert got out the '34 port and the Waterloo sherry, and pressed it upon the grave men who had come to show respect and not to sample vintages. He used to turn hot for years after when he thought of it. The fact that Marmaduke drank three glasses of port, and pledged the other guests, was no criterion of taste. When the time came to start, Rupert was angry and disgusted with himself and everything else.

As they were leaving the house the undertaker offered the customary gloves.

"No, thanks," said Marmaduke, stopping. "Brought a pair with me." Pulling them out of his pocket, he continued, "Old chap can't have left too much. Keep down the funeral expenses."

The dreary procession had hardly left the little village on its way to the cemetery, which lay through Odinton, when Marmaduke clapped his hand on Rupert's knee.

"Funerals and marriages—marriages and funerals," he said. "Following the old governor to-day; and in two months' time I'm to be married again, my boy! What d'ye think of that?"

Outside, the chief of the undertaker's staff could be seen walking, his professional solemnity flickering into a fat smile as he waved his black paw to some acquaintance, or raised his hat to a customer of his employer's, with an obvious pride in the turn-out. Rupert cursed him silently but deeply. The trappings of the dismal buffoonery of the funeral show revolted and sickened him. Marmaduke's voice sounded to him like a demon's screech in some operatic inferno. When he realised that the spoken words had a meaning, and what that meaning was, he turned to his companion with a look of horrified amazement. He said nothing.

The coach passed slowly through Odinton. Through streets black with the shuttered windows of the shops, closed out of respect for the dead man.

"Thought that would surprise you, my boy!" continued Marmaduke. "I'll tell you all about it. Keep your mind off your grief. Hey? You remember that girl Lily Costa— Katie's sister, you know, a schoolfellow of the girls'. You said there was nothing in her—and, by gad, you were right. But she took my fancy. It's astonishing how that girl took my fancy! She ain't pretty, and she ain't much better than a fool. But she took my fancy. I made up to her people. Of course they were only glad to be taken up by me. After a bit I made up my mind to pop. They live up the river at Teddington, and I went there for a few days' stay. One morning I was out in the garden with Lily, and I popped. 'Why, Mr. Redfern,' said she, 'we all thought you were after Katie!' (That damned fool, you know.) So I said, 'No, darling. I want you. You *do* love me, don't you?' 'Oh no, Mr. Redfern,' she said, 'not a bit,' and then she ran off. I told old Costa about it; he hasn't got too much money, you know, and, of course, he was furious, and said he'd talk to her. So the next morning after breakfast he came to me with Lily, and said, 'I've spoken to her, and the dear girl *does* love you. But you took her by surprise. And she is *so* shy. Take her, my dear boy, and be happy.' So I stood ready for her to fall into my arms. But she fell into her father's, and howled like the devil and all, damn her. She's *so* sensitive, and can't bear the thought of leaving her people. I'm going to settle 40,000 upon her. Of course everything will have to be altered now."

As the man was chuckling and jabbering, the slow, solemn toll of the funeral bell boomed out. The hearse drew up to the cemetery gates. The procession entered.

DISINTEGRATION AND PREPARATION

UPERT conveyed the news of Marmaduke's intended

JLV marriage to Laura in time to prevent her from offering her services as housekeeper. She dined with the men on Saturday night, and was entertained with a repetition of the naive story of the widower's wooing.

On Sunday morning Marmaduke went to church. He rarely missed this tribute to respectability. He was fond of exercising his light tenor voice in the Psalms and hymns, and, by his unrestrained tones, of attracting attention which he mistook for admiration. He had been in great form at the funeral service, and lifted up his voice in the little cemetery chapel till Rupert longed to throttle him.

During his absence the brother and sister and Celibate Sarah sat in conclave to consider the future. Rupert's was so far clear that he had but the one way open — to proceed to his admission as a solicitor and to husband the little capital he took from his father's estate until such time as he might be able to get a managing clerkship. When he had taken the Law Tripos, and been articled to Chapman and Starling, it had been understood that Marmaduke was to buy him a partnership when he was sufficiently experienced. But, of course, that was all over now.

The discussion perforce centred in the best course for Laura to pursue. With no expectation or wish that his suggestion should be adopted (for he knew how rarely two of a family can live comfortably under the same roof), Rupert offered to share the expense of a small establishment, if his sister cared to live in the suburbs of London.

But Sarah had succeeded in sowing a seed of suspicion in Laura's mind that he might endeavour to benefit himself at her expense; and, as is the case with most stupid people, Laura prided herself on seeing through meannesses that had no existence. She declined the offer with an emphasis which could not but betray her thoughts.

"Well then," said Rupert, "what do you think of doing? You know your income will be under *£200* a year; and though you can live comfortably enough on that, it will have to be in a very different style to that which you are accustomed to."

"Well I never, Rupert!" cried Laura. "Do you think you're the only one that's got any sense? Sarah and I have thought it all out. I'm going to take a little place in the country, where I can keep fowls and all that sort of thing."

"Ah! me dear. That's it!" said Sarah. "We doan't want no men humbuggin' about. I can't dew wi'm. Le'ss yew an' me sattle down som'ers nare Frogsthorpe, wheer my sister, Peggy Noddyfield, live. An' yew kin hev yar ducks an' chickens, an' fare as happy as the daay is long, wi' me to look arter ye. Theer's a small house ta let at St. Meery's-on-the-Fen as I ha' heerd on—oony about saven mile from Frogsthorpe. It's just arposight the simmingtairy, an' ta see the funerals a-gooin' out an' a-gooin' in, wha' it's quite amewsin', I'm shore. "

"Oh, don't talk of funerals, Sarah," said Laura, bursting into tears.

"By Jove, Sarah," said Rupert, "you haven't forgotten your Norfolk twang."

"Well, that doan't sigerfy now the old guvnor's gorn," said Sarah. "Lor', when he wuz alive, I wholly had to mind my tongue. He wuz on to me in a minute if he heerd me a-speeakin' brooad like, soo I allust had to speeak finicky like for fare o' gettin' into the old waay. But Lor', now he's gorn, that all come nateral, an' a sight comfortabler, an' Miss Loora doan't mind, dee yew, me dare?"

"Well, mind you don't catch it, Laura," said Rupert, laughing.

"I'm sure I don't care if I do," said Laura, still sobbing.

Rupert looked at the two women, and saw that their minds were made up, and that anything he could say either as to the Norfolk accent or their future residence would be treated with ignominy, so he said to Laura, "Do you think you'll like St. Mary's? It is as well to be sure, because moving's an expensive job."

"Did you ever, Sarah!" said Laura. "He seems to think that we can't be trusted to make up our own minds. I've told you what I wish," she said petulantly to Rupert. "You haven't anything to say against it, have you?"

"No. I only want you to do what will make you the happiest," he said. "And you think the country will do it?"

"I think so," replied Laura, somewhat softened by Rupert's words and manner, and forgetting her tears at the thought that she would soon be the real mistress and proprietress of an establishment.

"Then we'd better wind up things here as soon as possible," said Rupert, "and find out exactly what you will have."

Marmaduke, on his return from church, heard and approved the scheme. The further from London Laura was stationed the better would he be pleased. "I don't want any of 'em messing about my place," he said genially to himself. "Rupert's got enough sense to see that. But Laura's such a damned fool that she might be an infernal nuisance."

Before he left on the Monday morning, he selected a few of the best things in the house which he wished to have bought for him at the sale which would be made of the works of art, antique furniture, and plate.

"You can't afford to keep 'em, and I can afford to buy 'em," he said delicately. "So there you are. Now there's your mother's portrait by Watts. That's a nice thing. I'll go to a couple of hundred for it."

"We shan't sell the portraits, thank you," said Rupert.

"I'll make it two-fifty"

"No, I'm hanged if you do!" said Rupert. "If Laura won't have it, I'll take it myself."

"Well, if you're so cocky you won't want any help from me," said Marmaduke.

"Devil a bit!" rejoined Rupert. "You'll be too busy making your Lily love you. It would be unkind to expect anything from you." He was losing his temper. It was as well that Marmaduke's time was up. He went without an open quarrel; but letting it be clearly seen that he washed his hands of his first wife's family for good. He was the only connection they had who was in a position to help them. They knew that they had only themselves to depend on.

The house at St. Mary's was secured, and the old house closed; the old servants paid off, and the old relations of brother and sister, as bound by possessing a common home, altered.

After the sale, when accounts were passed, and the residue ascertained and apportioned, Rupert ran down from town to St. Mary's to see his sister fairly started on her new course. It was really a last farewell to the old life, and the knowledge that this was so joined with the memory of the past in making Laura's heart more tender than it had been of late. Rupert's stay was only to last two days, and these had mostly to be spent at Odinton in arranging various outstanding matters in connection with the estate.

The last night Rupert, Laura, and Celibate Sarah sat late.

"What a can't see," said Sarah, "is why Miss Loora can't hev the brass harself. What's the use o' 'trusties,' as ye call 'em. Why should yew an' Mr. Howard be barthered with har affeers? Can't ye just pay over the £6,000 and ha' done wi't?"

"Yes; I can't see why not," said Laura.

"Suppose you marry and have children," suggested Rupert.

"Lor'! She oan't niver marry. Will ye, me dare?" said Sarah. "She doan't waant noo truck along o' min."

"Well then, suppose she were to die," said Rupert "(you know we must consider everything in business, however cold-blooded it seems), and left the. £3,000 to someone, and it could not be found. I should have to find it or be sold up."

"Why, you know, I shall leave it to you," said Laura.

"Thank you, dear," answered Rupert. "But then, there are George, Ted, and Reggie. Who'd look after their interests?"

"Wha niver mind about them," said Sarah. "They had theer's in the ole guvnor's lifetime. Now dee yew let Loora hev the brass."

"Look here," said Rupert. "I don't like discussing these things with you. Why don't you run up to Odinton and see Strainer, Howard's partner? He'll explain the whole thing to you."

"Well, that fare cur'ous to me," said Sarah, "as the gal can't dew as she like with har owan."

"It isn't that," Rupert answered wearily. "You'd better both go and see Strainer. Then he can tell you all about it."

"Aah! But Rupert," said Sarah, "we all know as the pore ole guvnor worn't azackly all theer afoor he died."

"Don't suggest such a thing if you have any regard for Laura," said Rupert angrily. "The will was made some time before he died. If any doubt arose as to his mind at the time, Laura might lose the interest on the 6,000, and merely share with me and the other boys. I must say that I fully believe that father was perfectly sane up to the last moment of his consciousness. Don't you ever dare to bring up the thing again."

"Lor'!" said Sarah. "That a oan't. That ouldn't dew noo-how."

D

"I mean to have my money put into what I like," said Laura, speaking loudly.

Rupert looked at her with surprise. Her cheeks were flushed. It was a cold night, and spirits were on the table.

"All right," he answered. "See Strainer, there's a good girl. It's much better that you and I should not talk about these things. You know very well that I shall always do all I can to please you."

"I'm sure you will," said Laura, rising and going clumsily to him. She imprinted a fat kiss upon him and sat down again heavily.

"Then yew'll dew what ye can to git ole Howard ta let har hev the brass," Sarah persisted hopefully.

"Oh yes, I'll do what I can," Rupert answered, seeing it was hopeless to explain further.

"Thassee," said Sarah. "Mix yarself another glass, an' we'll drink success to all on us. Maake Loora one tew. Tha'ss a parrishin' coold night."

It was in the early hours of the morning that the three said good night. Laura was maudlin with sisterly sentiment. Her effusive caresses were almost repulsive as she said "goo' night" again and again. Sarah looked cheerfully on. She knew that these outpourings of affection were too tremulous to last.

"I don't like the look of Laura drinking so much whisky," said Rupert as he got into bed. "But the poor old girl has had a trying time. Sarah will look after her, I'm confident."

And so was Sarah.

END OF THE PROLOGUE

I TWO OLD MAIDS ST. MARY'S-ON-THE-FEN is built upon one of the many bluffs, or headlands, that stand as lofty landmarks here and there about the wild expanse of marsh through which the River Saelig runs down to the great confluence of the waters of Norfolk and Suffolk near Herringhaven.

The greater part of it is still old-fashioned and picturesque. The new printing and engineering works, and the still more hideous modern villas, are congregated about the railway station. A new-comer passes with delight from the station road to the old market-place—a spacious square that surrounds the splendid Norman church with dusky red brick and tiles and quaint misshapen gables. The church has the peculiarity of being less old than its vast square tower of flint, and can lay claim to notable carving about its stone doorways and windows. The churchyard is enclosed by a wall of immense thickness, whence the fall is sheer to the north to the level of the marshland, a hundred feet below. The abbey that once occupied its site was strong to defend itself from the wild Northmen when they brought their long ships up the salt water that covered the flats for miles higher up the estuary, and left colonies that were to spread till all the blood of the marshlands became strengthened and brisked by intermarriage with the hardy invaders.

In former years the coach road from

London to Herringhaven ran through the town, and the taverns in and about the market-place boast of a magnificence of accommodation for man and beast that wears the shy retreating look of fallen grandeur.

The society of the town is composed of the clerical element, printers, maltsters, shopkeepers, the pettifogging lawyers of provincialdom, and some few antiquated ladies to whom the days for payment of the dividends on government securities are the red-letter days of the year. They are all saturated with the self-satisfaction of provincialism. The clerical set patronise the maltsters and printers; the maltsters and printers the shopkeepers; and all are unanimous in despising the hearty, noisy throng that enliven the sleepy old city on market days, and bring it beeves and grain out of the plenty of the land. The lawyers despise or patronise nobody from whom a shilling may be got, unless haply a moment's introspection lead them to despise themselves.

The female annuitants hold themselves apart. They are "ladies" in their own estimation by virtue of an exiguous independence. But their means do not permit them to vie with the hospitality of those who have attained to commercial success. And as their blood is no better than their neighbours' (their sole claim to superiority resting on their ability to exist neither toiling nor spinning), those who have made themselves well-to-do by dint of hard work are not disposed to submit to the airs which these aged tabbies give themselves. Therefore do they wrap themselves up in their old silk dresses and spun-silk shawls, and are warmed by the inner consciousness of, at any rate, the feelings of aristocracy.

But little of the stir of the outer world penetrates to East Anglian towns of the smaller class. The local papers devote more space to the marriage of Miss Susan Caxton to Mr. John Grains than to the death of a reigning monarch. The St. Mary's athletic sports are reported with notes critical and explanatory. But Henley and the 'Varsity boat race are passed by without mention. The fact that Miss Claybrooke has won a prize at the Trawlhaven poultry show eclipses in local importance the American attempts on English trade. The draper's new window surpasses the affairs of the Empire in interest.

About a mile up the Ipswich Road is a semi-detached houselet called "The Limes." It was hither that Celibate Sarah conducted Laura Claybrooke when the old house at Andersham was sold. The Limes was full large enough for the two women and a little country-girl for a servant, when one could be got to stay more than a week, which was of rare occurrence. Bits of furniture, pictures, and knick-knacks from Orford House were scattered about the rooms. Laura, in sole possession of this domain, seemed to herself more "Miss Claybrooke" than ever. Sarah looked on the whole concern (including Laura, the asthmatical toy terrier, and the fowls) as her own.

Five years and a half had elapsed since Rupert paid his first visit to the Limes. And still the 6,000 was in the hands of the trustees, to Sarah's disappointment and Laura's chagrin. The former was anxious to dip her fingers in the fund, and the latter thought it an insult to her dignity that her income should be controlled by anyone other than herself. For during the period elapsed Laura's dignity had increased and multiplied. Her Miss Claybrooke moods were more frequent and pronounced. The weakness of which Rupert had seen signs had grown upon her. And this, together with her constitutional tendency, had rendered her disgustingly gross and unwieldy in habit for a woman of her age. Her fat was soft fat, and as she moved she shook and swagged like an elephant. Her complexion, which had been delicate and clear, had become coarse and rubicund. Her round face and broad snub nose looked swollen. Her hair and eyebrows had grown thin and faded. Her weak, watery eyes still more weak and watery. Sarah, too, had laid on flesh. But hers was a hard, solid formation. She had no waist, and her rear view gave the idea of a huge porpoise. For her shoulders were bowed, and her back of the shape which dog fanciers denominate "roach." Her face had puffed up hard and mottled, and had a greasy shine on its blended tints like the outside of a German sausage. Her hair was scanty, and was growing white. Her little pig-eyes seemed smaller than ever. A set of false teeth, a little too large, stretched her thin lips thinner, and were not only false, but were honest about it.

As Laura's weak intellect grew weaker from self-indulgence, Sarah's power over her was trebled and quadrupled. But in spite of the lapse of time, and of Sarah's incessant scheming, Laura still had the germs of good nature and natural affection in her. The coolness that had arisen between her and Rupert on his failing to arrange matters so as to hand over the trust fund, had died. The affection of sister for brother was still alive, and capable of being nursed to strength. Over and over again Sarah had hinted that then was the time for her to exercise her power of appointment, and to make a will leaving.£3,000 and all her other worldly goods to her faithful companion. But Laura could only be induced to give her an interest for life in £1,000. The rest of her property she had bequeathed to Rupert.

Laura's birthday fell in July, and it was Rupert's custom to send her down a salmon for her birthday dinner. As the women were sitting down to breakfast on the morning of the anniversary, the fish was brought up from the station.

"I thought he wouldn't forget me, though you said he would," said Laura, delighted. "Open the basket, Sarah, and let's have a look at it."

Sarah undid the basket. "That whoolly stink!" she said.

"Well I never!" said Laura. "It must be the basket. He'd never send me a stinking fish, I'm sure. Dee you think he would?"

The long association with Sarah had tainted Laura's speech with traces of dialect, and the broad Norfolk accent was not uncommon on her lips. As for Sarah, she had seen much of her sister in the country, and spoke pure Norfolk.

"Lor'! I doan't know," answered

Sarah. "I rackon he 'ouldn't be tew pertickler."

When the salmon was taken out, it answered for itself. The weather was very hot, and the result screamed to heaven.

"That warmin' of a booy," said Sarah. "If I wuz yew, I 'ouldn't hev narthen moor ta dew wi' him."

"It's not his fault. The weather turned it," said Laura, half crying.

" Tarned it! Tarn yar granny!" retorted Sarah disdainfully. "Tha'ss noo good tellin' me that wuz sweet when that wuz bote, 'cos I know ta worn't. He thote as ta wouldn't fare quite so bad, an' yew'd eeat it an' git pisoned. I know he want yar brass. The tooad!"

"Oh, nonsense!" said Laura. "But there's letter inside. Le'ss see what he say."

"Noo good, I'll bet a sixpence," grunted Sarah.

The letter was of surprising import.

"Dear old Laura," it ran. "I'm sending you off a salmon as usual, to wish you many happy returns. I hope you'll enjoy it."

"Injy it!" interrupted Sarah. "Wha tha'ss enow ta tarn yar inside! I oony hoop as we shan't git the feeaver."

"' I expect,'" continued Laura, reading again, "' you'll be surprised to hear that I have decided to leave town, give up the law, and try to earn my living with my pen. I've got some reviewing through Harry Lyndon, and have already had two or three tales accepted by good papers. Now I want you to put me up for a week or so, so that I can look about for a small cottage right out in the country. Perhaps Sarah may know of one out Frogsthorpe way. If you'll have me, I'll run down at the end of the week, when I can explain things to you more fully than I can in a letter. Love to Sarah.'"

It will be seen from this that Rupert had no idea of the esteem in which he was held by Sarah, or the way in which she spoke of him.

"Well, that booy's impidence git oover me!" said Sarah. "O' coorse yew doan't want him livin' in these parts. Whativer can be the rayson on't? He've done some'at, I'll bet a penny. And want ta git out o' the way, soo theer!"

"Of course my house must be always open to my brother, Sarah," said Laura. "And I must ask you not to speak of him like that. I 'spex he's ill. You must git the best room riddy for him at once, and I'll write and tell him that I shall be glad to hev him for as long as he can stay."

"Wha I've noo paatience wi' ye," said Sarah testily. "But I s'pooz tha'ss noo good a-talkin' sense. But dee yew mind my wuds. Yew'll be sorra foor't. Doan't yew maake noo mistaake. Yew'll be whoolly sorry foor't. An' doan't yew saay as I niver warned ye."

Sarah started to do her mistress's bidding, but turned as she reached the door.

"Ooh!" she said. "Theer's one thing I want ta speeak tee yew about. Tha'ss that Bessie." (Bessie was the little country-girl of the time, who acted as general servant at the Limes for *is. 6d.* a week and her keep.) "What thet gal eeat 'ud keeap a fambly. I doubt we shell ha'e ta git rid on har. Yew mind that pudden I maade yisterdaay. I thote I'd shaame har out o' har hoggish waays; an' whin she took it out I saay, 'Yew can finish that pudden if ye like'—an', would yew believe it?—blaame me if she di'n't saay, 'Thanky, mam,' an' took an' eeat the lot."

"Well I never, Sarah!" said Laura. "Whatever made you say such a thing? Why the gal will be ill."

"Not har!" replied Sarah. "Ye see I thote I'd shaame har. But I rackon she can't hev noo shaame in har. But *she* oan't be ill. She'd bust harself, an' then want moor."

"Well, give her her breakfast," Laura suggested, "and then we'll think about sending her home. Girls are so difficult to git now. I'm sure I doan't know why. "

"It's the mothers' fault," explained Sarah. "They doan't think the laazy wenches ote ta dew narthen nowadays but jest set an' stuff 'emselves. Theer wuz that gal Bina. I oony axed har ta rub out four blankets an' nine or ten sheets afoor brekkust, an' she wrote hooam to har mother, an' she come an' whoolly gi'e me a mobbin', an' took the gal away then an' theer. She ote ta ha' been prarsecuted, an' I would hev if ta hadn't ha' been for bringin' yar naame up as yew di'n't faancy."

"Well, call Bessie," said Laura.

"Bessie!" called Sarah. A growing healthy-looking girl of sixteen came.

Sarah cut off two thin slices of bread and butter and poured out a cup of tea. "Theer's yar brekkust, Bessie," she said. "If yew want any moor yew must ax foor't."

"Thanky, miss," said poor Bessie, who knew the formula, and that she would cause as much sensation by asking for more as did Oliver Twist.

"And now little Fiddy Fi Fi must hev *his* brakfast," said Laura, fondling her terrier. She took some puppy biscuit in her mouth and chewed it. Then removing it from her lips fed the dog, repeating the process till it was satisfied.

"Now I'll go and feed the fowls," she said. "Will you bring down the water and then see about Rupert's room?" she asked Sarah, who, exhausted by her diatribe against modern servants, had postponed leaving the room.

"Yis, me dare," said Sarah. "Though I wish he worn't a-comin'. I rackon I'd best cook this hare fish. That 'ull dew ta grease Bessie's innards with."

Laura had devoted the greater part of the last five years to obtaining a prize strain of Dorkings. Out of her *£200* a year or so her chickens cost her a good. £50. But she was anticipating the time when they would pay. Sarah grudged every farthing spent on them. But her greed and ignorance were eager for the large profits she believed might be made out of show poultry. "Anyways, that's better'n har marryin'," she said to herself. "An' help ta keeap har at hooam along o' me."

"I wonder what Rupert will think of my fowls," said Laura, as she complacently surveyed some of her best pullets and cockerels. "Dear boy, it will be quite a treat to have him here for a bit. I'm sure he sent the salmon off all right, and the weather turned it. It's a shame for Sarah to speak of him as she do. I must tell her that I can't do with it. It's too bad. He never done her no harm.

I wonder what's the matter with him. Hallo! There's Tommy weak on his legs. Sarah! Sarah! Tommy's weak on his legs. Bring the strychnine pills down when ye come," she shouted, as she saw a cockerel squatting on the lower joints of his legs, apparently unable to rise.

"I'm a-comin'," screamed Sarah from the house.

"She oan't be aable ta speer much for that warmin' if he want it," she muttered, as she sought for the pills. "Har fowls eeat up all she ha' got ta speer, an' I'd raythcr they had it than him. Well, if he must come I s'pooz he must, for I doan't seem as if I could fare ta help it. " II RUPERT AT this period of Rupert's career it seemed as if it had L been decreed that all the male issue of William Claybrooke should prove failures. Rupert had made a good start. He had been head boy at Odinton Grammar School and captain of his college boat at Cambridge. He took a fair degree, and after his three years' articles with Chapman and Starling had expired, he qualified as a solicitor without trouble. He was popular with the firm, and as soon as he was on the Rolls they offered him a managing clerkship with a generous salary, and at the same time raised no objection to his practising on his own account. Taking it all round, it looked as if he ought to make a very comfortable income for a bachelor. But there were many reasons why things were not so bright as they looked. His whole nature was antagonistic to the dreary routine of a solicitor's office. And, in addition, he found that many of his private clients seemed to entrust their business to so young a man with the idea that he might be persuaded to do dirty bits of work which they knew no firm of good standing would touch. Others expected their work to be done on the cheap, or on the understanding that the costs should be got out of the other side if possible, if not, none were to be charged. One of the reasons why solicitors are (with some honourable exceptions) more contemptible than other men, is that whereas God makes other men (with some dishonourable exceptions), clients, as a rule, make solicitors. There would be no quibbling, no underhand work done in a lawyer's office if it were not praised as smart by some employer. Lawyers would not deserve their character for falsehood if they refused to tell the lies with which they are instructed. This does not apply to many London firms whose standing is that of old family solicitors, and among whom some of the most trustworthy and straightforward men living may be found; but it does apply to most firms whose chief business is litigation, and to quite nine-tenths of all solicitors whose practice lies in little provincial towns. The principal, almost the only work for lawyers in a town like St. Mary's, for instance, is county or police court, and either of these would have corrupted Bayard in a fortnight.

Rupert could have borne the work he had to do for Chapman and Starling at the commencement of his managing clerkship. But in the fourth year it was thought advisable by the firm to hand over the affairs of a brewery to him. This entailed attending at the various "changes" of tenancy of the publichouses in the trade of that particular brewery, and necessitated his mingling with some of the foulest blackguards unhung. Some of the publicans were, he found, very decent fellows. But their hangers-on were to a man a deplorable set of shameless frauds and foulmouthed, foul-minded parasites. The whole *entourage* of the inner life of "the houses "—the perpetual standing and accepting drinks—the irregularity of meals owing to the wild uncertainty as to the time at which a bit of publichouse business would either commence or finish (and it is by no means unusual for a "change" to last from six in the evening till midnight, and then have to be postponed because the outgoing or the incoming tenant is too drunk to sign the necessary documents)—the applications at the police courts, where every constable, sergeant, or inspector connected with the case had to be bribed to lie or tell the truth, according to the necessities of the matter from the point of view of the brewery—everything, indeed, connected with the sordid business began to be a strain upon his temper and his health, both moral and physical. He would have given up his private work if he could have afforded it, and waited till such time as Chapman and Starling might offer him a partnership; but a tendency to extravagance in living had been encouraged during the years of his intimacy with Redfern. There is no more fatal thing for a youth than association with a wealthy man who is all promise and no performance. Every attempt to gain independence is met with "My dear fellow! Why do you want to bother? I'll see you are all right when the time comes." No doubt the highest kind of nature would shake itself clear of patronage of all kinds. But Rupert was but a boy at the critical time; and, at any rate, had no such claims to superexcellence. He liked good dinners, good music, spare cash, and the irresponsible ease of life that he found at Redfern's in "the Long." When his independence did come, and his intimacy with the rich man terminated, he had acquired tastes and habits which might not have materially injured his worldly welfare had Redfern kept his promises, but would never have given his soul the chance to cleanse itself that he met in the life which was destined for his ordeal.

As it was, he found that his outgoings exceeded his income. Without being vicious, he had the habits of the ordinary man about town; and his refinement of feeling rendered it a matter of course for him to indulge his appetites with the greatest delicacy, and consequently with the greatest expense. He was a good-hearted youth, and liked his friends to share with him. He lent a ready ear to tales of trouble. He was especially prone to be imposed upon by women; and a kind of quixotism in this respect was a heavy tax upon him and his resources. He was unsuspicious, and it was difficult to force the knowledge on him that he was being deceived or treated unfairly; and he never failed to be surprised when he grasped the fact that he had been "done." Unfairness, lies, and treachery were things he could not understand. He was certainly ill fitted for the law!

His one qualification for his profession was his intellect. Intellectually he was at this time almost, solely guided in his opinions by the rules of pure logic. One of his greatest weaknesses was an intolerance of any decision or expression of judgment not based on strict logical deduction. Nothing roused his contempt more than a flaw in reasoning or irrelevancy in argument. It followed from this that when once perfidy had been proved to the satisfaction of his reason, he never forgot it. No plausible excuse weighed with him. The thing was proved—and there was an end of it. It also followed that he had been forced unwillingly into agnosticism and utilitarianism. With an intense "devotion to something afar," he was compelled to chill his emotional fervour in the cold chamber of his brain. And while he admired and reverenced the teaching of Christ, he could not accept the beliefs that go to make a theoretical Christian. He was (like most of us) a quaint blend of elements; and in all the world of whimsies against which he fought, it is questionable if there was anything more illogical than himself.

After less than a year's experience of brewery work, he was worn out with the deadly strain of it. He was sick and wretched at the meannesses of his private clients; the rogueries that he was employed to support. The know, ledge that his expenditure was greater than his income, together with certain complications in his private life (which form a drama of surpassing interest in themselves, and which may see the light of publication after the death of one of the *dramatis persona* concerned), increased the nervous tension—the wear and tear that were making an old man of him before his time. His health broke down. He got better and went up to the office again. Worries accumulated. A bill he had given for an old Cambridge friend, also a solicitor, matured, and fell to him to take up. He could not do it. In all the world there was no one to whom he could look for assistance. His health broke down again, and this time his medical adviser warned him plainly that he must give up the life he was leading, get into the country, avoid all worry, and live as simply and as primitively as possible. "If not, my dear Mr. Claybrooke," said Dr. Mayor, who was a humanitarian as well as a general practitioner, "I tell you candidly that you won't last two years without some serious brain trouble."

A slight disagreement with Starling on his return to the office gave him an opportunity to end his clerkship. He took it, decided to throw up the sponge as far as London was concerned, and try his hand at literature in some quiet country spot. He had always had a fancy for writing, and had tried his hand at it both at school and at Cambridge. One of his principal friends, Harry Lyndon, had made a name for himself in the world of letters, and promised his aid in the new scheme of life which Rupert had decided to adopt. Rupert still believed in promises. He sold up everything he had, and after clearing off his debts found himself with barely fifty pounds in hand.

To some men the outlook would have been discouraging. But Rupert was a man who dealt in extremes. Moderation at that time of his life was impossible for him. He worked and played with equal vigour and excess. He never seemed to have enough time in town, and it became natural to subsist on a diet of the compressed elements of life. To him the country had a great charm. He thought that there he would be able to develop his emotions more at ease. He would be able to read life in the complete edition, instead of the short bare statement of facts which was only of use for cramming purposes, and deleterious at that. The prospect of having to "rough" it held no terrors for him. Though he was fond of good living, he could enjoy simplicity with equal keenness. He was a thorough sportsman, and loved the country so dearly that he had never really felt at home in London. His big, athletic frame called for more exercise than it was possible for a Lincoln's Inn solicitor to obtain, and he thought that this had something to do with the breakdown of his health. He had a great tenderness for his sister, and did not distrust Sarah's show of regard for him. It was natural that he should turn to the Limes for a home when his change of profession and residence was decided upon. His spirits rose and his worries vanished when the arrangements were complete, and he looked forward to the new life as to a holiday in which he might gain health, peace, and, perhaps, ultimately fame and wealth. He had been successful in getting a few short stories accepted through the introduction of Lyndon, and as yet knew nothing of the heartbreaking monotony of the courteous printed forms that come back, so politely, but with such deadening persistency, from editors to unknown writers.

Confident of his abilities, and apparently secure of a trifling income from the reviewing work he had mentioned in his letter to his sister, he went down to St. Mary's full of hope and courage. His future seemed to him more roseate than it had ever done, for literature was always the mistress of his love, though law had for him the fascination of continual dramatic interest that it has for those whose imagination can vanquish the dreary routine of the office. What he objected to was that all the legal dramas were of the sordid, realistic school—a mixture of Ibsen in his later style and Eugene Sue.

Besides Harry Lyndon he possessed a friend who was more faithful. This was old Socrates, a magnificent dark brindle bulldog, with champion blood all through his pedigree. He was quiet and good-natured, as nearly all bulldogs are, and loved his master with all the strength of a steadfast heart and keen intelligence.

The summer was one of exceptional heat, and to avoid the discomfort of travelling during the fiercest hours of the sun, Rupert caught the newspaper train down from Liverpool Street, and arrived at St. Mary's before ten in the morning. He had not written to say what train he was coming by, and decided to defer going to his sister's house for an hour or so. He slung his luggage on to the King's Head omnibus and directed the driver to take it up to the Limes, and deliver the message that he himself might be expected in a couple of hours. He took his Eureka camera with him, and struck through the town, past the old church, down to the river, and out into the country lanes ablaze with hedge-roses and honeysuckle.

"By George," he said to himself, "the place reeks of copy. I ought to do some good work here. Look at that old chap in the smock! He's a sketch in himself. I'll snap him. He'll be worth half-a-guinea anywhere, eh, Sock?" Old Sock grunted and wagged his tail. Rupert patted the old fellow and started to sing Schubert's *Rosen aufder Heiden.*

The two hours passed rapidly enough. He felt stronger and better already when he rang at his sister's door.

A horrible yapping was his first welcome, at which old Sock grunted contemptuously. He had too great a sense of his own dignity even to prick his ears at the sound of a pestilent little dog's wrangling.

Presently the door opened and Laura "galumphed" out, followed by Fido.

"Well, my dear boy," she said, " and how are you? But whatever brute is that? Here, Fi Fi."

She seized the snappy little beast up in terror.

"He won't hurt anyone, old girl," said Rupert, kissing his sister. "Make friends, Sock."

The old dog walked slowly forward, sniffed, and lifted his great jowl.

"Pat him, Laura," said Rupert.

Laura put her hand timidly down, and Sock licked it. All the time the little beast was yapping and straining to get down.

"Wha Lor' dare me," said Sarah's voice inside the hall. "Taake that ogly brute away, for goodness saake!"

"Hallo, Sarah, how are you?" cried Rupert. "Come and make friends with the old chap. He won't hurt you."

Partly reassured, Sarah came out on to the doorstep, wiping her hands on her apron. Sock sniffed gingerly at her as she came forward. A low, rumbling growl sent her in quicker than she had come out.

"Ooh whativer shell I dew?" she screamed.

"Quiet, you old fool!" Rupert chid his dog. "He doesn't like you, Sarah. It's funny, for he nearly always takes to anybody that's fond of me."

"Well, that dew fare cur'ous then," said Sarah. "And tha'ss a fack!"

"Take him round to the back, dear," said Laura. "I can't have him indoors because of Fiddy Fi Fi, my prashus. But we'll soon find a stable for him."

"Why the dog's as quiet as a lamb!" cried Rupert.

"If he come in the house I'm a-gooin' out, and tha'ss all about it," said Sarah. "Whativer yew want wi' sech a brute git oover me. He fare enow ta tarn anybardy's inside."

"Oh well," said Rupert, "I'll soon find a place for him." More vexed than he cared to show, he led the dog round to the little backyard and shut him in. Then he went indoors.

"Well," said Laura again, "and how are you, old boy? And whatever's the matter? But you must be famished. Hurry up dinner, Sarah."

In the country the wholesome custom of dining at midday still very generally prevails. Sarah went off, and Laura kissed her brother again.

"It's good for sore eyes to see you, dear," she said. Her eyes were liquid with tears. Her habits made it hard for her to restrain her emotions. "But you don't look up to much. Dee you think I'm any fatter?"

"I wondered when that was coming," said Rupert, laughing at the question, which was a stock inquiry of Laura's. "I don't think you are any thinner."

But as he looked at her bloated form his laughter died on his lips.

"You don't look very well, either," he continued, "in spite of your colour."

"It's my heart," answered Laura. "I get such horrible attacks of palpitations sometimes."

"Hum-m-m!" muttered Rupert, recollecting the partiality to stimulant he had noticed on his previous visit to the Limes. "Well," he said, "you must come out driving and walking with me in my search for a cottage. I'll soon cure your palps."

He had only briefly sketched out the reasons of his coming, and his plans for the future, when Sarah came in with the dinner.

"Theer!" she cried. "I knowed as yew'd fare ta like a biled batter pudden an' graavy. Yew're a reg'lar Noorfolk domplin', I 'specks, saame as iver. Come on, bor. Them as eeat the moost pudden shall hev the moost meeat."

When the old-fashioned dinner was over Laura took Rupert out to inspect her fowls. Sarah busied herself in gathering raspberries to take into the town to sell. "Tha'ss arly foor'm," she explained. "An' I doan't see why Miss Loora shou'n't maake a penny like other folk."

As a matter of fact it was Sarah that had the pennies, but neither Rupert nor Laura was to know that.

Laura hardly liked the early sacrifice of her dignity, and suggested to Sarah under her breath that the gathering might be dispensed with for once; but Sarah replied, "Wha whew's he? If he doan't like it lar him lump it. *Yew* hain't done narthen soo as yew ha'e ta hide. What did he want to start sa early foor? Wha soo's he shou'n't be follered!" She only ceased her insinuations on being treated to a dose of her employer's "Miss Claybrooke" manner.

The afternoon passed pleasantly and quickly, and after supper, when the whisky was on the table, the question of Rupert's future abode was mooted.

"I only want quite a tiny place," he said, "near the marshes, so that I can get a little wild-fowl shooting."

"Well then," said Sarah, "my sister Peggie hev a little cottage ta let tha'ss right down by the ma'sh, but a doubt ta 'oun't be good enow for the likes o' yew."

"Dee you mean the little one at the corner?" asked Laura. "That would never do. Why I don't believe Rupert could stand up in it!"

"I should like a quaint old place like that," said Rupert. "Let's go over and look at it to-morrow."

"That 'ud dew pore Peggie a bit o' good," said Sarah, who knew Rupert's good heart and played on it. "She can't git no rent out o' them Herons. It's twelve pound a yare, an' tha'ss a'moost all they ha' got ta depend on."

"Don't they pay their rent, then?" asked Rupert. "Why doesn't she turn them out?"

"Har husband oan't dew't," said Sarah. "They oony paay five shillun at a time when they hev a fancy."

"Shall we go over to-morrow, Laura?" said Rupert. "I haven't seen old Peggie for years. She's got a boy, hasn't she?"

"Aah! That she hev," replied Sarah, launched on her favourite topic. "He's my gardson, Bartie is; an' I fare whoolly proud o' him, though some fules dew say as he's innercent. Yew should jest see the corfins he maake! He's larnin' the undertaakin', an' he've got the wood for his father's an' mother's corfins a'riddy agin they want 'em. He's"

"Yes, dear," broke in Laura, in answer to Rupert, and anxious to stop the flood of eloquence with which Sarah loved to overwhelm everyone on the subject of her "innocent" godson. "We'll drive over if it's fine. Will you order the butcher's tax-cart, Sarah? He only charge five shillun a day."

"Oan't Peggie fare somethin' proud if Maaster Rupert come ta be har tinant!" said Sarah. "Lor'! Theer oan't be noo hooldin' on har. She'll dew ivery moortal thing yew ax har."

"So she ought to," said Laura. "I'm shore we've been very good to you and yours, Sarah. Mother frequently made her little presents, and you know as I've often sent her some o' my ole things arter I'd done with 'em."

"Aah! That yew hev, me dare," said Sarah.

"Well, I believe the place will do," Rupert said. "It will have to be a very funny hole if it won't."

The conversation wandered off to old times and old friends. By bedtime Laura was maudlin and tearfully affectionate.

"Goo' night, me dear old boy," she said, giving Rupert a slobbery kiss. "But 'member, if you can't ger on there'll alius be a hooam here for you."

III RUPERT'S REFUGE THE next morning Sarah rose at five without disturbing her mistress, and went down to the town to see her godson Bertie. She found him on the point of leaving his lodgings for his day's work.

"Lor', aunt!" he said. "Yew gi'e me right a tarn! An' how dee yew fare?"

"Now, Bartie," said Sarah, "dee yew mind what I tell ye. Yew can't goo ta wark till arter brekkust. Yew must git on yar bicycle an' goo oover ta yar mar, an' tell har as Miss Loora an' har brother Rupert be a-gooin' oover theer ta-daay, an' Maaster Rupert think o' taakin' the little cottage, soo she'd best clane it up a bit."

"Yis, aunt," said Bertie. "Maaster Hubert be a-gooin' oover, an' Miss Loora think o' taakin the little cottage,

"Wha drat the booy! He *dew* fare half sorft, an' tha'ss a fack," said Sarah impatiently. "Hare. Dee yew waait. I'll write it down." She scribbled her message in pencil on the back of an old envelope. "Hare," she said, "take an' give this ta yar mar, an' look sharp, theer's a good booy. Gi'e me a kiss."

"Yis, aunt," simpered Bertie. "I'll look out."

"Ooh yew be a-gooin'," said Sarah sharply. "Tha'ss a rum thing ta me," she said to herself, as she walked home. "He fare right quick at maakin' corfins an' grindin' awaay at that ole ammonium, but now an' thin he doan't fare noo better 'an an innercent. I must hev a h'arin' with Peggie about him, for he's me owan dare booy, an' he *dew* love his ole aunt."

It was a bright summer morning, with a pleasant stir of wind from the northwest, when Laura and Rupert set out from the Limes on their way to Frogsthorpe. Sarah had insinuated her views to Laura on her return from her visit to Bertie. "Yew doan't want ta put him off of it, if he faancy it," she said. "Peggie's somethin' pore, as yew know, an' that 'ud dew har a bit o' good. If he find arter a time as he doan't like it, he can give it up. 'Sides that'll be useful ta know what he's a-dewin' on, an' Peggie oan't let narthen escape har, I'll bet a sixpence."

"Well I never, Sarah!" replied Laura. "You think of everything. I never did!"

Both brother and sister were in high spirits as they drove through St. Mary's—across the old bridge over the Saelig—along Cootham Dam, and up to the high land between the level of marsh at St. Mary's and the wider sweep of fen stretching from Frogsthorpe clear away to Broadwater. A compromise had been effected as to old Sock. During the day he was to be kept in an outhouse, except when out in the town or country lanes with his master; but at night he was to sleep in Rupert's room, according to his custom. On the morning of the excursion he was seated in a high state of delight (between Laura and his master) in the butcher's tax-cart.

When the open country was reached, Rupert lifted up his voice and sang from sheer lightness of heart. The spirit of youth was upon Laura as she drove. She turned and kissed her brother. "Dear old boy," she said.

"By George!" said Rupert. "This is better than London."

The upland hay was carted; but here and there peeps of the marsh afforded vignettes of lightly clad labourers tossing or loading the marsh hay. The buzz of the clipper sounded sweetly in the shimmering air, as it crescendoed with a breath of favouring wind or died away in a calm. Presently the lanes grew heavier, and at a sudden turn round a well-timbered plantation, Hockingham Church, majestic on its eminence, came into view. Laura pointed it out with the whip.

"There!" she said. "Round that church, to the left, past Frogsthorpe Church (where you see that clump of trees), and about half a mile on, is where Peggie live. Do you think you'll like the place?"

"Like it!" answered Rupert. "My years in town seem like a waste of life. What can the rush of the city—the incessant toil and moil of litigation (or society, for the matter of that) give, to compare with the lovely peace and wildness of this? I admit there is a charm in going down Piccadilly or the Strand on the top of a 'bus when the theatres are closing, especially on a rainy night. The lights are so wonderful, and the magnetism of humanity so fascinating. But the charm of that as compared to this is as Liszt to Mozart; as Ibsen to Charles Lamb; as fever to sweet health. "

"I'm so glad you like it," said Laura, without the faintest comprehension of his meaning. "It will be nice if you come to live here. We shall often see each other; for it's only a sixpenny fare from Duckingham to St. Mary's, and you will always be welcome at my house. Always."

As she said this she drew herself up, and assumed an expression of mingled kindness, importance, and satisfaction. She was fond of her brother; but the words "my house" left a sweeter taste in her mouth than did Rupert's name.

"Thanks, old girl," said Rupert, a little amused at the touch of pomposity in her tone. "You may be sure that IH often run over, and I'll soon cure your palps. Why you're looking better already."

But he thought to himself, "It will be devilish hard, though. You can't tell your sister she drinks. And I'm almost sure that's at the root of the mischief. But it must be stopped somehow. God help me! It's bad enough in a man; but it's a million times worse in a woman."

From Hockingham Church hill the view extended over fen and water clear away to the northern horizon. All about the flats the huge black sails of Norfolk trading wherries stole in and out, seemingly amongst the kine, grazing on the rich marsh levels. A number of smaller white specks, moving more quickly along the network of rivers, betrayed the whereabouts of some local yacht regatta. The labourers met with in the fields or stodgy lanes began to wear an amphibious look; the blue woollen sweater of the fisherman being seen as often as the check cotton shirt; and knee boots and great woollen stockings (even on that warm summer day) telling of trudges in watery places, and of fears of ague and rheumatism. Herons flapped slowly high overhead, and hornpies (the local name for the green plover) were seen searching for wire-worms among the swede tops, which as yet looked sparse in the even rows along the black soil.

Past Frogsthorpe Church, down Turkey Cock Hill (haunted by the ghost of a gobbler), along the low road skirting the marsh, and there, in the midst of tall willows and stunted bullace and apple trees, the tiny remnant of the once splendid Noddyfield Estate lay before the househunters.

The little clump of three cottages known as Noddyfield Corner stands at a point or spit of low-lying land projecting out into the marsh. At the southern end, Peggie and her husband, the blind basket-maker, had their dwelling. The middle tenement was occupied by the Heron family, consisting of the old man, his three sons, Jack, Bob, and Gilbert (aged respectively twenty, nineteen, and seventeen), and his daughter Bertha. They had moved in from the smallest cottage at the northern end on Bertha's return home from a situation after her mother's death. The third cottage was a tiny little place, consisting of a small livingroom and a larder downstairs and two sleeping-rooms upstairs, in only one of which was there room to swing the proverbial cat. There was a false attic, which had been used as a bedroom in the years gone by. But the local authorities had lately forbidden it to be utilised in any way for the occupation of human beings. If they had done their duty they would have condemned the whole cottage. A bakehouse adjoined; but there was no intercommunication indoors between this and the cottage proper. This was older than the other two dwellings. In the living-room the great baulks stretched across bare and unsquared. The main baulk was hardly five feet ten inches from the brick floor. The premises, together with a strip of garden on the other side of the lane which ran past the three cottages, were rated at *£2* per annum, worth 3, and to be let at *£6.*

As Rupert and Laura drove up to this domain, a little dumpy woman stood at the iron gate giving ingress through a tall quickset hedge to the garden of the first cottage. At the approach of the pony trap her eyelids flickered rapidly over her pale eyes, and her hands jerked spasmodically in ridiculous, marionette-like gestures. Her grey hair was drawn tight back over a head that was narrow and low in front, and rose to a bulge at the back of the crown. Her face was wizened, and her deep-set eyes small and piggish, like Sarah's. Her mouth was small and mean, and her lips pursed in a quaint pouting, as if shaped to say "puff." Her nose was aquiline, like her sister's, but was pinched. Her body was so long that it seemed a mystery where she kept her legs, and the porpoise-like appearance of Sarah's back was reproduced in her in an exaggerated form.

Behind her stood her blind husband, a tall, stalwart man, with a countenance which would have been noble but for a coarseness of the nose and a horrible rheumy right eye. A handsome white beard and moustache imparted a dignity to the lower part of his face, and an erect carriage spoke of a vigorous old age. He had little of the appearance of blindness.

"Wha Lor' dare me!" said Peggie. "This be whoolly a sapparise! I fare right pleeased ta see ye. An' Maaster Rupert, tew! Wha I sh'u'd hudly ha' knowed ye! Phillup, dee yew goo an' taake the poona oover ta Mr. Reed's and put it up. An' tell Mrs. Reed as Miss Claybrooke ha' brote har brother oover, an' ax har for a jug o' har hooambrewed. Wha come in, dew!"

"How are you, Peggie?" said Rupert. "I should have known you anywhere. Glad to meet you, Mr. Noddyfield." He shook hands with the pair.

"Thanky, sir," said old Noddy. "Saame ta yew." The blind man advanced and laid hands on his guest. He felt him all over. "Aah!" he said. "Yew're whoolly a fine figure of a maan. As fine a gennleman as iver I see. "

"Whativer be yew a-dewin' on, Phillup?" said his wife. "P'raps Maaster Rupert doan't faancy yar fumblin' on him like that."

"I don't mind," said Rupert, laughing. "Especially to win such a compliment from one who should be a judge of a fine man. But can't I take the pony over? Can Mr. Noddyfield manage it?"

"Lor', yis!" Peggie simpered. "He allust put tew our little dickey afoor that hanged itself. He's nigh as handy as a maan what can see, an' not half soo interfarin'. Dee yew be a-gooin', Phillup. Come in. Wha come in, dew; I'm right pleeased ta see ye."

Rupert followed his sister and hostess along the garden path that led to the back door. When there are two outer doors to a marsh village cottage, the front is for formal visits only. As this was a surprise party, strictly informal, according to local etiquette, Peggie naturally led the way to the back.

On Philip's return the object of the visit was mooted, to the intense gratification of the Noddyfields, who had thought Sarah's message too good to be true. Peggie armed herself with a key some six inches long, and bulky in proportion, and led the way round to the empty cottage, which had already been cleaned and scoured on the receipt of Sarah's note.

The first thing that became apparent was that to be able to enter this mansion upright, Rupert would have to submit to decapitation. He bowed to the lintel, and to the inevitable, and went in. The quaint little shanty pleased him. The bare baulks, sanded floor, and big, open fireplace were picturesque in his eyes. It was summer, and he could not see the damp steaming up from the ground, between the seams in the brickwork. The facts that he caught his head against the main baulk, and had to go up the corkscrew staircase sideways and bent double, were as nothing compared to the charm of the old-fashioned structural arrangements. Even the squalid little door that opened out from the staircase into the living-room found favour in his sight. He could always make friends with country folk, he said, and he wished to live among them as one of themselves, for the purpose of "copy"—a magic word which had an awesome effect on his hearers. They did not know that it is only the tyro in letters who is always talking of copy, and never finding it. The old hand never mentions the thing, and gets as much as ever he can do with.

"An' I'm shore," said Peggie to Laura, "anything as Phillup an' me can dew, we shell be proud an' happy ta dew; willin' and welcome. He've oony got ta saay the

F wud. Lor'! ta think as we sh'u'd iver hev a Mister Claybrooke for our tinant!"

"Aah!" said old Noddy. "That maake my ole innards rumble wi' deelaight!" A dark saying, but well meant.

As the party emerged from the cottage, Bertha Heron passed by on her way to her own back door, which was reached by a circuitous route, down the lane, and round the end of the empty cottage.

Bertha was then twenty-four years of age. Tall and lissome as a willow wand, and graceful as a panther. Her face was delicately moulded, of a pure oval shape. A thin, straight nose, with thoroughbred, quivering nostrils, divided a pair of large blue eyes, Scandinavian in hue, but truly pastoral English in beauty of expression. A well-formed mouth, not small enough to be mean, nor large enough to be coarse, with sufficient curve in the upper lip to render it enticing, and with a full promise that told of soft delights, had laughter lurking in its every line. Her teeth were small, even, and as white as new milk. Her cheeks were so clear in cream and pink as to almost give an impression of transparency, an impression which leapt to life in spying the little ears which peeped beneath hair that had the light and rich fulness of golden autumn. The idea born of her presence was not only that she was beautiful, but that she was pure and good. And (rare complement of those qualities) a brain owner as well.

Rupert's eyes glistened for an instant. Then the dissimulation that is the attribute of unacknowledged love checked him.

Bertha passed with a smile and a pleasant "good morning," and was gone.

Rupert had the discretion to ask no questions.

On the way back to the Noddyfields' cottage Laura said, "I think Bertha Heron looks better than she did." And by this Rupert knew that the lovely girl would be his neighbour if he took the little place he had just inspected. That settled it.

"Aah!" said Peggie, in reply to Laura. "She look well enow. But tha'ss amaazin' ta see how she goo about. Collars, an' cuffs, an' a fall, an' a light blouse an' all! I doubt sech waays can't come ta noo good! Wha she might be a laady the waay she git harself up!"

A desire to defend the girl against all ill speech—against ill of all kinds—suddenly set Rupert's blood galloping. He was a chivalrous fellow and he knew it. So he put it down to that. Again he had the discretion to say nothing, but he thought Peggie was a scandalous old fool. Dissimulation, unrecognised even by him, led him to make further inquiries, and to raise an objection or two which he knew would be easily overcome. But the hamper which former experiences had induced Laura to bring over from the Limes for dinner had not been unpacked before the bargain was closed, and Rupert had agreed to take the cottage and garden at the rent of *jQ6* a year.

Before the good-byes were said it had been settled that he should enter into residential possession on the following Monday week.

HIS COMING TO FROGSTHORPE, AND AN ADVENTURE THE purchase of the few articles of furniture necessary to make the cottage habitable made but a small inroad on Rupert's little capital. Laura set him up with bed-linen and crockery. A bed and bedding, a chest of drawers, a table, one armchair, and two or three diningchairs, formed the greater part of the requisites that had to be bought. He still had his old college ornaments, his little Broadwood, and other goods and chattels which accumulate even in a bachelor's possession, and when the fitting up of the cottage was complete the interior was both pretty and cosy. The piano, the shields, the short oar, the first boat colours, and the multitude of photographs of Cambridge groups seemed out of place in the homely lime-washed room. But their very incongruity had a charm. The cottage was ready to receive him before the time fixed for his taking possession, and he had painted over the one outer door the title he had chosen for his splendid residence, "The Castle. "

"Ooh, dare me," Peggie said, when she saw it. "It's quite amewsin', I'm shore!"

By the eventful Monday all Rupert's belongings had been housed at "The Castle," and it only remained for him to go over with his gun and old Sock.

The ten days or so which he had spent at the Limes had been too fully occupied by journeys to and from Frogsthorpe, and by getting his week's reviewing done, for the spirit of mischief to have the chance to stir up strife between brother and sister. But it was with a good heart that Sarah sped the parting guest, and said good-bye with much protestation of good wishes. She witnessed the affectionate parting between Rupert and Laura without a pang. She knew how to wait.

"Goo'-bye, dear old boy," Laura said, kissing Rupert fondly. "I hope you'll be happy and successful. But remember that there will allust be a hooam for you here. Allust."

Both felt some emotion, and showed it according to their respective natures. The woman by tears and loving words, the man by an affectation of careless indifference that often conceals a deeper feeling than ostentatious sentiment.

The handiest way from St. Mary's to Frogsthorpe is to go by rail to Duckingham, and then, after crossing the bridge over "The Cut" at Dingleton, and turning sharp off to the right along the railway, to follow the line till a stile is reached affording access to the marshes. Thence the path is plain, along the wall of the Fleet Dyke. With the hope of picking up a duck or teal on the way (for it was now the first week in August) Rupert had postponed his departure from the Limes till evening, so that he might cross the marshes at fall of dusk, or " between the lights," according to the picturesque language of the district, for it is then that the fowl come out into the dykes to feed.

He swung over the stile on to the marsh way, and after cocking the hammers of his gun, started along the Fleet, eager to kill his first fowl of the season. Old Sock trotted quietly along the edge of the dyke, proud in the consciousness that he knew a gun and its uses, and was no mean retriever—an unusual accomplishment for a bulldog.

There is no finer grazing land in England than the lush marsh levels in the valleys of the Thorwater and Saelig; and in the summer innumerable stock are turned out to fatten on the flats. Young bulls, as well as the quieter bullocks, may often be seen stamping and roaring mutual defiance, and the unwary foot-passenger has not unfrequently an unpleasant experience when the hot weather has rendered the stock irritable. Few women care to cross the marshes by themselves at this time of the year; but as the way round to Duckingham is four miles by road, as against a mile and a half by the Fleet Dyke, timidity is sometimes constrained by expediency. These things were known to Rupert, but as he supposed, immaterial to him, and he pursued his way, intent only on the chance of a shot.

The evening was cloudy, and the afterglow of the sun, over Rushingham to the north-west, was hidden. It was barely possible to see from gate to gate, and the stock not yet couched on the grass for their night's rest loomed through the dim light like indistinct phantoms. A parcel of hornpie swept overhead, uttering their wailing cries, in their evening flight up to land. A snipe bustled up in front of old Sock, and went off calling "pee-ink" in shrill staccato. Rupert did not care to fire at the hornpie, for fear of frightening any fowl that might be about; and the snipe was too small and too quick for a shot in the gathering gloom.

His ears were strained for the rustle that would prelude the rise of a duck from the water. But he was to have no luck of that kind. He had travelled half the distance across the marshes, when his hearing thrilled tensely at a shrill scream. "Help! help!" came the piteous appeal from somewhere in the invisible marsh ahead. It was a woman's voice, and a sullen snorting roar proclaimed the nature of the danger. Before the second cry of "help" was uttered, Rupert was running at his best speed; and as he ran he shouted, "All right! I'm coming! Heel, Sock," he added to the old dog, who had pricked up his ears and was galloping with the heavy roll of his breed in advance of his master.

"Help! Oh, for God's sake, make haste!" came through the grey dimness, and urged him not to relax his speed. On to the next gate he ran. To slip the chain off the hook staple was the work of an instant, and without waiting to close the gate again (a heinous offence in the eyes of a marshman) he continued his rush to the rescue.

Then he saw.

A girl was cowering down by the edge of the dyke, and on the top of the wall, within six feet of her, a young bull stood roaring and tearing up the turf with his hoofs and snorting furious threatenings. As Rupert ran towards the brute it lowered its head, and seemed about to risk the descent to the water in pursuit of its victim. There was no time to lose. Rupert stopped, raised his gun to his shoulder, and emptied his right barrel at the near flank. A roar of rage and pain followed the report. The bull swung round to meet the attack. The girl still cowered, shuddering, hiding her eyes in her hands. As the bull charged, stung rather than injured by the small shot, old Sock created a diversion by running forward and leaping at its head. He missed his aim, and the bull stopped to take summary vengeance on his nearest enemy. Rupert's left barrel was loaded with larger shot, and before his brave dog could be hurt, he let the bull have it again in the flank, and shouted to Sock to come to heel. That did the business. The No. 3 shot at close range crashed through the hide like a bullet, and with another roar of pain the bull stumbled, recovered itself, turned, and shambled off into the marsh, followed by a deep bark from the excited dog, who reluctantly obeyed his master's voice, and ran to meet the praises and caresses which were his due.

Rupert hurried forward to the girl. She had not moved. He sprang down the wall and touched her. Her form seemed familiar in its graceful outlines.

"Come," he said, "it's all right now; you're quite safe. Old Sock and my gun have driven off the enemy."

The kneeling girl took her hands from her face. It was Bertha Heron.

Rupert did not stand aghast. His voice did not stick in his throat. He did not feel that the one great love of his life was before him. He had done that so often that the feeling may have been worn out. But his heart *did* give a leap of delight at the girl's beauty. And he said to himself complacently enough, "Gad! here's a stroke of luck!"

He raised his cap, held out his hand, and said, " May I help you up the wall? I'm awfully glad that I was so lucky as to be near enough to hear your call."

Bertha was still faint with her fright, but she rallied with an effort and took the hand extended to her. "How can I thank you?" she said. "If it had not been for you I might be *there* now." She pointed to the dark surface of the dyke and shuddered.

"Please don't say anything more about it. I did nothing more than ease off a couple of cartridges. Here's the hero," Rupert said, patting old Sock. "He *did* risk his life for you. Make friends, Sock. You're not afraid of bulldogs, are you?"

"Oh no," she answered, laughing, "I'm not afraid of bulldogs. It's the bull without the dog that I don't like."

Old Sock looked gravely up in her face, and then gave an extreme token of his favour. He raised his bulk up on his hind legs, placed his muddy paws against her dress, and licked her hands, wagging his stumpy tail the while.

"Down, Sock!" said Rupert. "He'll spoil your frock."

"Oh no," laughed Bertha. "I can't afford to wear anything that will spoil. He's much cleaner than my brothers are."

"Well, I'm glad you've made friends with him," said Rupert. "You know we're to be neighbours. May I effect an introduction? Miss Heron—Mr. Rupert Claybrooke." He held out his hand again, and again Bertha took it. This time she felt her fingers slightly pressed, and reddened as she said, "Oh, I've heard all about you. Mrs. Noddyfield has told everyone in the village of your coming. She's an old friend of yours, isn't she, sir?"

"Well, yes," said Rupert, cursing the old woman's impudence in claiming the equality of position that the term "friend" implied, but not seeing his way to explain matters without seeming arrogant. "But never mind that. What I *do* mind is your base ingratitude. You said you wished to thank me—and now you call me 'sir.'"

"But I think I ought to," Bertha replied. "You know we're only poor folk, and you are a gentleman."

"If you call me 'sir' again," said Rupert, " I'll fetch the bull back."

Such pleasant fooling soon placed the pair on a friendly footing, and they were laughing and chatting freely when they arrived at the marsh end of the loke.

Bertha paused at this point. "Would you mind," said she, "if I went on first, and you followed five minutes after? The village people make so much out of nothing, that there would be all kinds of talk about us to-morrow if we were seen going up together. And that wouldn't be nice either for you or me."

"Well, I do mind," said Rupert, "for it will shorten the chance I have of really making your acquaintance."

"Don't you think you've done that sufficiently already by saving my life?" asked Bertha a little coquettishly.

"Oh, please don't say anything more about that," said Rupert. "Of course, I'll do as you wish. Good night," he added, holding his hand out.

She took it, and again fancied she felt a pressure.

"Do you know," said Rupert, holding her hand, "I love that bull. I'll look him up to-morrow and pour oil on his troubled wounds. If it had not been for him we should not have had half so pleasant a welcome to our new quarters. Should we, Sock?"

Sock wagged his tail and grunted.

"Good night," said Bertha. "If you won't let me thank you aloud, you can't help my being grateful inwardly. And I am. Indeed I am. I do hope you'll be comfortable, but it must seem very strange to you. So lonely, and such a poor place. You'll let me do anything for you I can, won't you?"

"I don't think I shall be lonely *now"* said Rupert, stressing the last word, and again bringing the colour to the girl's cheeks.

She left him after patting Sock on the head and accepting a kiss from the old dog.

"She's a devilish nice little girl," said Rupert, when he had watched her disappear in the darkness. "How the deuce she evolved herself in this out-of-the-way place is a mystery to me."

When the five minutes had elapsed, he sauntered up to "The Castle," produced his ponderous door-key, and let himself in.

"Damn!" he said, as he cracked his head first against the lintel and then against the main baulk of the livingroom. He lit a match, and then a candle, and finally got the lamp alight. Then he flung himself into a chair, and said to himself, "Well, here's a home of my own again; and from what I've seen already I think I'm going to have a really good time in it—or near it," he added thoughtfully. "She's a devilish nice little girl."

There was no blind to the tiny window between the door and the staircase, and the white curtain which had been put up allowed the light from the lamp to stream across the loke, so as to be plainly visible to the Noddyfields in their cottage. Rupert had hardly got his boots off and his slippers on, and laid out some cold provisions sent over from the Limes, when there came a sound of footsteps, a knock at the door, and a deep rolling voice asking, "Is anybardy at hooam?"

"Come in; come in," said Rupert.

The door opened and showed his landlord and landlady on the threshold. Peggie was winking with all her might. Her little thin lips were distended in what was meant for a pleasing smile.

"Well, hare ye be, sir," said old blind Noddy. "My missus 'ouldn't gi'e me noo peace afoor we come round to ax if theer wuz anything as us could dew for ye."

"You see, Maaster Ruput," said Peggie, simpering and winking furiously, "a thote ye must fare straange like, all alooan by yarself, wi' noobardy ta look arter ye, nor dew for ye, nor narthen."

Peggie had spruced her husband up in his best chapelgoing coat and waistcoat. She herself wore her secondbest skirt. The best she only donned when the occasion was of sufficient solemnity to justify a white petticoat beneath the old black silk; a gift of Rupert's mother thirty years past.

"No! I'm getting along capitally, thank you," said Rupert. "But I'm glad you've come in. Won't you sit down and have some supper?"

"Wha' noo, I thanky," said Peggie, simpering more than ever. "We di'n't come for that. That 'ud be nice dewin's, I'm shore! But I wuz worrited ta knoo how yew wuz a-gittin' on. Come yew on, Phillup. Le'ss leeave Maaster Ruput ta his meeat."

"No! Please don't go," said Rupert, and after receiving the amount of pressure that village etiquette demanded, Peggie consented to take what she had come for.

"Doan't gi'e me but a mossel," she said politely. "I doan't fare hongra, a mite."

Rupert set the chairs and produced additional plates and accessories. "Jes' as if he'd been at hooam hare for yares an' yares," as Peggie said with admiration. Philip was led to a seat, and then the meal began.

The blind man's system of feeding was primitive. He disdained the use of a fork, and held his meat steady with his left hand, while he got at it with a knife in his right. He conveyed the morsels to his mouth with his fingers. His bread was mixed with his meat and pickles, and all went to the same place by the same means. The result must have resembled Huck Finn's "barrel of odds and ends," where all the flavours "got swopped around."

Peggie, on the other hand, lay claim to being "city bred," by virtue of having been born within two miles of Odinton, and she fancied it was the correct thing to peck at her food.

"Did Seerah bile this hare beef?" she asked. On being answered in the affirmative she said, "Then it's a pity as she di'n't bile it a bit moor. Tha'ss a'moost raw in the middle. Lor! Look a' the blood a-oozin' out. I'll tell ye what. I'll pop it in my copper for ye ta-morrer if ye like."

"Hode yar row an' ate yar wittles," said old Noddy, who was enjoying himself. "Tha'ss bewtiful! Tha'ss got the goodness in't. Ta bain't all bu'nt up like yar cookin'."

"To tell you the truth," said Rupert, "I like my meat underdone."

"Soo dew I," murmured Noddy, with his mouth full. "But a can't orfen git it."

"But that can't be whoolsome," persisted the little old woman, who had thoughts of a surreptitious slice or two.

But she was fated to be disappointed, and having professed no appetite, and being taken at her word (owing to Rupert's ignorance of country " serciety " manners), she was forced to leave it to her husband to represent "Ozier Cottage" worthily; which he did to a marvel.

"Yew'll escewse me," he said at the second helping, "but I likes my meat cut thick. Suthin' ta chew at soo's yew can feeal yew ha' got some'at atween yar teeth. Not little slithery shaavin's."

"Ah! you're like Tennyson and the mutton," said Rupert, laughing, as he carved an inch slab and put it on the old man's outstretched plate.

"Aah! Tha'ss moor like it," said Noddy, wiring in afresh. "I doan't fare ta knoo the naame, but in my oopinyeron the gennleman's right."

When the meal was over, Rupert passed his pouch, and the men lit up.

"That might be convaynient," said Philip, puffing hard to get a fair start on his pipe, "if a toold ye how we fare ta manage about hare. Theer's a poost ivery daay esceptin' Sundays. That come about ten in the moarnin' an' goo out about half arter tew in the arternewn. The poost box is a holler slit in the gre't ellum what stand agin the chutchyud gaate."

"An' the butcher come for orders o' Wensdays," broke in Peggie, "an' bring the meeat o' Friday arternewns. Yew want ta mind he doan't bring moor 'an what yew oorder, as he fare wery fond o' dewin'. I allust maake him taake a knife an' cut a bit off in the cart if ta come ta moor 'an half-a-crown. I allust baake of a Friday, like other folk. An' I'll cook yar bit o' meeat for ye willin' an' welcome."

"I don't think I shall have to trouble you," said Rupert, to her chagrin, "but it's very kind of you to offer."

"Then about waashin'," continued Peggie. "I doan't s'pooz as yew'll hev that done at hooam. Now *I* waash ivery foortnight of a Monday, when my husband waash hisself an' chaange his shut. An' I'll dew whaat yew ha' got, willin' an' welcome, an' oan't hu't ye with my chaarge. That yew maay deepend. I ha' done yar sister's waash iver since she come ta live at St. Meery's, soo that 'ull tell ye as I can dew it prarper."

"Thank you. That will suit me very well," answered Rupert, a trifle weary of the conversation.

"Then," said Noddy, "I doan't knoo if yew be chutch or chapel. *I* allust goo to chapel on a Sunday, moornin', arternewn, an' evenin', an' o' Wensday nights. But the missus an' Bartie goos ta chutch. The missus plaay the ammonium, an' Bartie he ha' fixed up a some'at ta blow the bellers. Chutch is at elaven, an' tha'ss hare one Sunday, an' at Tarlham Chutch the next."

"I never go to either," said Rupert blandly. "My temper is not strong enough to stand it."

"Aah, tha'ss what I saay about chutch."

"Aah, tha'ss what I saay about chapel," said Noddy and Peggie respectively and simultaneously.

"Well, we won't have a theological discussion," said Rupert, laughing. "As long as people do as they like, and let me do as I like, I don't mind."

"A hoop yew bain't a Carthlic, or a Jew," said Noddy, to whom the terms were synonymous. "I must saay as in my opinyeron the Prim'tive Meth'dises git as nare right as can be."

"Narnsense," said Peggy.

"No, no," answered Rupert, replying to Philip's question, "it would be difficult for me to explain to you exactly what I am."

"But whativer'll yew saay if the paarson call on ye, as he's sartin ta dew," said Peggie, holding up her hands in expostulation. "An' yew—whew used ta plaay the ammonium sa bewtiful at Odinton Schewl! I hooped yew might ha' took a sarvice now an' agin."

"I've touched nothing but the piano for years," replied Rupert. "And pray don't let the parson call if you can possibly help it. Tell him I'm a Buddhist, or whatever you like."

"Well I niver," said Peggie, shocked, but not yet free from the glamour of the name of Claybrooke. Old Philip heard the term and pondered over it, but failed to come to any comprehension of its meaning.

Rupert puzzled his guests still more (perhaps not altogether unintentionally) by opening his piano and singing, "There is a green hill far away," "Thus saith the Lord," and "But who may abide," and as a finish the leading part of the Evening Hymn from *Hansel and Gretel.*

"I'll tell ye what," said Philip to his wife, as they walked the short distance home. "I rackon he's a Carthlic, an' doan't like ta saay soo."

Peggie shook her head and primmed her lips suspiciously. "I doan't knoo what ta maake on't," she said. "Whativer dew Miss Loora think? An' what 'ud his pore mother ha' said if she'd ha' heerd him?"

Rupert had said nothing of his adventure on the marsh. But he had laid the foundation for a scandal on the first evening of his arrival. Nevertheless he went to bed in sweet unconsciousness, and slept the sleep of peace of mind and placid hopefulness.

HIS NEW LIFE THE sweet country air, breathing through the open window, brought light and refreshing slumber to Rupert's still jaded nerves. He woke at daybreak feeling a health that he had not known for years. He rose at once, with none of the inclination for lazing in bed that accompanies the first awakening of a townsman. The morning was grey, and the sun only just hinting his advent over the hills of Duckingham, right across the marshes to the north-east. Rupert got his gun, filled his pockets with cartridges, and stepped out into the loke, down to the public way along the wall of the Fleet Dyke. Old Sock trotted at his heels, sniffing up the scent of the earth joyously. He had been somewhat upset on the previous evening by being banished to the bedroom, but the sight of the gun, and the idea of an early bath in the dykes, dispelled all clouds of mortified rancour he may have felt.

Even the early-rising country was still asleep. The birds were chirping muted notes within the thick cover of the hedges, and their subdued twittering emphasised the quiet and peace of the hour of dawn of an August day.

There was a heavy mist rolling along the marshes before a north-east breeze. But above this the streaks of amethyst and yellow to windward, against a grey-blue skyline, foretold a cloudless sunrise that would soon dissipate the quivering film of the fens.

Sport was brisk for once. A couple of snipe, a mallard, a smea, and three water-hens gave a promise for the shooting qualities of the marshes that was hardly justified. By the time that Rupert had got to the embankment the sun was up and the water-fowl dispersed. When he turned his steps homeward a greater spirit than that of sport was at work, gathering its allies, the wildness, mystery, and beautiful solemnity of the lonely marshes, to influence his nature.

In spite of his inexorable logic, he had the sensitive temperament of an artist, and the majestic calm of the hour and place had more power to sway his thoughts, his credence, his *vxq* (that undefinable something that a materialist can only explain by heredity, and then to no one's satisfaction but his own), and even, indirectly, his action, than all the syllogistic deductions of the exact sciences. He could not accept a Divine Spirit as proven. All the arguments were against the existence of an active intelligence, personally directing the affairs of the universe. Asked if he believed in "God," he would at this time have answered that he did not understand what was meant by so vague a term. He could only define God as the answer to the question "why?"—the universal reason of all things. If this were what was meant, he believed in its existence; but that it was, as yet, a riddle unsolved.

But here by the Fleet, with the golden sun rising into sight and waking the breeze to rustle the dyke reeds, driving off the damp fog, lighting up the dewdrops upon the thistle bloom till they flashed and quivered with glittering radiance, calling the pigeons to cry to their mates that it was time to go to the feeding-grounds, bidding the larks rise and soar till the marsh was as full of rippling song as of light; here, where the reflection of the sky in the dykes gave a more vivid blue minute by minute, and the springing warmth called out the moist odour from the meadowsweet and unfurled the yellow petals of awakening lilies; here there seemed some mystic aura round and about the lovely loneliness that was inexplicable by any rules of reason, any analysis of test-tubes, or discovery of dissecting knife—something that was not of man, and that filled his heart with reverence and devotion to the "unknown God."

He stood some minutes in an aesthetic ecstasy which was only broken by a cheery sound from landwards. "Ha hao, ha hao, ha hao," sang Bob Heron the cowman, calling up Farmer Reed's cows for the morning milking. Rupert saw the placid animals pass slowly on to the wall and through the gate which their attendant held open. Their great udders sagged pendulously, and every now and then a drop of milk fell from their repletion.

The moment of the spirits of the marsh had passed, but a new graft had been made on the stock of Rupert's consciousness. And it would depend both upon the culture and the climatic fortuities, or to speak without the veil of metaphor, upon the character of Rupert's temperament and fortunes, whether it would bring forth fruit, and of what quality.

He hurried to catch up the herdsman. "Good morning," he said pleasantly to Bob, as he ranged alongside.

"Moarnin'," was the rather sullen answer. "You be a straanger in these parts. "

"I've just come to live in one of Mr. Noddyfield's cottages," Rupert explained.

"Then a rackon yew be our neighbour," said Bob more civilly, "bain't ye?"

"I'm afraid I don't know who you are," said Rupert, smiling, "so I can't say."

"My naame's Bob," answered the youth in a tone of surprise.

"Yes. But Bob what?" asked Rupert, repressing an inclination to laugh.

"Noo; Bob Heron," replied Bob naively. "The Wattses live t'other eend o' the willage, an' warks for Billy Reed. I warks for Bob Reed."

"Yes. You're right, then," said Rupert. "I am your neighbour."

"Well, Mr. Claybrooke, my sister saay as yew saaved har from Jimmy Taxon's bull larse night, an' yew whoolly lar him ha'e't wi' yar gun. Ha! ha! ha! Sarve the right. I hoop as yew oan't ha'e ta paay foor't. Old Deeapun he pratty nigh kilt one larse yare, an' he niver had ta paay narthen. Noo moor a 'ouldn't if I wuz yew. None of us oan't puff, yew maay depend."

"I'm not afraid of that," answered Rupert. "The bull was shot in the public way, in defence of human life. No action for damages would lie."

"Ole Jimmy 'ould if he got the chance," grinned Bob. "But, Lor', yew doan't waant ta pay noo regard ta him."

"I hope your sister is none the worse for her fright this morning," said Rupert.

"She fared right as ninepence larse night," Bob answered. "I hain't seed har this moarnin'; I shorn't see har till brekkust."

"She's not an early riser, then," said Rupert, for the sake of saying something.

"Not if she can't help it she bain't," Bob replied. "A gre't laazy wench I calls her."

By this time the two had reached "The Castle," and Bob went on to the farm, while Rupert went in.

The world went very well with him that morning. "I must go about and make acquaintances after breakfast," he said to himself. "I'm sure there's lots of copy to be got. I may as well begin with the Herons."

Persuading himself that it was for literary purposes only that he desired to cultivate a better acquaintance with the family next door, he went round to see if he could find any of them in the garden, a piece of land which was well overlooked by Peggie's scullery window, the latter having been built out beyond the line of the houses for the express purpose of affording the landlady a peep-hole into her neighbours' and tenants' affairs.

Old Heron had a workshop and a cowshed in his garden adjoining the loke, and from the former of these came the sound of a voice, crooning in unmelodious intervals, accompanied by intermittent hammerings.

Rupert remembered that he wanted to borrow a hammer. He pushed open the gate of the cartway leading to his neighbour's garden, and swinging round to the left, found himself against the open door of the workshop.

In the midst of frowsy paint-pots, rotten old pieces of timber trimmed and untrimmed, some pig-potatoes, a broken wheelbarrow, rusty tools of all kinds, shavings innumerable and filth indescribable, a lad of seventeen stood at a small space he had cleared on the carpenter's bench. Before him lay a quantity of empty cartridge-cases. Beside these were a number of new caps, some wads, a flask of powder, and a bag of shot. In his hand was a round piece of stick, cut to fit the empty cases, and close by lay a slim bit of steel, like an ice-pick. Every now and again he took up an empty case, placed the discharged cap over a small hole in the bench, applied the steel to the inside detonating iron of the cap, and with a tap of the hammer knocked the exploded cap into the hollow beneath. He then carefully recovered the detonating iron, inserted it in the case, pressed in a live cap, placed the case over the rounded stick, stood this upright on the bench (cap uppermost), and with another tap of the hammer drove the cap into place. The cartridge was now ready for reloading.

Interested in this primitive but effective method of recapping, Rupert stood silent for a space. Young Gilbert (for it was the third son who was thus busily engaged) was too occupied, and was making too much noise in endeavouring to sing a totally unprintable song concerning a cobbler, a sailor, and the sailor's wife, to notice the strange footsteps. He was a merry-looking lad of about five feet eight inches; sturdy and wiry. His eyes were those of a sportsman, but were alternately keen and unintelligent; an alternation frequently seen in Norfolk, where there is so much shrewdness associated with so much simplicity and ignorance. The face was moulded roughly on the same lines as Bertha's, but was coarse and entirely lacking in the refinement and purity suggested by the girl's features. Yet there were possibilities in it which made the observer think that there was material for something more than the average rough brutality of the marshlands. The dark eyebrows over blue eyes were typical of the mixture of Danish and Scandinavian blood found about the marshes; and even a casual inspection of face, ears, and neck showed that Gilbert was no fanatical advocate for soap and water.

Rupert guessed the way to the boy's heart would be through guns and gunning. He had his double-barrel under his arm, and knew that a strange fowling-piece serves as a subject for conversation and an object of interest everywhere where two or three are gathered together in the name of sport.

"Ahem!" he preluded. "Good morning," he said, when the lad looked round with a start at his cough. The shyness of hobbedehoyhood extends to manhood in the case of village males. Gilbert was no exception to this rule, and, moreover, he instinctively regarded everyone with the appearance of a gentleman in the light of an enemy, likely to become unpleasantly inquisitive and inconsiderate in the matter of poaching.

"Moarnin'," he answered sullenly. "D'ye waant anythin'?"

"I was going to ask you to lend me a hammer," said Rupert. "But that can wait. I see you are loading up some cartridges, and expect you are as fond of a gun as I am. If you've nothing better to do, I should be much obliged if you would come on the marshes with me and show me where I may shoot. I shall be glad to lend you my gun if you'd like to try it; and I've got plenty of cartridges."

"I hain't got noo licence," said Gilbert suspiciously.

"But that doesn't matter here, does it?" asked Rupert, laughing. "There's no one about on the marshes, and I don't care a hang if you've got a licence or not. You know I'm your neighbour. And two sporting neighbours ought to make friends."

Now Gilbert had promised to devote the morning to getting up the crop of early potatoes in old Peggie's garden. But the sight of the admirable breechloader, together with an inherited dislike to work of all kinds, at once destroyed any lingering intention he may have had of keeping his promise.

"Wha', be yew Mr. Claybrooke?" he asked eagerly. "Bartha ha' toold us about yew larse night. If yew'll come along o' me I'll just tell faa'er as I'm a-gooin'."

Rupert followed the boy to the back door of the Herons' dwelling. It was open. The room was furnished with no unnecessary splendour. It contained a plain deal table, four Windsor chairs, and a wooden armchair. A Dutch clock ticked on the wall. Bertha was not present. But in the armchair, against the fire (for the fire was kept going on the hottest summer day), an old man sat crouching. His left trouser leg was turned up to the knee, and he was slowly rubbing some sticky, yellow unguent into his leg. He had suffered with a bad ankle for years. His stick was ready to his hand when he should rise, for he walked with difficulty. The likeness was strong between him and his boy. If anything, the old man's hair, beard, and skin gave an impression that he was the owner of more dirt than even his son could claim. Unwashed breakfast-things stood about the table. Jam-pots appeared to do duty largely as cups and saucers. A reek of cooked bloaters and shag made the atmosphere of the room rich and rare.

"Faa'er," said Gilbert, "hare be Mr. Claybrooke. He waant me ta goo a-shewtin' along o' him, an' he's a-gooin' ta lind me his gun. Dee yew look ar it. Bain't it a bewty!"

"Booy," replied the old man, apparently addressing the fire, "wharabout ole Peggie's taters? Yew toold har yew'd ger 'em up this moarnin'."

"I'll make that all right, Mr. Heron," said Rupert. "Tell her he's with me. She won't mind then."

At the sound of Rupert's voice, the door leading from the kitchen to the staircase opened, and Bertha appeared, radiant in her fresh beauty. She seemed to light up the whole dingy room.

"Good morning," she said cheerfully to Rupert, giving him her hand, which was taken and necessarily pressed; a performance which heightened her colour and increased her beauty.

"Why, Gilbert!" she cried. "Fancy bringing Mr. Claybrooke into this dirty hole! I'm ashamed you should see it like this," she added to Rupert. "But Bob hasn't been home to breakfast yet, and I can't clear up till then. Gilbert and Jack will make such a mess."

"Tha'ss right! Put it down to us," said Gilbert. "Ivery bardy knoo as it's yar laaziness. An' that ole "(he nodded his head at his father) "maake moor muck 'an all on us. Slobberin' ole warmin'!"

"I'm sure there's nothing to be ashamed of," replied Rupert. "You don't feel any the worse for your adventure, I hope?" He spoke almost tenderly.

"Not a bit, thank you, and thanks *to* you," said Bertha. "Father, have you thanked Mr. Claybrooke yet for saving my life last night?"

"Tha'ss a nice thing la goo a-shewtin' o' folk's bulls," grunted the old man. "Ha'e ye got any bocca?" he asked, for the first time showing a lively interest.

Rupert jumped at the chance of winning the old fellow's favour. He pulled out his pouch of goldflake. "Help yourself," he said. "I've plenty more indoors."

"Thanky, sir. Yew're a gennleman," said old Heron, carefully emptying the pouch. "Aah! That dew smell somethin' fine, that dew! Tha'ss whoolly a good bit o' bocca. That that be!"

"Hare! Gie's a bit," said Gilbert, making a grab at his father's hand, as he was slowly stowing his acquisition away in a brass tobacco-box.

"Yew doan't waant none o' this hare," retorted the old man. "Our maaster saay he ha' got planty moor. Yew waant ta ax him."

Bertha's lips were opened to expostulate, but she caught a glance from Rupert and remained silent.

"Come on," said Gilbert. "Tha'ss noo good paayin' noo regard ta him. He fare half sorft, an' tha'ss a fack!"

Old Heron paid no attention to his son's compliments, but smoked placidly on. Rupert and Bertha looked at each other, their eyes telling their mutual desire to remain together. "Don't think the worse of me," hers said appealingly. "As if I could," his answered. "I'm so sorry for you when I see what you have to put up with."

"Come on," said young Gilbert again from outside, where he was pointing the gun which Rupert had surrendered to him at imaginary marks. "I knoo wheer theer's narely allust a snipe or tew."

With a sigh and a last glance at Bertha, Rupert followed him out.

Two hours sufficed for a tour round the level of marsh on which, according to Gilbert, it was safe to shoot. "Tha'ss ole Gully Barkland's," he explained. "An' all yew ha' got ta dew is ta paay for a pint or tew for him now an' ag'in. "

A couple of snipe formed the meagre bag. Gilbert handed them to Rupert, saying, "Hare, dee yew taake 'em. I doan't care a mite for 'em. Bartha'd oony bile 'em, an' faa'er hev the brooath!"

To prevent the iniquity of boiling

snipe Rupert took them, but insisted on giving the smea and water-hens he had shot in the early morning in exchange. He had entirely succeeded in winning the boy's heart, and Gilbert offered to go with him whenever he wished.

On the way up the loke, a shrill, screaming noise was heard, which became articulate as the sportsmen advanced.

"Geelbut! Geelbut! Geeeeeel-baaaaaart! Drat the booy! Hare be all my 'arly taters a-sp'ilin' in the land, an' if theer come a raain they'll all git theer second growth. Young warmin'. Wheeriver can he ha' got tew, Bartha?"

Bertha's voice was heard in explanation, and old Peggie retired mumbling. "Phillup," she was heard to say, "hare be Maaster Ruput been an' took young Gilbut down ta ma'sh when he ote ta be foorkin' my 'arly taters. Yew'll ha'e ta speeak tew'm about it."

"Speak tew'm yarself," said Noddy. "Yar tongue's long enow, I reckon."

"An' soo a will," said Peggie. "An' wha'ss moor, I'll speeak ta Miss Loora if he interfare like that. I can't dew wi't. "

Her clicking syllables grew fainter as she retired round her scullery window.

"Hark a' th'ole "said Gilbert, chuckling. "Doan't she whoolly mob!"

He had accepted the offer of "a pint," and after effecting the exchange of the birds the two went on up the Turlham Road in the direction of the "Grey Mare. " Old Peggie's cottage stood at the corner of the road, and as they passed the old woman was weeding in her front garden.

"Good mooarnin', Maaster Ruput," said she. "An' how are yew? Bewtiful mooarnin' ta be shore. What! Hev yew been a-hevin' of a shewt? A hoop yew've had good spoort."

The treacherous old hag looked up and simpered.

"Hum-m-m," muttered Rupert, after he had returned her greeting. "Rather a *volte-face.* I'm afraid that old woman is a humbug."

The "Grey Mare" kitchen was full. Old Gully Barkland and Deeap-un Reed represented the marshmen, Jack Heron the poaching interest, Neetch Jinnis the fishermen, and Hoppety Sam the loafers. The labourers were greater in numbers, but less in interest. Pontifex, Mrs. Pontifex, and Edith Norton were respectively the host, the hostess, and the hostess's daughter by a former irregular connection.

Old Gully and Deeap-un were wizened grey-headed veterans, bent with lumbago and ague, contracted at "flighting" time on cold, wet, winter nights. Neetch Jinnis was a bluff, hearty, russet-faced man, who said little, but drank a great deal. He had the reputation of a Don Juan in the village, and deserved it. Hoppety got his nickname from the halting action which his club feet entailed. It was only necessary to see Pontifex and his wife to know that the name of the inn was the better horse. The man's little meagre figure was surmounted by a small face in the midst of bushy black whiskers and beard. He looked like a wren in an ivy bush. His wife would have made three of him. Her buxom maturity was round and rubicund. She seemed the ideal of an honest, straightforward, kind-hearted countrywoman. The last epithet she deserved, for she did more good actions than many a more moral woman. Edith was flower-like in her freshness—a typical innocent, pure country beauty to look at.

Rupert greeted the assembled company, and Gilbert whispered information concerning them in his ear— information which was more accurate than complimentary.

"I'm right glad ta see ye, sir," said Mrs. Pontifex, when she had learnt the identity of her new customer. "What can I git for yew?"

"I see our maaster out with his gun this mooarnin'," said Deeap-un, "an' I saay ta myself, I saay, 'Aah, he'll be a-comin' up ta the Meer at dinner-time ta paay his futtin'.'"

A chuckle of approbation greeted this hint.

Rupert ordered drinks for the crowd. "Yew're a gennleman, sir," was the audible comment.

"Yew'll be welcome ta shewt oover my level whiniver ye like, sir," said Gully. "An' I wish ye luck."

"Saame hare," said Deeap-un. "I'll show ye my ma'shes. Theer's a nice lot o' pa'tridges a-comin' on, an' tha'ss the best spot for snipe an' fowl on the whool Chetbridge level. But that maan's bain't noo good at all." He pointed derisively at Gully.

"He fare tew greedy, he dew," continued Deeap-un, chuckling. "He shewt the young things afoor they ha' got wings. He can't hit 'em flyin'."

"Blust! noo! I bain't noo shot," said Gully, who shared with Deeap-un the honour of being the best shot for miles round. "I especk our maaster'll whoolly larn us the waay ta shewt."

"Yew fare lucka," whispered Gilbert. "Tha'ss right what he saay. His level is the best, but ta bain't iverybardy as he let goo on. Will ye taake me with ye sometimes?"

Reassured as to this, the boy subsided quietly into a corner. He was shy with adults, even of his own station, but though he spoke little in their company, not a word or action of theirs escaped him. After a night's "settin'-in" (a local name for a beer orgie) he could repeat what each person in the room had said and done. He would have made an admirable reporter.

When the beer had been brought in the mugs were filled. All the villagers raised their drink solemnly to their lips, and, looking at Rupert, said, "My bes' respecks." Then they drank.

"Well, sir," said Mrs. Pont (as she was usually called by those who were not sufficiently intimate to call her "Melia"), wiping the porter from her mouth with her apron, "an' how dee yew like these parts?"

"Oh, very much, thank you," said Rupert.

"Tha'ss caapital!" said Gully. "We're pore, but jolly."

"Aah!" said Hoppety, "but we ha'e ta wark some hud! We can't goo about injyin' of ourselves like gennlemen."

"Wark!" sniggered Gully. "I'll sweer the oony wark as yew iver dew is washin' out yar inside! Tha'ss a mooartal pity as yew can't dew as much for yar faace."

"Wha' dee yew knoo about it?" asked Hoppety sullenly. "Look arter yar owan stock, an' let mine be."

"Yew hain't got none, bor," said Deeap-un, chuckling. "But if they had whaat they used ta hev at Chetbridge when I wuz a booy, yew'd git stocks enow, an' tha'ss a fack!"

"Come, come," said Mrs. Pont, who had a partiality for Hoppety, second only to her affection for Neetch Jinnis, and who found traits in each which reminded her of the late lamented Juicy Joe. "Leeast said sunest minded, an' a long tongue maake a sore skull."

"Lor, Melia," said Hoppety, "I doan't paay noo regard ta that ole He's innercent, he is. Pore ole"

"Well, I must be a-gooin'," said Gully.

"What!" cried Deeap-un, "an' leeave all that bare! Set ye down. We'll maake a settin'-in on't,"

But first one, and then the other had to go, and, last of all, Hoppety and Neetch (having drained the last drop) took their departure, and left Rupert with the landlady and her daughter. He stayed with the intention of having a chat with the hostess, to whom he had taken a liking. He was sorry when she left him to go and see about the dinner. Edith remained, and, on her mother's departure, rose and took a seat close beside Rupert.

"Tha'ss whoolly hot," she said, smiling up in his face.

"Lovely weather," replied Rupert, not feeling quite at ease, and not in the least knowing what to talk about. "Won't you have some more stout?" he asked, by way of saying something.

Now in Frogsthorpe the offer of a glass of stout by a man to a woman has a peculiar significance.

"Thanky," answered the girl. "This weather maake ye somethin' dry, doan't it?"

She went out, and returned with a glass of the porter that is called stout in Norfolk hedge ale-houses.

"That maake ye waant ta set unner the hidge, doan't it?" she said, touching his hand. "Lor'! How sorft yar skin fare!"

He laughed, and touched her cheek. "Not so soft as yours," he said.

"I heerd about yar resky o' Bartha Heron," said Edith. "I rackon yew think a sight o' har, doan't ye?"

"I hardly know her," said Rupert disingenuously. "I only sent the bull off, and it was too dark to see clearly."

"I can't dew wi' har," said the girl. "She fare tew consayted. She niver come up hare for a glass o' stout, nor narthen."

"Well, that's her loss, isn't it?" said Rupert. "But perhaps there's more attraction for a man than for a woman where you are."

"Git along wi' yar narnsense," said Edith, in a state of high delight. "I'll tell ye what! If ye like ta come up hare arter dark, I'll goo for a walk along o' ye."

"You're awfully kind," Rupert replied. "If I possibly can I will. But I'm not sure if I shall have time."

H

"Wha yar time's yar owan, bain'tit?" asked Edith. "I've got some work to do. Writing, you know," said Rupert.

"Wha', dee yew write taales an' sech like?" said the girl, laughing.

(The idea of anyone making a living out of story writing always aroused amusement in the village.)

"Yes, that's my work," he answered, with the want of reticence of a beginner.

There is no profession to which the tyros vaunt their adherence so much as to that of letters. It is possible to sit in the company of a barrister, enjoying the recent delivery of his first brief, without having the contents of that brief thrust down one's throat at every turn of the conversation; or to lunch with a doctor on the day of his first case without hearing all the symptoms and their treatment at his hands. But the young author who has just got his first bit of stuff taken by some accommodating publication (that has not the faintest intention of paying him for it) can talk of nothing but "copy," and, if he gets the chance, will anticipate the publication of his tale (or whatever it is that he has got accepted) by reading or recounting from memory the wonderful work, to anyone who is so unwary as to mention books or writing in his presence. Rupert only followed established precedent in telling an ignorant country-girl, whom it could neither concern nor interest, that he made his living by his pen. He also had authority for not disclosing what a very precarious living it was as yet.

Bertha looked upon him as something bizarre. He rose in favour with her.

"Well," she pleaded, "yew doan't waant ta dew noo wark ta-night."

"Would you really like me to come?" said Rupert, unaware of the small amount of speech necessary in the country to prelude amorous action.

He was taken aback to find a soft pair of arms flung round his neck and a pair of rosy lips pressed to his. Mere rudimentary politeness required that the kiss should be returned.

"Theer!" said Edith, panting. "Now ye knoo a should, doan't ye?"

"But will your mother let you go?" he asked, still sufficiently master of himself to endeavour to escape the invitation.

"Wha she'd like ta goo harself," said Edith; "but I axed ye fust, di'n't I?"

There was no way out of it but one. Rupert took it.

"All right," he said, "111 come. What time?"

"Sune's it's dark," replied Edith. "Goo'-bye." She held up her mouth again. Mortal flesh and blood could not resist. Rupert kissed her again. "Good-bye," he said, and went out.

"Well I'm hanged!" he said to himself. "I must get out of it somehow. What a little minx it is! And what an extraordinary family, if she's right about her mother. And she ought to know. My search for copy will land me somewhere if I'm not careful. Blow the thing!"

Revulsion had set in, and he went home to his midday meal in a state of self-disgust. But marsh air and exercise would not be denied. He fed mightily, and his foreboding left him.

VI

"FAMA VOLAT" APARCEL of books had come down for review by the morning post, and it was Rupert's intention to get through two or three of them during the day. But as soon as he had cleared the table, lit his pipe, and settled down to read, Deep-un appeared on his way down to "ma'sh" to inspect the stock under his charge, and offered to show the whereabouts and extent of his level. This lay beyond Gully's. And the peregrination of it was slow. For the old man loved to tell tales of his sporting adventures, and stopped at the scene of each, while he related the details with elaborate particularity. It was tea-time when the return journey had been negotiated, and by the time the solid country meal had been got through with, the sun was glowing a subdued amber, and the shadows of the trees stretched long athwart the land.

Rupert settled himself comfortably, and proceeded to consider what course he should pursue with regard to the promise he had made the fair Edith of becoming her escort in the lonely country lanes, when darkness had added to their solitude.

In his younger days he would, perhaps, have had little hesitation in falling in with the code of morality accepted in the village. For the girl was winsome, and was clearly no innocent country maiden whose heart might be broken, or reputation tarnished, by the dangerous nature of the proposed excursion. But he was no longer a boy. The aimless wantonness of youth was passed. Self-respect made him reluctant to keep the appointment. Although he had ridden his passions with too loose a rein, he had never done wrong to any woman. And it had been he, rather than the objects of his boyish fancies, who had been the sufferer from them. Had Edith bided her time, and had there been no Bertha Heron, he might possibly have been won by persistent subtle cajolings. Had she delayed the boldness of her attack till such a time as would have enabled her to push it home, she might have carried the post by storm. But the opportunity given him for reflection, after she had disclosed her plan of campaign, enabled him to decline to be drawn out into the open, and to strengthen his position against future assault.

Before his first pipe was smoked out, her chance was gone, never to return. With an emphatic "No! I'm d d if I do!" Rupert arranged a pile of books on the table beside him, tore a number of strips of paper as markers of quotable passages, sharpened his pencil, opened his notebook, and settled down to a night's work.

But the result of an insult to her beauty by neglect is the same in a rustic lass as in a classical goddess. Inasmuch as he had thwarted her by refusing to compromise himself, she determined to report that he had made overtures to her which had been repulsed.

"'Strew's Gord," she said to herself, "if he doan't prewve as he cou'n't help it, I'll put it about as he axed me ta set unner the hidge with him, an' a 'ouldn't. If he di'n't meean narthen, what did he paay for that glass o' stout for arter the others had gorn? I doan't knoo the meeanin' o't, an' tha'ss a fack. But I bain't a-gooin' ta hev noobardy asultin' o' me like that, even if he be a gennleman. A pratty gennleman, livin' in a mucky ole shud like that!"

In deciding on his future line of conduct to the girl, Rupert made the fatal mistake of forgetting that, simple as the Norfolk villagers are in all that does not appertain to their daily life, in matters plainly human, and intelligible to them by use and habit, they are both shrewd and suspicious. They are so accustomed to lies and deceit that overwhelming proofs are necessary to convince them that no injury or slight is intended to them when they have fancied something of the kind is meant. The very worst method of persuading them is to overact ingenuousness. And Rupert's scheme of explanation was radically hyperhistrionic.

He went up to the "Grey Mare" in the morning expressly to put matters on a satisfactory footing with the girl. Edith saw him approaching, and persuaded her mother to let her have him to herself. She tripped into the kitchen as he entered.

"Well, yew sarved me a pratty trick!" she cried. "I gart my hat on, an' wuz all riddy a-waaitin' for ye. An' then yew niver tamed up. Wha'ss the meeanin' on't?"

"My dear little girl," said Rupert, "the fact is that it will never do for you and me to go out together. It would only lead to unhappiness for both of us. You are a nice and pretty girl, and I don't want to have any ill done to you on my conscience. I'm sure you know what I mean. And I'm sure, too, that you only asked me to go for a walk with you because you pitied my loneliness, and wished to be kind to a stranger. And I like you, and thank you for it. But I should be a blackguard if I took advantage of your kindness."

Now this was altogether too clever; the fear lest her honour should come to harm at his hands too obviously assumed.

"I'm shore I doan't want yew if yew doan't want me," she said a little tearfully. For both her inclination and her pride had received a check.

"Please don't think that," said Rupert. "I'm only thinking of what's best for you. Forgive me, and have a glass of stout to show you do."

She had the stout, but drank it with an inward reservation.

That evening, when the kitchen was full, the story of how the "furriner" had wooed Edith, and been repulsed, was told and told again with infinite gusto. It was considered so dainty a tit-bit that it was all over the village the next day. No one thought it necessary to tell him of the rumour. Why should they? It was not deemed to reflect upon him seriously in any way. But its pith lay in the failure of a stranger "gennleman" to secure favours of a daughter of the soil. It increased the feeling of superiority over all "furriners," which is a pleasing attribute of every true son of the marshes. Even had the story been disgraceful in village opinion, it would have been quite foreign to village etiquette to give its subject a chance of refuting it, and so do away with an admirable topic of humorous conversation in a place where such topics are scarce.

So Rupert continued to pass his days in shooting, reviewing, and copy hunting amongst his new acquaintance, in a state of unconsciousness of what was being said behind his back. Had he been cognisant of the rumour, it would have troubled him little, but for one thing.

Among the first to hear of it was Bertha Heron. Young Gilbert came chuckling home from the "Grey Mare" on the night that saw the birth of the story, and gave one of his accurate reports to his sister, embellishing it with notes, critical and explanatory.

Bertha had been born and reared at Duckingham, a village on the other side of the marshes much frequented by summer visitors, who drive over from Herringhaven to see Duckingham Lake, one of the loveliest of the meres of East Anglia. The inhabitants of Duckingham are of a much higher civilisation than the marshmen, and are blessed with a school which is one of those called voluntary, and conducted on old-fashioned lines. It is not a nursery of rudeness and irreverence after the manner of the Board Schools. In Bertha's time the mistress was a Miss Fathom, a lady who taught the children the rules of honour and fairness, subjects which are not deemed worthy of a place in the national curriculum. Bertha's naturally sweet disposition and keen intelligence throve in the kindly soil of her surroundings. She necessarily attracted the notice of her mistress, and obtained a share of attention which was perhaps more than in fair proportion. From pupil she became assistant teacher, and thus came into still closer contact with Miss Fathom, whose interest grew into an affectionate friendship as the girl budded into bloom. At the age of seventeen she obtained a position as nursery governess at Richmond. Once again fortune favoured her. For her employers were people of small means, but considerable culture. They took a fancy to their nursery governess, and soon began to treat her as one of the family. Sir Austin Feverel was of the opinion that woman will be the last thing civilised by man. But in writing this he may be presumed to have referred to the passions and instincts of women. Not to their capacity for acquiring the habits and formalities of culture. For in these respects, women, far easier than men, will rise above their station if chance favour them. Thus, by the fall of circumstance, Bertha had come to have the gentle ways, elevated thoughts, and delicacy of taste that combined with her beauty to make her worthy of the love of any man. During her absence her mother, father, and brothers moved from Duckingham to Frogsthorpe.

Whatever refinement there was in the Heron family was centred in Bertha. The boys were rough, uncouth, and uncleanly in person, and they embraced the worst characteristics of the marsh people with avidity. Gilbert was the only one that seemed to possess even the possibilities of improvement. He, being the youngest, had fallen under his sister's sway before she left home more than his brothers had done. But during the time she was away he had retrograded greatly, and, unless chance once more threw him under her influence, there was little likelihood of his emerging from the state of brutishness into which the grossness of the example of the marsh people had plunged him. All three boys were children of Heron's old age, and when the removal to Frogsthorpe was effected, the father was too old and feeble to exercise any salutary influence over them. The mother was too careless to concern herself in the matter. A sound thrashing every day of the week, and twice on Sundays, might have saved them from becoming what they were. But the old man had neither the strength nor the energy to administer this. He rather fell in with the more degraded life, and had become as bad as his sons, or worse.

Bertha's consistent progress up the ladder of civilisation received a check at her mother's death. The news of this, and of her father's helplessness (which came upon him after a stroke of apoplexy), constrained her as a matter of duty to give up her situation and return to Norfolk to tend her father in his weakness.

She found things worse even than she feared. Her brothers treated her with insolence and ingratitude, and, in the face of the hard and dirty work she did for them, they cast it in her teeth that she was living "like a laady" at their expense.

Two years' endurement of the Frogsthorpe life had told upon her, and in place of the cheerful brightness which had once been her prevailing expression, there was too often the shadow of care and misery upon her features.

For two years she had not been the recipient of a word of courtesy. For two years no man had raised his hat to her. (For a grin and a patronising nod is the salutation of Frogsthorpe males for the females of their species.) For two years she had seen nothing in the village resembling a gentleman. The coarse wooing to which she had been subjected in the early days of her return home so disgusted her that, finding the public road was no protection to her, she rarely left the immediate precincts of the cottage and garden.

Love of man had never come to her yet.

It was not a matter for surprise that her very soul leapt up at the meeting with Rupert, and that hopes and fears chased through her when she recognised the pressure of her hand and felt herself thrill at the touch.

"Oh, I don't believe it!" she cried, when Gilbert had finished his admirable narration. "He's not like they all are about here. He couldn't have done it. I know he couldn't."

"Wha' dee yew know about it?" answered the promising youth, grinning. "Did ye think he wuz a-gooin' ta be yar faancy maan? Why shou'n't he ax the gal if he've took a likin' tew'r? A rack-on a maan's a maan all the warld oover; an' gennlemen bain't much diffrun from pore folk."

Bertha knew better than to continue the discussion. She knew the horrible, coarse banter which would be flung at her if she showed any personal interest in Rupert. Her heart told her rightly that the story was a lie. But she was troubled within her mind. She longed to see him and ask him. But she felt the indelicacy, the impossibility, of such a course.

"I'm sure he's as good as he is brave and chivalrous," she said to herself. She had already begun to clothe him in the garb of a hero.

It is a fortunate thing for us men that love can transform the object of a woman's affection in her eyes. God knows, the average man needs a cloak of some kind to wear in the presence of the woman he loves. The pity of it is that it is too often the wrong woman that fits it on him.

For the next day or two Bertha had no opportunity of speaking with Rupert; but within a week after Gilbert had made her feverish with unrest and anxiety she became feverish indeed. She felt weak and dizzy, and her whole body was racked with pulsing pain.

There was an epidemic of influenza in the village, and Rupert had already gained a reputation for magical powers of healing by the use of a clinical thermometer and by judicious doses of salicine. He had studied medicine by way of amusement in London, and during his own illnesses had been attended by an able doctor, who made no mystery of the secrets of his profession, and who liked to talk on medical subjects with anyone who showed an intelligent interest in them. It had thus come about that in certain disorders, such as influenza, rheumatism, gout, and nervous complaints, Rupert was better posted than the average country practitioner; for that worthy man seems to cease all endeavour to lessen his ignorance or to keep himself versed in modern treatment when once he has left his hospital behind and settled down to physic a number of constitutions that are more bovine than human.

Under any circumstances country people are loth to call in any doctor except the club doctor; and women are debarred from clubs by precedent if not by rule.

On hearing of his sister's illness, Bob Heron said, "Shall a ax Claybrooke ta hev a look at ye, an' bring his little finical 'mometer what tell him wha'ss the matter wi' ye? He fare good-natered enow. I rackon he'd come."

The Heron boys saw nothing indecorous in the idea. And they would resent having to bear the expense of professional medical advice. Bertha was quite alive to the strangeness of the suggestion, but she wished so much to speak to Rupert, and her brothers pressed her so hard, that she consented.

"All right," said Rupert, when Bob explained the case to him, "I'll be round in a minute."

"It's a bit unusual," he thought; "but if she doesn't mind, I'm sure I don't. She's a devilish nice little girl!"

In two minutes he had run upstairs, smashed his head against the low staircase door, sworn, got the little glass tube, and hastened round to the Herons' back door.

On his being asked to enter in reply to his knock, he found no one in the kitchen but Bertha and Gilbert. He had expected to see the old man, sitting grunting over the fire, to chaperon his daughter. But he had gone some distance on a wheelwright's job.

"How good of you to come," said Bertha. "I wouldn't have troubled you but that I feel so helpless, and the boys pressed me to let them ask you."

"That's as bad as thanking me about that blessed bull," said Rupert, laughing. "But," he added seriously, "I'm sorry to hear such a bad account of you. May I feel your pulse?"

Bertha flushed, and held out her left hand. Rupert laid his dexter finger upon her wrist. It is to be feared that her pulse was not a true indicator at that moment.

As had been said, Gilbert was shy; and, in addition to his shyness, he had a predominant idea that it was the correct thing for him to leave his sister alone with any adult visitor she consented to see. This made him eager to leave the room. "I'm just a-gooin' ta the shop ta cleean my gun," he said, and was off before any attempt could be made to detain him. The eyes of Rupert and Bertha, now left alone, met. Gilbert's shyness appeared to be infectious. Both looked embarrassed; but clearly the best thing to do was to ignore the awkwardness of the situation and behave as if there was nothing singular about it. Rupert did so.

"Rather fast," he said, referring to the pulse. It was galloping with more than fever.

The more difficult test remained to be put. He took the thermometer from its case and knocked the mercury down.

"Please put this end under your tongue," he said. "There. So. Now close your mouth till I ask you to take it out again."

For the life of her, Bertha could not help laughing.

"Don't!" cried Rupert, laughing too; "you'll break the glass and hurt yourself."

It would be difficult to imagine a more ridiculous position for a young couple (with a leaning to mutual love) to be placed in. Bertha couldn't talk, and Rupert's usual readiness had quite deserted him. What he wished to say he felt he must not. The girl's charm increased by proximity, and words of tenderness were rebelliously demanding utterance. If he spoke at all he knew that he would make a fool of himself.

Two minutes passed in a silence that was both eloquent and uncomfortable. Then, with a little sigh of relief, he said, "Now let me have it, please."

Bertha removed the instrument from her lips and handed it to him. He would have loved to kiss it. But the girl's laughter, no longer repressible, saved him.

"By Jove!" he said. "103! You must go to bed at once. But first tell me exactly how you feel." "Yes," he said, when the symptoms had been described, "it's influenza right enough. Go to bed, and I'll send you some stuff. It's horribly bitter, but you mustn't mind that. Take it every hour till your head buzzes, and then let me know. I don't suppose you've got any whisky in the house. You must have some. I'll send some in with the other stuff. I think you'll be better to-morrow, but the most important thing of all is bed."

"But who's to cook the boys' dinner?" asked Bertha. "I can't go to bed, I can't really."

"You must," persisted Rupert. "Hang the boys' dinner! Let 'em cook it 'emselves. I give you my word that if you don't do as I tell you, you will be seriously ill; and then it may not be a question of bed for a day or two, but for weeks, or even months. Come, promise me you'll go."

She promised, feeling a strange delight at the solicitude displayed by her amateur physician.

"Then good-bye for the present," said Rupert; "I'll come in after dinner, and get one of the boys to take your temperature again; and if the pain in your head is no better by then you must have a mustard-leaf on the nape of your neck. "

He nearly said "dear neck."

"Good-bye," said Bertha, "and thank you so much."

"If you knew what a Good-bye," said Rupert, making a hasty exit.

"I shall get fond of that girl if I'm not careful," he said to himself querulously. "But I can't avoid her now, poor little thing. I must get her right first. Now about those boys' confounded dinners. Gad! I have it, if my old woman is still at mine."

Old Mrs. Barley was still poking about "The Castle," and with a little pecuniary persuasion he easily prevailed upon her to prepare a suitable meal. He himself got some Brand's extract out of his store and made some beef tea for the invalid.

With the exception of Gilbert, the male Herons took their dinner sullenly. It was more plentiful and of better quality than they were accustomed to, but they swore at Mrs. Barley, who paid them back in their own coin. They went upstairs and swore at Bertha, to show their superiority. They scowled at Rupert when they met him, to show their independence. "Traatin' us like wuckhus! Whew's he a-interfarin'?" they asked with sublime inconsistency, seeing that it was at their own instance that Rupert had been called in at all. Gilbert alone showed some signs of natural affection for his sister and of gratitude to Rupert, but he was already beginning to look upon his neighbour as a friend.

At four o'clock Rupert again made a little beef tea, and went round to the back door, that was acquiring a quaint fascination for him.

As the sound of his footsteps rang into clearness on his rounding the northern corner of the block of buildings, old Peggie popped her head up and peeped out of her scullery window.

"Phillup," she called softly, "hare be Maaster Ruput a-gooin' round to the Herons ag'in. Dee yew come an' sharpen yar lugs ag'in the winder. Yar h'arin's keener'n mine."

The back door was open, and Rupert found Gilbert rubbing away at the barrel of an antiquated muzzle-loader with a handful of sand.

"Will you please go up and ask your sister if I may see her," said Rupert, who had changed his mind as to letting one of the boys take the afternoon temperature.

"Aah!" said Gilbert, and went.

Presently his voice came down through the staircase door: "Bartha saay will ye please come up."

"Blaame my ole heart alive!" whispered old Noddy. "He be a-gooin' upstairs ta see Bartha. Nice dewins!"

"Dewins!" hissed Peggie, simmering. "Sech dewins oan't dew in *my* house! Yew'U ha'e ta give 'em nootuss."

"Let a be, let a be," replied Noddy, who thought that payment of rent was a cloak for all latent irregularities. (And Sarah's complaint that the rent of the Herons was not paid was as erratic as most of her statements.)

"I rackon Maaster Ruput want a some'at tew amuse hisself with."

"Wha 'tain't a week since he wuz arter Edith Noorton," said Peggie. "Miss Laura'll ha'e ta hare on't. He allust wuz a one for the gals, but he ote ta think hisself above sech as them."

"Aah! yew doan't knoo narthen about it," sniggered Noddy. "A petticut's a petticut, whether 'tis o' silk or calicoo."

"That'll dew," said Peggie tartly, "yew want ta stretch yar lugs 'stead o' mardlin'."

But Noddy stretched "his lugs" to no purpose.

"Le'ss goo upstairs," said Peggie, "an' listen at the wall of har rewm. We might hare some'at."

Rupert bent his head and went quietly up the narrow staircase. Gilbert met him at the top. "Tha'ss Bartha's rewm," he said. "Yew'll find har in theer."

"Yes. But you'd better come in too," said Rupert, afraid of alarming the delicacy of the girl by being alone with her in her bedroom.

Gilbert could not see the necessity for this. He felt shy and awkward, and he wanted to get back to his beloved gun. But he did not wish to disoblige his new friend.

"May I come in?" asked Rupert, tapping lightly at the door.

"Yes. Come in," answered Bertha. She had heard the words spoken outside, and was grateful for a thought which would have been considered squeamish by her brothers, and foolish by the other male villagers, who could only have attributed Rupert's anxiety and care to one motive.

He half repented having come when he saw her. Her delicate beauty was so fresh and enticing as she lay upon the pillows, that he felt an undesirable tenderness well up in his heart. Fever had given her a brighter colour than usual, and this flushed still higher when her eyes met those of her visitor, who could not conceal his thoughts from appearing in the glitter of his look.

He passed to the bedside and took her wrist.

"I've brought you a little more nourishment," he said. "You must try to take it after your mouth has told its tale to the thermometer."

He treated her with such a strictly professional air that she began to feel more at ease.

"How kind he is!" she thought. "I wish he would let me tell him how grateful I am for all his goodness. Perhaps I shall be able to show it some day. So strong, so gentle, so thoughtful, and so clever! I'm sure it isn't true about that girl Edith. I expect he's fond of someone in his own station of life. And yet—and yet Well, his eyes *do* look as if he liked me. Me! In this hole!"

She was a little better, and felt less pain. She began to thank him. But he laughed, and said she was not to talk.

"You must have some more beef tea to-night," he said. "Keep on taking the salicine every three hours now. And in the morning I hope you'll be almost well. But don't get up till I've seen you. Good-bye."

They had been so intent upon their own thoughts, that neither had noticed that young Gilbert has stolen downstairs, and was again scrubbing away at his old gun in the kitchen.

A few minutes before Rupert left the room, old Peggie said to Philip, "Can't ye hare narthen?"

"Noo!" he answered.

"Then I'm a-gooin' round," said Peggie.

Her little legs stumped down, taking each step at a toddling leap. She got to the Herons' back door just as Rupert started to come downstairs.

"Wheer's Bartha?" she asked Gilbert.

"Upsteers, abed," answered the boy gruffly.

Rupert's descending footsteps were now audible. Old Peggie commenced to wink, to screw up her little pig eyes, and to purse her lips. She slithered behind the staircase door.

When Rupert stepped into the kitchen, she toddled from behind her screen.

"Good arternewn, Maaster Ruput," she said. "And how are yew?"

Her formula of salutation had become so habitual that she was rarely able to dispense with it. But she continued, "Whativer hev yew been a-dewin' on?"

"Damn!" swore Rupert under his breath. "Now there'll be lies spread about that poor girl!" He said aloud, "I'm glad you've come in, Mrs. Noddyfield. Miss Heron is laid up with a sharp attack of influenza, and ought to have a woman to look after her. I've left her some medicine and told her the treatment. But of course she can't nurse herself properly. Now I'm sure a good-hearted old lady like you will be only too glad to help. Good-bye."

He effected a skilful retreat before the old woman had time to recover from the effects of his coolness.

"Well!" she muttered. "Of all the beer-faced impidence! Innerferlenza, indeed! If tha'ss right, tha'ss ketchin', an' I doan't want none on it! If ta bain't—well, I know as much as I want tew ariddy. But it oan't dew. I must hev a h'arin' about it, an' tha'ss a fack!"

Later in the evening, as Rupert was writing, the sonorous rumble of old Noddy's voice came to his ears.

"Is anybardy at hooam?" it growled.

"Yes. Come in, Mr. Noddyfield," said Rupert.

"Be that dorg o' yarn quiet ta-night?" asked the old man, as if Sock had periodical fits of ferocity.

"He's all right," answered Rupert a little testily. "What does the old fool want now?" he murmured.

"Could ye spare a minute or tew ta come round an' see the missus?" asked old Noddy on entering. "She'd ha' come round ta yew, oony she fare narvous o' yar dorg."

"Oh, all right," said Rupert; "I'll be round in a minute."

"Thanky, sir," replied the old man, and took his leave.

Rupert did not feel comfortable. He knew he had been guilty of an indiscretion, and was annoyed at its discovery by so evil-tongued an old woman as Peggie. He was far more concerned for Bertha than for himself. It was quite immaterial to him in what esteem he was held by the village people. But a girl's good name is fragile. And Bertha's self-respect and aloofness would render her a piquant prey to the foul beaks of the village hoody crows. He determined to do all in his power (even to the extent of utilising his social position, an act of snobbishness he would never have dreamt of perpetrating for his own sake) in order to prevent harm from coming to the girl, who seemed so sweet and pure. He damned young Gilbert for leaving the bedroom. He damned himself for not observing his exit. But most fervently did he damn old Peggie for her inopportune appearance on the scene. When he got round to Ozier Cottage, he found Peggie and Philip sitting in the kitchen looking mighty pleased with themselves.

"Here I am, Peggie," said he. "What do you want to say to me?"

"Well, Maaster Ruput," simpered Peggie, winking furiously, "yew'll escewse an ole 'oman what knowed ye whin ye wuz a baaby, an' ole enow ta be yar granny, let alooan yar mother. But yew're a straanger in these parts, an' doan't knoo the folk like me an' Phillup; an' I dew assure ye that yar sister is soo respected in the willage that I shou'n't like noobardy ta put the grin ontew ye. Soo I thote yew'd escewse me for a-tellin' on ye."

The old woman paused for breath.

"Drive ahead," said Rupert, guessing what was coming, and raging inwardly.

"Well," continued Peggie, "I see yew a-comin' downsteers nex' dooar, an' yew said as yew'd been a-givin' Bartha Heron medsun. Now she bain't 'speckable! She'd a drefful name at Duckin'ham afoor she went ta Lunnon, an' she bain't likely tew ha' come back any the better. An' even the doctor doan't like a-seein' on har by hisself. She used ta goo on the yachts, an' we all knoo what that mean for a gal." (It speaks well for the character of the Londoners who make holiday on the Norfolk waters, that a country lass has only to get the name of having been on a yacht, to lose any last shred of reputation she may have been fortunate enough to retain till then.)

Rupert confined himself to Peggie's statement about the doctor.

"Why?" he asked, laughing. "Is he afraid she'll tempt him to deadly sin?"

"Yew dooan't want ta maake a mock on't," sputtered Peggie, colouring with indignation. "I'm a 'speckable married 'oman, an' I'm a-speakin' for yar good. An' yew say she ha' got innerferlenza. How dee yew knoo ta bain't some'at else? I allust fancied she might git into trouble. An' the folk 'ull call ye the 'quack doctor' an' what not! An' yar sister soo respected in the willage!"

"Come, come," said Rupert, "let's get to the point. I know she's got influenza from the symptoms and from what this little thing tells me "; he held up the clinical thermometer.

"Wha whativer might that be?" said Peggie, allowing her curiosity to get the better of her indignation. Rupert explained its uses.

"Wheer d'ye put it?" asked old Noddy, sitting up with an eager air.

"Under the tongue," said Rupert.

"Can't she talk when she hev it?" inquired the old man, with a great show of interest.

"No," was the answer.

"Blarm! I whoolly wish yew'd try my missus's tempitewer now an' ag'in," said Philip. "Will ye lend it tew us?"

"Wha hoold yar narnsense, dew!" cried Peggie, infuriated.

"But be yew shore?" she asked Rupert, holding her head on one side and blinking and smiling sourly. "Sure of what?" said Rupert. "Be yew shore ta be the innerferlenza?" "Yes, quite." "Be yew sartin shore?"

"Yes," said Rupert, driven to desperation, which alone excused him, "littorally shore!"

The terrible paronomasia acted as a stimulant. After that he felt that he would prove equal to the occasion.

"Then dee yew let me goo inta har room for ye," said Peggie. "Yew can't be tew keerful. Now I'm a 'speckable married 'oman, an' arter I wuz married Paarson Mottridge kep' a-comin' hare o' Wensdy nights when my husband goo ta chapel. Arter tew or t'ree times, I say ta him, 'What dee yew keep a-comin' hare for o' Wensdy nights, Mr. Mottridge?' 'Wha ta see yar husband, Mrs. Noddyfield,' he say. 'Now yew knoo that bain't true,' I say. 'Yew knoo my husband allust goo ta chapel o' Wensdy nights. It's me yew're arter! An' I'm a 'speckable married 'oman, an' doan't want none on't. Soo dee yew ha' done!' I say. An' he went off with a flea in his ear. Then theer wuz Widder Barley (she what wark for yew now). Well, Phillup fared ta goo an' see har afoor we wuz married. An' when we *wuz* married I heerd as we wuz prashus nigh bein' stooned down the Tarlham rooad, 'ecos o' what folks said o' my husband an' har. An' I went an' axed har, an' she wuz as 'speckable a married 'oman as me, oony har maan wuz did!"

Rupert cast a glance at old Noddy. The blind man seemed aware of it, for he winked wickedly with his better eye and grinned.

"Yes, yes. Very creditable, no doubt," said Rupert. "But you'll remember that I asked you myself to go up and see the girl. Did you go?"

Peggie thought it best to ignore the question.

"Soo," she started again, "if any woman want help, dee yew dew it t'rew me. Then narthen can't be said. Yew mind what I toold ye about Paarson Mottridge when I wuz fust married. He kep' a-comin'"

"By all means," said Rupert. "Then will you take the thermometer? I've shown you how it should be used. Take her temperature at eight in the morning, and let me know what it is."

"We're all pore folk about hare," objected Peggie, "an' we doan't want noo 'mometers. We can't affoord 'em, an' we can't dew with 'em."

"But it won't cost anything," cried Rupert. "Here it is all ready."

"We're all pore folk," repeated Peggie, "an' we can't dew with 'em."

"Oh well," said Rupert, "then I must ask her brothers. Don't let her get up till I know how she is in the morning."

"We're all pore people," repeated Peggie, "and we can't affoord ta lay abed all day a-dewin' narthen, same as gentry."

"Then if you don't believe I'm giving proper advice, why don't you send for a doctor?" asked Rupert.

"An' whew's ta pay him?" asked Peggie. "We're all pore folk about hare, an' we can't affoord noo doctors."

"Confound it then!" burst out Rupert, at the end of his patience. "Leave the girl alone. I'll get old Mrs. Barley to do what's necessary. Good-night.... But I must say one thing. No one knows of my visit this afternoon but young Gilbert, Miss Heron, and we three. Gilbert will hold his tongue, I'm sure. If there's any scandal about it, I shall know whom to thank.... And, yes, by Jove, whom to repay."

"Yew doan't take it amiss, I dew hope," said old Noddy.

"Oh no, I like it!" said Rupert, turning on his heel and leaving the room.

Philip rose and followed him. He caught him up at the garden gate. "Yew doan't want ta pay noo regard ta har," he whispered. "Har tongue goo like a t'roshin' machine. That fare ta daaze me whoolly at times. D'ye knoo any way ta stop it?"

"No," answered Rupert. "But I advise you to find one. For if I hear that anything gets abroad about this, I'll make you both repent it. But," he added, as he thought what the blind man probably had to endure, " I'm sorry for you."

"Aah!" groaned Noddy. "An' soo yew may be. Tha'ss a pity, arter all, as I di'n't hev Polla Barley. Peggie Chin*daffy* wuz har name. I orfen think as that ote tew ha' been *Vrimivaggy*. But I'll dew what a can. Blarm! If a young gennleman like ta amewse hisself"

"No! Confound it!" said Rupert savagely. "There's nothing of that kind. The girl's a good girl, I'll swear."

"Well, I'm glad yew find har soo," said old Noddy drily. "Good-night t'ye. "

"What the devil do you mean?" cried Rupert furiously.

"I niver meant noo harm, sir," replied Noddy blandly and innocently. "Good-night t'ye ag'in. I'll dew what a can."

"You'd better," said Rupert; "and don't you forget it." VII SARAH CALLS IN A SPECIALIST EITHER owing to the treatment, or because her fever was caused by something other than influenza (which the mere fact of Rupert's kindness had affected), Bertha's temperature was down to normal the next morning, and she was well enough to do without old Mrs. Barley's assistance. Gilbert brought round the news and messages of gratitude in more or less garbled form. And Rupert, on being satisfied that he could do no more, sent in the rest of the Brand's extract and betook himself "down ta ma'sh" with his gun.

Although by the marshes Duckingham is the nearest station to Frogsthorpe on the St. Mary's line, Willowby is nearer by the highway, and has the additional advantage of being on the St. Mary's side, for which reason the fare is less by that route than the former. It was to Willowby that Celibate Sarah preferred to travel when on the way to her sister's. For, as she said herself, "she wuz whoolly afeared o' the bullocks down ta ma'sh."

Since Rupert had left the Limes, Sarah had made little progress towards the accomplishment of her designs. Indeed, she seemed to have suffered a setback. For the renewed association with her brother had revived Laura's sisterly affections. This being so, and feeling herself at a nonplus, Sarah went over to Frogsthorpe to consult Peggie on the morning after the latter had had her "h'arin"' with Rupert.

There was in Turlham (the next village to Frogsthorpe) an aged crone named Sally Young (more commonly known as "Granny"), whose powers of witchcraft were devoutly believed in by all the neighbourhood, and in whom Sarah herself had implicit trust. If any reliance at all can be placed on country report, the old hag had given many evidences of powers difficult of explanation by the recognised laws of nature. And thirty years ago she was famed throughout the eastern counties for black sorcery.

Sarah proposed to persuade Peggie to accompany her on a pilgrimage to the witch's hovel, and endeavour to obtain advice or whatever more material assistance might there be purchasable. As she travelled *via* Willowby, she escaped meeting Rupert on the marshes. And while he was stalking a parcel of hornpie on Cock-na-hay Marsh, Sarah and Peggie were exercising their cunning on greater game.

The two sisters would have made an interesting study for a gynecologist. Though Peggie was ten years the elder, and her hair white, her skin wrinkled, she was much younger in manner and appearance than her sister. In the Norfolk marshlands no one is considered more than middleaged till well on in the eighties. In Peggie's eyes she was still in the prime of her life. She simpered and she skipped like a giddy marionette; and her whole bearing was ludicrously incongruous with the drawn face and the *old* malevolence which dwelt in her eyes.

Sarah was on a larger scale—more self-contained and quieter. Both the sharp Norman faces and small, thin mouths were hard and cruel, and alive with treacherous cunning. Peggie might have been the offspring of Puck and Sycorax j Sarah, of Judas Iscariot and Jael.

"Well, how ha' yew been a-gittin' on?" asked Peggie, when the greetings were over and old Noddy sent out for a walk.

"Wery moderate! Wery moderate indeed!" answered Sarah. "She fare that aggerawatin' I could give har a good clout o' the lug if a dars't. Since that warmin' of a booy come down she oan't hare narthen ag'in him. 'Blood be blood,' she say, 'an' a hadn't ote ta leave my brass away from him.' Tha'ss why I ha' come over. Look yew hare, Peggie! Yew've got ta git him inta trouble somehow, soo's she'll tarn ag'in him."

"He! he! he!" simpered Peggie. "He's a-dewin'; he's a-shovellin' up the muck for his owan grave. The whool willage ha' put the grin on tew'm oncet; an' now he's a-dewin' better'n iver. Look yew hare! I'll tell ye what!

He "Peggie bent forward and poured forth the scandal that had been accumulating concerning Rupert, Edith Norton, and Bertha, ending up with a dramatic account of how she "whoolly give him a mobbin' larse night."

"Then yew acted like a fewl!" said Sarah encouragingly. "Yew di'n't want ta put him on his guard. He doan't want ta think as yew're a spy upon him, an' tha'ss what yew ha' got ta be. An' if yew can't say narthen moor ag'in him from what ye know, I rackon yew'll ha'e ta dream some'at. Git that theer will altered I must, for Bartie's sake as well as my owan. An' yew want ta help!"

"Yew've noo call ta be afeared o' me not helpin'," said Peggie, "but doan't goo a-puffin' to ole Phillup. He's whoolly a rum egg, he is, an' he might goo ag'in us as like as not. He's that wexed wi' Bartie for allust a-playin' on the ammonium wheniver he's at hooam. He say the hymns an' chants sour on his innards."

"Now theer's another thing," said Sarah. "Is ole Granny at Tarlham now?"

"Aah! now yew want ta knoo tew much," said Peggie, blinking and shaking her head. "Noobardy can't niver tell wheer the ole witch is. Did ye want ta see har?"

"I thote as yew an' me might goo an' ax har if she can see what's a-comin'," answered Sarah, "an' if she can l'arn us a trick or tew. I got a bit o' brass out o' Laura's cash-box larse night when she wuz droonk, an' I can make it wuth the ole 'oman's while. 'Sides, if I can git the will altered, she may be able ta give us some stuff as ull stir things up a bit."

"Yew knoo somethin', yew dew!" was Peggie's admiring comment. "Wait yew hare till I ha' got my bonnet on, an' we'll goo ta oncet."

"Wheer's Ruput this moarnin'?" asked Sarah. "He doan't want ta knoo narthen."

"He've took his gun down ta ma'sh. He oan't knoo as yew've been hare if ye goo back by the top rooad. Come on."

Within handy distance of the "Grey Mare" was a small hovel, so old-fashioned as to have its walls of baked mud beneath a rotting thatch. The two rooms of which it consisted were of fair size as to area, but were barely six feet in height. Each had but one small window, diamondpaned and dilapidated. Through the ceiling between the rooms a dark space here and there showed where the lath and plaster had given way. Anyone walking in the upper room would have to mind his footsteps or fall through. A table, a few wooden chairs, and one armed settle stood in the middle of the living-room. There were no outward and visible signs of the wealth with which common report credited the witch. The whole den and its surroundings were as sordid as such weird haunts usually are. Old Granny, when at home, loved to sit on a three-legged stool, crouching over the fire that was vestal in its vitality. The patch of garden between the road and the hovel was overgrown with burdock, hemlock, sheep's-parsley, hogweed, henbane, fennel, and bindweed. There was a fine specimen of the deadly nightshade near the door, with a heavy hang of its luscious, black cherry-like fruit. Desolation and mystery made the place their home, and even the sun seemed wan and unwholesome within that dreaded territory of evil.

Sarah and Peggie hushed their voices as they came near the gateway that had no gate and hesitated. The wind from the marsh turned chill to the women. They shivered. "Le'ss goo back," suggested Peggie, "she's at hooam. Har dooar's oopen. I doan't half fancy gooin' in."

Even as she spoke a guttural cackle came from the door.

'' Come one, come tew;
Booth must taste the witch's brew.
Up the path and t'rew the dooar,
The way yew ote tew ha' come afoor.
What yew're seekin' is hare ta find,
For the black man favour the black man's kind,
An' Peggie an' Seerah be booth ta his mind.

"Hech! hech! hech! Peggie an' Seerah! Seerah an' Peggie! Come on, 'bors. I've been a-waitin' for ye. Doan't ye be narvous of ole Granny. Come yew in, my pratty bewties, an' set ye in the devil's kitchen."

Peggie advanced timorously, blinking and shaking. Even the more daring Sarah felt qualms of dread as she approached the entrance to the hut.

No stage manager could have set the scene better than its natural presentment. The old crone, on her threelegged stool, cowered over the fire. Her square face was harsh, and wrinkled over with furrows of age and dirt. The cheekbones were high, and "padded over" with no "flash and fat." The skin drew to dim hollows beneath them. Her iron-grey hair, coarse and hard as a pony's mane, hung a wild tangled mass over her shoulders, and shaded her shrunken chest, which was bare, and open at the neck like that of a plucked gobbler. Her eyes were sunken beneath grey eyebrows, but were black and full of evil glowing fire. Her yellow lips bunched over her toothless gums with an ever-varying expression that seemed the very genius of sinister mockery. Her skeleton hands, stretched to the warmth of the blaze, were taloned with a filthy growth of nail, and were ever tremulous with senility, or strung to a pitch of nervous vivacity during the eager and dramatic gesticulation with which the old woman was wont to accentuate her croaking syllables. From a sooty hake a large iron boiler hung over the fire. Some saucepans and pots stood about in the glowing wood embers and on the hearth.

As her visitors stepped fearfully into the room, the witch bent her head round to peer at them, and her hair fell and formed a screen from the fire that left her features shadowed in the dim light of the room.

"Hech! hech! hech!" chuckled Granny again. "I knoo what yew ha' come arter. But yew want ta git me my brooath fust.

'' A quartern o' gin, a quartern o' rum, A quartern o' whisky, a quart of ole bare.
I'll bile 'em, an' stir 'em, an' drink when they hum,
Then I'll read ye the riddle that brought ye both hare.

"Git along wi' ye ta the 'Grey Meer. ' An' when ye bring 'em back, I'll lar n ye... I'll lar n ye!"

The liquors were fetched and heated till the reek of their steam made the very atmosphere seem drunk. Old Granny watched it boil and boil. Then, when but little more than a pint in all was left, she took a small stone bottle from the cupboard and poured a few drops of a syrupy green liquid from it into the bubbling mixture. "Aha!" she chuckled. "Yew can't buy that! Yew can't buy that!"

The contents of the saucepan now frothed up in a smooth grass-tinted foam, and hissed against the iron sides that confined it. Granny raised the saucepan, swirled its contents round in three quaint, involuted curves, and streamed the stuff into a brown earthenware jug. With this in her hand she swayed herself, and danced with jerking, grotesque steps round Peggie and Sarah, who sat shuddering in a terror of excitement. Then she stopped; spat thrice; stamped thrice; bowed north, south, and west, and with a burst of cackling gibberish lifted the frothing liquor to her lips. She swallowed the scalding mixture at a draught. And as she did so, her eyes gathered increased fire, her cheeks grew smoother and plumper. Her

K whole frame seemed to fill with vigour as she drank. After the last drain, she hissed—

"I'm a-gooin' inta one o' my trances. Dee yew mind what a say then, or else"

She fell back into the arm settle before her sentence was complete. Her lower jaw dropped, and her eyes stared open and glazed with blank unconsciousness.

"Christ!" screamed Peggie. "She's dead!"

But as she spoke, the witch's tongue (protruding through the toothless gums, which were exposed by her open mouth) quivered, and a curious clucking, choking noise sounded in her throat. The guttural sounds increased in rapidity and intensity, and presently articulate words were formed and spoken. But horrible to see and hear with no movement of the pendulous lower jaw.

"The fire 'ull fade, but will not die
Till a day onseen by the witch's eye.
A white soul won, and a black soul lost,
Afoor iver the last o' the deeaks be crossed.
Cruelty, artfulness, greed o' pelf,
A heart as false as the black man's self.
A proper net
For the devil ta set.
But the meshes o' Faate
Are booth small an' great.
An' the fish may git
T'rew the nettin' yit."

The scraping, choking syllables ceased. Her tongue quivered for a little space and then was still. Sarah and Peggie remained motionless, spellbound by the horror of the thing. Some five minutes elapsed before there was any sound in the room save the leaping burst of burning wood and the sough of the wind in the trees and verdure without. Then the witch quivered and shook with sharp convulsions. Her mouth closed, her eyelids flickered, and with a groan she sat up in her chair and turned to her visitors with sly consciousness in her eyes.

"Well," she said in her natural voice, "did ye mind what a toold ye?"

"Ooh dare! ooh dare!" said Peggie. "Yew give me sech a tarn that I cou'n't mind narthen!"

Sarah said nothing. Her nerves were stronger than her sister's, her interest keener. The doggrel was written on her memory, but she had no intention of admitting the fact. She meant to puzzle out the meaning of it for herself as best she could.

"Then my time an' trouble's wasted. Blust ye!" grumbled the witch. "Anything moor yew'll ha'e ta pay moor for. "

Sarah pulled out two sovereigns and handed them over. "I want yar adwice," she said, "how ta part brother an' sister. D'ye want me ta tell ye anything?"

"I knoo moor'n yew can tell me!" grinned Granny. "But yew'll ha'e ta give moor goold foor't. Goold, and what I like ta ax. An' taake th' ooth. Hark tew't."

Sarah took the oath the witch required, then Granny leant forward. "Listen hare!" she said.

Events will show the development of her scheme. It was with revived confidence that Sarah left the hovel to go by the high road to Willowby, while Peggie toddled back to Noddyfield corner.

VIII

"LOVE! WHOSE COUCH IS ON THE MAID'S SOFT CHEEK!" THAT night Rupert worked late, and it was past midnight when he crept up the little corkscrew staircase to his bedroom. He had hardly blown out his candle and settled himself to sleep, when the thunder of heavy knocks at the outer door roused him to excited wakefulness. He leapt from bed and thrust his head out of the window. "Who's that? What's the matter?" he cried.

"Faa'er's took wery quare," answered Gilbert's voice. "Bartha say, please would ye come at once?"

Rupert flung on some clothes and hurried downstairs. He found the boy still waiting on the doorstep, clad in nothing but his shirt. A fine drizzle was falling, and the poor lad shivered as he said, "Come in the front way. The dooar's oopen."

It was only necessary to step over the low privet fence that divided the flower gardens to get to the Herons' front door. The parlour was in darkness, but a bead of light shone in the kitchen at the back, thrown by a candle from upstairs down through the staircase door. Rupert followed the boy in and ascended the stairs. As he passed Bertha's room on the way to the larger sleeping-chamber, in which the old man and his three sons shared a couple of beds between them, he thought of his yesterday's experience, and tenderness for the girl, and disgust at old Peggie's impertinence fought for the mastery in his mind. Tenderness won. He felt pleased that Bertha should have sent for him.

The whole family were assembled in the double-bedded room. Jack was still in the bed which Gilbert had recently left. His eyes were closed, and he paid no attention to what was going oh round the other bed. But he raised himself heavily to curse Gilbert when the boy got his shivering body between the bedclothes again.

Bertha was standing by her father's bedside, holding a glass of whisky to his lips; while Bob, on the other side of the bed, supported the old man in his arms. A badly burning candle cast a feeble light from the mantelpiece. The deep shadows and the sickly glimmer afforded a scene such as Rembrandt alone could paint.

As Rupert approached, Bertha involuntarily held out her unoccupied hand. "I'm so glad you've come!" she said, as he took her hand and pressed it. "You are so kind. I hoped you would not mind my sending Gilbert for you!"

He would have liked to assure her that to do anything she asked was a delight to him. But the time and place made love-making incongruous. He took the candle from the mantel and held it so that the light fell on the old man's face. Beneath the covering of dirt it was ghastly white, and there was blood and foam upon the lips. His breathing was heavy and laboured. Rupert felt his pulse. It was irregular and fast, but strong. The forehead was cold and clammy.

"How long has he been like this?" he asked.

Bob answered. "He wook me up a-snoortin' about ten min't agoo, an' when a spook tew'm he di'n't say narthen. Soo I lit a cannle an' hollered for Bartha. He doan't knoo what ye say, nor narthen."

"What has he had to take?" asked Rupert, looking at Bertha.

"He *would* finish up about a quart of soup," she said, "and he'd had three cups of tea just before."

"Any beer or spirits?" said Rupert.

"Did he have anything when he was out with you?" said Bertha to Gilbert.

"I oony see him hev free pint o' stout," said the boy. "But I worn't with him all the time."

Rupert asked Bob to hold the old fellow up higher. He did so, and the breathing grew less laboured.

"Do you know me, Mr. Heron?" asked Rupert.

The old fellow made no sign of comprehension. His eyes were partly closed, and he seemed unable to use his limbs.

"Try him with the whisky again," said Rupert.

He sucked at the glass and drank a good part of it.

"Now try him with some water."

Bertha filled a cup with pure water. The old man smelt at it and clenched his teeth.

"Drink it, father," said his daughter, "it will do you good."

He resolutely declined to do any such thing.

"Ah!" said Rupert. "Can you hear what I say?" he cried, speaking loudly close to the old man's ear. Still he gave no sign.

"Open his eyes," Rupert said to Bob. He remembered Mr. Begge's test of unconsciousness, and resolved to apply it.

Bob lifted the eyelids, but there seemed little or no intelligence in the eyes. Rupert took the candle and drew the flame across, close to the stolid eyeballs. They blinked.

"Try the water again," said Rupert.

"Do drink it, father," pleaded Bertha, holding the cup close to his lips.

"What is't?" said the old man at last.

"Only water," she replied. "It can't do

you any harm."

"Whisky! Whisky!" gasped the old fellow.

"Throw the water on his head," said Rupert. And it was done.

"Blust!!!!" roared the invalid, immediately recovering the use of his voice in its completeness and swearing horribly.

"There! You see it's done him good already!" said Rupert blandly. "If he gets worse repeat the treatment. Don't give him any more spirits. He'll be all right. There's nothing to worry about."

"But what is it?" begged Bertha. "I thought he was dying before you came. I was dreadfully frightened."

"He's overloaded his holding capacity," said Rupert euphemistically. "He'll be all right in the morning. Never mind his groans." (For he had been groaning horribly all the time.) "That's only discomfort. If he gets worse send round for me again. But I don't think you'll need to."

All this time Jack was snoozing placidly.

"But whar about me?" asked Bob. "Wheer can / sleep? I can't git into that mucka bed ag'in."

"You must get in with Jack and Gilbert," said Bertha.

"Blust!" roared Jack, suddenly waking up. "I'm damned if he dew!" But Bob proceeded to follow his sister's advice.

The three boys were already in bed together, and the old man, finding that no more whisky was coming his way, had sunk back on his pillow.

"Good-night," said Rupert.

"I'll show you down," said Bertha, "there's no light downstairs."

"Please don't," replied Rupert, " you ought not to risk the night air after your touch of illness yesterday." "Let me come," she pleaded.

It was all very irregular, but the boys didn't care. Indeed they were already asleep, and Rupert could not persist in his refusal. He felt his whole nature yearn to cherish this jewel on a muck heap.

Bertha preceded him downstairs with the candle. In the parlour he said, "Don't come any further, don't come to the door into the night air, pray don't. Good-night, I'm so glad you sent for me."

Bertha put the candle on the table. "Good-night," she said, holding out both her hands, "and thank you so much."

Rupert took her little hands in his—they trembled and communicated their quivering magnetism to him. He kept her hands and pressed them. She made no effort to free herself. Rupert's heart beat more and more riotously. He looked at her. Her eyelids were drooped. He could see the rapid rise and fall of her breast. She seemed to incline to him. And, with a mighty wave of passion, love overwhelmed all barriers of prudence or propriety. He drew her to him, and with a little sigh of content her head dropped to his bosom.

"Bertha! Bertha!" he whispered fiercely. "Bertha darling, I love you!"

She threw her arms about his neck, and their lips met and clung.

"Oh Rupert," she said, when her mouth was free again, "I've loved you since I saw you first, but—you!—me! —poor me!" she said, sobbing.

"Hush, my dearest," he said, kissing her again and again, "but you must run up to bed now. I can't let my girl get cold, and you *are* my girl, are you not?"

"Always and always," she answered, raising her eyes and meeting his with a fervour of steadfastness in them that awed him for the moment. "I am yours to do as you like with, to live for you or to die for you, and if my death were for your sake, oh be sure that I would go to it singing. Oh! my dear! don't go yet!"

But Rupert could not trust himself. His feeling for her was love as well as passion, and her entire self-surrender put him on his honour to take no advantage of what he knew to be innocence in the very furnace of passion.

"Yes, dear," he said, "I must go now, but we shall see each other to-morrow. Good-night, my sweetheart and my love."

"And oh! good-night to you, my dearest," said Bertha. He kissed her lips, her cheeks, her eyes, hair, neck, and hands, and tore himself away.

SARAH MAKES A MOVE THE nervous exhaustion, following on the excitement he had undergone, and the long hours he had spent without rest on the previous day, sent Rupert into a deep sleep almost as soon as he had returned to his bed. His heart was still beating tumultuously; his brain was still tense with the problems which the events of the night had presented for his solution, when the questions which perplexed him faded into vagueness and then into unconsciousness. The sun was high, and the day breeze spinning white, fleecy clouds along, when he woke on a bright morning. The weight on his mind at first puzzled him. And it was not till he had thrown off the bedclothes that the pregnant events of the small hours became vivid to him. Then at once he felt the clinging of Bertha's lips on his and the soft pressure of her form in his embrace. Three courses seemed open to him: to leave the cottage at once, and for ever; to apologise to Bertha for having offered and accepted love which could only lead to unhappiness; or to ask her to be his wife.

The first he at once rejected as being heartless, cowardly, and inconvenient; the second as being cowardly, impertinent, and disingenuous. There remained only the third.

He could not trust himself to see her daily, and to repeat the caresses (which would to a certainty be repeated unless the first or second course was adopted), without danger to the girl. No doubt the genuine love with which she had inspired him helped to guide him in his decision. And his reason leapt up to support his inclination—a common trick of the jade.

He asked himself what he could do better than marry her. The simple country life suited him, and was incumbent upon him. But it was a bit lonely. Bertha would be the very wife and companion for him. She had all the merits of the practical knowledge of the village girls; while at the same time she was a true lady in thought and manner. There was no one of his family he need consider except Laura. And he felt sure that he could soon persuade *her* that the marriage would be the best thing possible for him. Anyhow, he determined to make an opportunity during the day and ask Bertha to be his wife.

But the fates postponed his putting them to the touch.

As he was at breakfast (for his long sleep had made him very late) the post came in, and a letter from Sarah was handed to him. In it he was requested to repair to the Limes that morning with his camera. Laura was going to show some fowls and wanted to have them photographed. "And Miss Laura say, don't leave Sock at home. She've took quite a fancy to him."

He had just time to finish his meal and get together some hornpie and snipe, shot the day before, before he had to start across the marshes to Duckingham.

He did not like to go without seeing Bertha, so he took round his door-key to the Herons, to be given to old Mrs. Barley when she put in an appearance. But Gilbert and the old man were both in the kitchen with Bertha, and the eyes alone of the lovers had a chance of repeating vows and endearments. Ocular speech and a pressure of the hand were all that could be indulged in. But they served to ratify the understanding, and to set both hearts beating with amorous impetuosity. There was no time even for inquiries as to the old man's health, beyond the briefest, "How's your father this morning?" and "Much better, thank you." And though a good deal may be done by intonation, it is impossible to impart much tenderness to these phrases.

Laura met Rupert at the door. Poor Bessie (the servant who liked pudding) had been dismissed, and no other as yet found to take her place.

Old Sock was shut in the kitchen, while brother and sister went down to the fowl runs.

Sarah had not yet said anything to her mistress of the information she had gleaned from Peggie. That was reserved until the agenda of the day had done their work.

Rupert was in the act of snapping the crack pullet, when yaps, yells, and screams from the house struck on Laura's affrighted ears.

"Help! help!" screamed Sarah's voice. "Hare be that warmin' of a dorg a-killin' Fiddy!"

Rupert and Laura rushed indoors, and found Sarah seated in a chair, nursing the little terrier, whose eyes looked glazed, and who was panting and gasping painfully. Old Sock was standing in the middle of the scullery, looking as if he wondered what it was all about.

"Whativer's the matter, Sarah?" said Laura. "Here, give him to me."

She took the terrier in her arms, while Rupert got hold of his dog and chained him up. The old chap wagged his tail, transparently unconscious of guilt.

"Howiver ta happened I doan't knoo!" sobbed Sarah. "I s'pooz it wuz ta be. Yew must ha' left the dooar oopen," she said to Rupert. "For a'moost as sune as I went upsteers ta empty the slops I heerd a tarrible n'ise. An" I come down, an' see that gre't brute a-chookin' o' pore little Fi Fi in the coarner, an' a-worritin' on him like a rat."

"But he never hurts little dogs!" said Rupert.

"D'ye think I doan't knoo what I see myself?" said Sarah indignantly. "I rackon he ha' kilt him!"

Laura was in a state of tearful imbecility. She moaned, and kissed her dog.

"Let me look at him," said Rupert.

"Ooh, you can't do narthen! He'll niver get over it!" wept Laura. "He's dying now."

Rupert took the dog. There was a little moisture at the neck, but not a sign of a bite was to be seen anywhere.

"Aah!" said Sarah, "he's artful. He thote if he oony squeeged the life out on him ta wouldn't be knowed."

By this time Fido was recovering, and on being placed on the ground ran over to old Sock, who stood wagging his tail. Fido snapped at him, as was his custom with all big dogs, whom he knew to have too much self-respect to retaliate on one so much beneath their dignity.

Laura snatched him up with a scream. The bland old bulldog still continued to wag his tail, superior.

"Theer!" cried Sarah, "that'll tell ye! Fido ou'n't bark ar him nor narthen if he han't ha' hu't him!"

"Ooh," sobbed Laura, "he'll niver get oover it. What-, ever did you come down for with that great brute of a dog to kill my little prashus! Aren't you a-going to throsh him? Here, gi'e me a stick."

"Steady on, Laura," said Rupert. "I don't believe Sock touched him!"

"D'ye mean as I'm a liar then?" asked Sarah, turning very red in the face. "Look ar all that slaver! That must ha' come out o' yar dorg's gre't mouth!"

Rupert was puzzled. There certainly was saliva on the terrier's neck, but not the faintest mark of teeth. It was, moreover, quite contrary to Sock's habits to hurt small dogs. He had been known to run about with a toy terrier hanging on to his neck, paying no attention at all to the matter, and appearing to consider it an entertaining sort of game. Rupert distinctly remembered that Fido had been placed in the dining-room, and all the doors of the scullery shut. The thing was a mystery. A suspicion of Sarah lit, struggled to a faint flame, and went out, like the last match in a wind.

"I think you must have seen them playing," he said to Sarah.

"Plaayin'!" snorted she. "Then what wuz't took his breath away an' kilt him?"

"He isn't dead yet," answered Rupert. "Has he ever had fits?"

"Yes, he've had fits," said Laura, bringing on herself a glance of anger from Sarah.

"But that worn't noo fit!" persisted Sarah. "I tell ye I see that gre't brute a-hooldin' on him down, a-chewin' on him."

"Ooh," cried Laura, "he'll niver get oover it!"

"Don't be so silly, Laura," said Rupert, beginning to get annoyed. "He's all right again now."

And indeed there seemed little the matter with him.

"Well, you hear what Sarah say," argued Laura. "She can't be mistook. You ought to throsh your dog."

"Well, I shan't, at any rate," replied

Rupert. "Look for yourself, there's not a sign of a bite."

"Look a the slaver!" said Sarah again.

"Well, take him away," said Laura; "I never want to set eyes on him again. The brute!"

"Oh, hang the women!" said Rupert to himself. "I'll chain him up outside," he said aloud, "and when we've finished the photo I'll take him home."

"Ooh, I can't see about any more photos," wailed Laura. "I can't leave my prashus. You must come oover again without that dog."

"Yes," said Sarah; "whativer yew want wi' sech a dorg I'm shore git oover me. Gre't ogla brute!"

"All right, old girl," said Rupert to Laura, with praiseworthy patience. "Let me know when, and I'll come if I can; I won't stop now."

"If you think Fido's still queer, shall I ask Brown the vet to call, as I pass his house on the way to the station?" he asked, as he was leaving the house.

"He doan't want noo wet," Sarah interposed suddenly.

"No, thank you," said Laura; "he couldn't do no good."

"Good-bye, then," said Rupert. "I'm sorry that this has happened while I've been here, but I really don't believe that old Sock had anything to do with it."

"Then you call me a liar!" spat Sarah viciously.

"No, I don't say that. I think you are mistaken," Rupert answered; "but I can't make it out yet. I won't say anything more about it now."

He bent down and kissed Laura, whose eyes were now considerably more dazed and vacant than her dog's. She returned his kiss, and continued to rock her grief and to caress her dog in her lap.

"Good-bye," said Rupert to Sarah curtly.

"I bain't mistook, an' tha'ss a fack!" said that worthy; "an" if I wuz Miss Laura I'd see as yar dorg *did* git a t'roshin'."

Rupert said nothing in reply. He left the house, unchained old Sock, and departed.

"Come, me dare," said Sarah to her mistress, "dee yew hev a drop o' whisky. Yew must fare ta want it arter sech a shaakin' up. That warmin' of a booy! I knowed noo good wouldn't come along o' his bein' in these parts."

Laura passed by the insult to her brother. She drank and drank again, and for the rest of the day sat in a state of maudlin sentiment caressing Fido.

That night Sarah despatched a letter to Peggie which ran as follows:—

"Dear Sister,—I did what old Granny said, and got the dorgs together. But his dorg wouldn't do no harm. So I pinched Fido's tail, and made him yap, and then I throttled him and rubbed him up agin the old dorg's nose and mouth, but afore I could throttle him enow they come in, and now he fare right as ninepence; but I've give him one of old

L

Granny's powders in his milk, so don't be seprised if you hear of a death in the family. She'll put it down to his dorg. She fare whoolly flummoxed tonight. You'd better come over and see us o' Fridy next week and tell her all about him, and a little bit more. Let us know if you're a-comin'. Hoping this will find you well as it do me.

"Your affexnit'sister,

"sarah."

Fido died that night.

THE QUESTION THE more Rupert thought over the events of the morning and Laura's behaviour in relation thereto, the more puzzled and indignant he became. He knew well enough that her intellect was weak, but this did not excuse her imbecility or her injustice in his eyes. He forgot that she could not be expected to know the nature of his dog as well as he did, and that it was only natural that the evidence of Fido's condition, together with the assertions of the woman who had for long been the guiding influence of her life, should outweigh the opinion he had expressed. Her inability to see that a bite must have left teeth marks, her unwillingness to attempt to sift the facts, were exasperating to a man accustomed to form conclusions on strict grounds of reason. In his love of fairness and truth he grew unfair to his sister, and took a false view of her conduct.

His thoughts were centred upon her during the return journey to Duckingham Station, and it was not till he was on the marsh that he turned his attention to the other human actor in the scene.

"I'll swear Sarah was lying, and knew she was lying!" he said to himself. "Her indignation at my disbelief did not ring true. Her violent expression of it was bluff—pure bluff. Now what is her game? And how did that little brute get hurt? It's taught me one thing, anyhow—that she's not to be trusted, and that's useful to know."

As he walked along, little facts, unnoticed at the time of their occurrence, came to his recollection. He remembered his dying father's words, "Sarah—deceit—a devil!" and they gathered import. He remembered her eagerness to have the trust moneys handed over to Laura, and little by little he began to see light. But it was hard to change the opinion of years of habit. Since he was a child he had liked Sarah and trusted her. He regarded her with a certain patronising favour from the heights of his own intellectual eminence as an ignorant, simple-minded woman, with a practical ability that was of use to Laura. Straitened in circumstances as he was, and as, by his own fault, he had often been before, he had never cast an eye to his interest under his father's will that would fall in on his sister's death. He had no meanness or greed in his disposition, and it was difficult for him to suspect their existence in others, especially in one whom he had held in tolerant affection for so long. It is humiliating to find treachery and cunning where we have habitually expected honesty and simple-mindedness. But now that he was awakened to the nature of many of Sarah's past sayings and doings, the certainty that it was her desire to make mischief between him and Laura was forced upon him. And the motive could only be pecuniary.

The purpose troubled him less than the means taken to fulfil it. It grieved him little to think that Laura might not mention him in her will, but he was distressed at the idea that Sarah might cause a rupture in the love that had grown up fresh and sweet again since he had come down to the country.

"If I could bring any amount of evidence to prove that Sarah is deceitful, I doubt if Laura would believe it," he mused. "And if she did believe it, would she be any the better off? She's used to Sarah, and has a competence, even if she's robbed, as I now begin to think she may be. If I were to cause a breach between her and Sarah, what could she do? Although I'm fond of her I couldn't live with her always. She isn't fit to look after herself, and any new companion she found might very well be worse than Sarah. I'll be shot if I can see how I should be benefiting her in any way by exposing Sarah—even if I found irrefutable proof of what is now, after all, but a suspicion. If she turns against me through Sarah's machinations I must grin and bear it—and be satisfied with seeing that she is comfortable. And then!—And then!— It can't matter to her whom I marry!"

Sarah, Laura, Fido, and even old Sock, were swept away at the thought of his love. He was going to her. He quickened his pace. His thoughtful expression left him, and one buoyant and keen took its place. He looked about him. Over on Gully's level he saw Gilbert with his gun. "Now," thought he, "if only the old man has gone out I shall have her to myself!"

He found her alone in the kitchen. The door was open, and she started as he appeared on the threshold. He entered, closed the door behind him, advanced eagerly, and held out his arms.

"No! Oh no!" she said. Her beautiful eyes were suffused with tears. Timidity and sorrow spoke eloquently through them. But he was not to be denied. He caught her to him, and she was at once passive in his embrace.

"No, my darling?" he cried. "Why? Don't you love me any longer?"

He raised her chin and kissed her on the lips. She quivered with emotion as she clung to him a moment. Then she said, "Rupert, you know I love you. I shall always love you. But you must not love me. I am only a poor girl, and you are a gentleman. People would laugh at you for thinking of me. You could not make me your wife, and you would be unhappy if you made me unhappy, dear." (The old, old objection, so often raised, so rarely persisted in.)

"Not make you my wife? But that's exactly what I want to do," cried Rupert, kissing her again. "Bertha, dearest, will you be my wife?"

"You mustn't, dear," she pleaded. "Think of father and the boys, look at this place, and think who I am."

"I do; that's all I do think about," said her lover. "You are you and lam I; and soon you shall be I and I shall be you. Come, dear, I've thought it all out. Nothing could be better for me than to win you for my wife."

"But I can't leave father while he lives," said Bertha, beginning to sob. "The poor old man can't see to himself, and the boys do ill-treat him and swear at him so."

Rupert considered. He could not rise to the height of love sufficiently to suggest giving the old man house-room in his own place. He was over seventy. Perhaps he would be in the way as father-in-law. He was feeble and unlikely to last long. Rupert felt that he could wait. He could trust himself now that Bertha was his promised wife. He would not be so vile as to foul the flower he was to wear. He felt, moreover (a fact he had not realised in his self-communings of the morning), that a new strength had come to him together with a new health from the marshes. The emotional ecstasy he had experienced the first time he saw the sun rise on the marshes had been repeated more than once. He knew that his nature was becoming purer and stronger, and was expanding in the semi-consciousness of some great knowledge that was coming to him, whence, or how, he knew not. A trust in some invisible direction— some mystic *zeit-gheist*—was, little by little, gaining force in his idea of existence. As yet he hardly realised what was happening, but he knew that he could face and overcome temptations now that he would at one time either have fled from or succumbed to.

"Don't think me brutal or cold-blooded," he said, "but your father is an old man. Will you marry me when he no longer has need of you?"

"I will never marry anybody else," replied Bertha. "If you want me then you will only have to ask for me, for I am all yours."

"Then that's settled," cried Rupert exultantly.

"But you won't tell anyone yet?" asked Bertha.

"Why not?" Rupert inquired. "I mean to see plenty of you now. And you'll get talked about."

"I don't mind," said Bertha. "What do I care what the people about here say of me?"

"But your father and brothers?" said Rupert.

"Give father some tobacco, and the boys some powder and shot now and then," said Bertha bitterly, "and they won't care what you do. Any one of them would sell me for a gallon of beer. "

"Good God!" cried Rupert. "Let me take you away from them at once. They are not fit to live in the same house with you."

"I can't forsake father," the girl answered sadly, but decidedly. "Mother asked me to look after him, and I promised her I would."

"But suppose someone else offers the beer and baccy?" asked Rupert.

"Oh! I can take care of myself," Bertha assured him. "I've done so till now, and it will be all the easier now that Oh, my darling, are you sure that you won't regret it?"

There is a subjective eloquence and charm in lovers' endearments that never palls by reiteration. But half a dozen "darlings " and a few " dearests " are enough for the casual reader, and Rupert and his love may be left to themselves to enjoy the rest.

One more may, however, be written down as being material to these presents.

When Rupert left the kitchen he turned again, and standing in the passage outside, he said, "Good-bye, darling!"

"Well, I'm damned!" whispered old Noddy to Peggie at their scullery window. "Now we can make a guess at what they ha' been a-dewin' on by their selves for the last half-hour!"

"Disgustin' I calls it!" said Peggie. But she chuckled to herself, "Moor tales for Miss Laura, an' without me tellin' noo lies neither. Seerah'll be whoolly pleased!"

SARAH PAYS A VISIT, AND WHAT CAME OF IT

rHE death of her dog was bad for Laura in more ways

A than one. She had the old maid's passionate attachment to her pet, and was even more overcome at his loss than she had been at her father's death. The latter had been assuaged by the excitement of a new independence, but there was nothing to take her mind off the former. Nothing, that is, except drink. For the evil effects of her sorrow were greatly magnified by the excuse it gave Sarah to constantly press liquor upon her. "Hev a little drop moor, me pore dare," the woman said again and again, "yew need it. If ye doan't keep up, yar pore heart 'ull drip blood. Hev a little drop moor. That'll make ye sleep an' forgit."

Urged on thus, Laura drank herself into oblivion, and only came to her senses to be persuaded to repeat the horrible process.

Two days after the murder of Fido, Sarah again wended her way to Frogsthorpe. On this occasion her visit was as much to Rupert as to Peggie. She called on the latter first, and with many chuckles related the success of the first step in the course old Granny had mapped out. "Yew'll ha'e ta come oover ta-morrer, Tharsdy, 'stead o' Fridy," she said. "I want Ruput ta come o' Fridy, an' she must hare all yew ha' got ta tell afoor that. Is theer anything fresh?"

Peggie told her of the farewell outside the back door.

"Aah, tha'ss caapital!" grinned Sarah. "I rackon she'll whoolly give him a mobbin'. Be he at hooam?"

Peggie had just seen him leave the Herons' door, and said so.

"Then I'll just goo round an' hev a wud or tew along o' him," said Sarah.

Rupert looked up from his work with astonishment on hearing his gate open and seeing Sarah come up the garden path to his door. "Hallo, Sarah!" he said. "Come over to see your sister?"

He made no offer to kiss her as he had been accustomed to do since childhood.

"Well, I *hev* a seed Peggie," replied Sarah solemnly, "but I want ta hev a mardle along o' yew."

"All right; go ahead," said Rupert. "Quiet, Sock."

The old dog was growling. He never got over his first dislike of Sarah.

"Ooh dare! ooh dare!" began Sarah, bursting into an admirably acted fit of tears. "Yew'll ha'e ta kill that brute. Pore little Fiddy died the night he wuz bit, an' Miss Laura's pratty nigh craazy."

"Fido dead?" cried Rupert, astonished.

"An' noo wonder, arter what yar dorg did teVm," said Sarah.

"Now look here, Sarah," said Rupert firmly. "What he died of I don't know, but I do know that Sock never touched him."

"Well, I thote a did," said Sarah. "He wuz a-smellin, ar him, but I may ha' been mistook. Per'aps 'twuz a fit' but yew'll niver git Miss Laura ta believe't. She say yew ought ta shewt yar dorg, an' she expect yew will."

"I'll be hanged if I do," said Rupert "But why didn't you say it was a fit at first? Then Laura would never have blamed the old dog."

"I wuz soo frighted an' maazed," replied Sarah, "I hudly knowed what I wuz a-dewin' on; but please forgi'e me foor't. I di'n't mean noo harm; but what I want ta say is that Miss Laura is a-drinkin' harself into har graave, an' yew ote ta stop it."

"I thought so," said Rupert savagely. "Can't you do anything at all?"

"I *hev* tried. 'Strew's Gord I hev," wept Sarah. "I tode har she ote ta pay regard ta me, for I've sarved har faithful an' trew, though not a farden o' money ha' she give me since the ole guvnor died."

"What's that?" cried Rupert, amazed. "Do you mean to say that she pays you no wages?"

"Not a farden," repeated Sarah. "She's whoolly a rum egg, though yew mightn't think it. But doan't yew let har knoo I tode ye. I prarmussed yar pore mother as I'd niver leave har, an' I niver will—not if she niver gi'e me a farden."

"That's really very good of you," said Rupert, in doubt whether to disbelieve his visitor on this as on all other points, or to think that he had done her an injustice. "But didn't she pay any attention," he asked, "when you tried to stop her from drinking?"

"Norra mite!" answered Sarah. "She tode me ta mind my owan bizness, an' said as she wuz Miss Claybrooke, an' di'n't want noo imperence."

"But I've seen you offer her spirits," said Rupert. "Why did you do that if she is in the habit of taking too much?"

"Tha'ss soo as yew shou'n't suspeck narthen!" explained Sarah. "'Tain't a nice thing for a brother to knoo as his sister drink. An' I hooped I might be able ta git the better on it without yar help. But I darsen't wait noo longer. But for Gord's sake doan't yew let har knoo as I tode ye. Come oover the day arter ta-morrer without lettin' har knoo as yew're a-comin', an' if she be as bad as she be ta-day, yew'll be able ta find a 'scuse for speakin' tew'r about it."

"Do you think it was safe to leave her to-day?" asked Rupert anxiously.

"She oan't try ta leave the house," said Sarah. "She've sense enow ta knoo when she bain't fit ta be seed."

"Yes; but it would be an infernal nice thing if she should take it into her head to go out. And besides, suppose anyone calls! Here, you'd better be off back at once. You ought not to have come, but to have waited to see me over there. You should never have left her in that state. Why didn't you write? Oh, hang it all, look sharp."

"I did it for the best," wept Sarah. "She've been wuss since Fiddy died, an'"

"You can just get the 1.30 if you make haste," said Rupert. "I'll go across the marshes with you, as you are afraid of the stock. That's the shortest way. Come on."

The rapid transit of the marshes allowed little further conversation. "Fare ye well," said Sarah as she got into the train. "Then yew'll come oover the day arter ta-morrer. Doan't bring yar dorg. Yew'd best tell her he's kilt, if yew want ta hev any inferlence oover har. Yew"

The train moved off, and left Rupert to deliberate on the pleasant duty that lay before him—a duty which, from the very nature of it, precluded him from seeking assistance or advice in any quarter whatsoever. The knowledge that even if this were not so, there was none in the world to whom he could have gone for counsel or help, only made his thoughts more sombre, his disinclination to the task more pronounced.

He spent the one day's grace permitted him upon the marsh, and found there the solace for an unquiet mind that may be drawn from the majesty of the lonely land. Every day the peace, the beauty of the wild scenery, the tantalising murmur of the rushes (inarticulate to him, but ever seeming to strive to become intelligible), became of greater influence in moulding his character. There is no God in bricks and mortar, in the rush and turmoil of London traffic, in the cynical selfishness of London life; least of all in the petty details and senseless quibbles of Lincoln's Inn. But here, in the very lap of nature, Rupert was unconsciously coming to the knowledge that there is a God—" or something very like him. " He could not yet formulate the new sense of unseen power. But it was sufficiently real to enable him to gain comfort and strength from it. And the great love that had come to him out of nature's purity, untricked with any gauds of affectation, tended to bring him down from the conceit of his intellectual vigour to the simple trustfulness of primitive life.

While he was preparing for his ordeal in this mediaeval way, Peggie was instilling the belief in her brother's utter worthlessness into Laura. Sarah had prepared her mistress for the visit and for the flood of scandal.

"Peggie's a-comin' oover ta see ye, me dare," she said. "She've a someat ta tell ye as I think yew ote ta knoo on. She di'n't want ta come, but I tode har 'twuz har dewty. An' though that'll wex har cruel, she's a-gooin' ta oopen yar eyes."

Laura had by this time been fully persuaded by her companion, not only that her dog had been killed by Rupert's, but that it had been done with his knowledge and contrivance—a story ridiculous to anyone capable of gauging probabilities, and an event trivial enough in the occurrences of life to have a vital effect on their issue. But an old maid's devotion to a pet animal is not based on reason. And Laura, even more than other women, was incapable of weighing evidence, or of following a line of argument. Her temper was soured, her nerves shaken, and her passions excited by the drink that was always being offered to her. Rupert had not been over to see her as often as she had expected, and Sarah easily induced her to attribute this to neglect or indifference. She listened to the farrago of lies from Peggie without any notion that before accepting them as facts, she ought, in fairness, to hear what her brother had to say in answer. The tale was craftily told her under the pledge of secrecy. She saw no impropriety in giving this pledge, in listening to the foul slander under the veil of confidence, or in forming what opinion she was capable of forming without reference to the golden rule *"audi alteram partem."*

When Peggie went she left Laura under the impression that Rupert had made himself a laughing-stock, and discredited the sacred name of "Claybrooke" by the ineffectual wooing of Edith Norton, by reckless exhibitions of quack medicines, and lastly, by getting entangled in an intrigue with Bertha Heron, who was notorious throughout Frogsthorpe and Duckingham.

"For the whool willage knoo as he's yar brother," said Peggie, "an' yew want ta be soo keerful in the country! Now when I wuz fust married, Paarson Mottridge he kep' a-comin' ta see me o' Wensdy nights, when Phillup goo ta chapel. An' I say ta him, 'Now I'm a 'speckable married 'oman, an' '"

"Yes, yes. We know all about that," broke in Sarah, who was anxious lest Laura's mind should be diverted from the consideration of Rupert's iniquities to any side issue. "What you want ta dew, Laura, is ta tell him that yew ha' heerd as he've been seed a lot along o' them Herons. An' tell him what yew ha' heerd about Bartha. Yew doan't want ta mention Peggie's name, as she've made ye prarmuss not tew. An' yar naamin' on't 'ull be enow ta put him right."

Rupert and Laura were both intent upon each other's regeneration when they met on the following day. The situation was not without its humorous side if the sordid character of the rest of the dramatic interest could be eliminated. Both brother and sister had braced themselves for combat with the respective evils in their respective ways. But one was sad and earnest—the other indignant and petulant.

Sarah opened the door to him. "Yew'll find har in the dinin'-rewm," she said. "Yew'd best see har alooan. I thote I'd better tell har as yew wuz a-comin', or she might ha' been tew droonk ta unnerstan' any moortal thing. But she fare soober this moarnin', and is espectin' on ye."

Laura had been priming herself for the interview, and was scarce as collected as Sarah made out. Her large, puffy cheeks were painfully flushed; her pale blue eyes red and watery when she exchanged kisses with Rupert.

"I thought I'd come over and say how sorry I am to hear of Fido's death," said he.

"So you ought to be," said Laura, bridling. "If ever I catch hold of your dorg I'll do the same to him!"

"Well, I can't help it if you believe it was Sock," replied Rupert. "But I'm sure he had nothing to do with it."

"It's no use talkin', I s'pooz," said Laura. "We can't bring him to life again. But I'm glad you've come. Will you have anything?"

"He can't have let him be killed willingly!" she thought to herself, as she looked at his frank face, clouded with a sympathy which even she could see was genuine. "Sarah's wrong there. I wonder why she hates him so!"

"No, thank you," said Rupert, in answer to her offer of hospitality.

"Then I will," said Laura, rising and mixing herself a drink.

Before Rupert could seize the opportunity this gave him, she continued, " How are you getting on in your cottage? I hope you don't see nothen o' those Herons. You allust was a fool about gals, and that Bertha is a downright bad lot."

This was not done so diplomatically but that Rupert smelt a rat. He knew old Peggie had been from home the

M day before. He knew Sarah had seen her sister on the Wednesday. He put two and two together.

"Ah," he said, "you've been hearing lies from old Peggie. There is not a better girl in England, nor a purer, than Bertha Heron."

"That's what you allust thought of all the gals you ha' got mixed up with till you found 'em out," said Laura, unfortunately with some truth. "I've no patience with you. Here's this gal, as is knowed as a thorough bad lot, an' I'll be bound she'll turn you round her little finger. A nice thing for me. Everybody about there know me as Miss Claybrooke."

"I assure you that you are mistaken as to that," said Rupert; "very few of the villagers know anything about you. But that doesn't matter. What does matter is that that venomous old woman has been spitting her scandal after I warned her against doing so. I told her I'd make her repent it, and by Jove I will!"

"I never said it was Peggie," said Laura, "and everybody know me there."

"Don't let us quarrel about it, dear," rejoined Rupert. "Your mind has been poisoned, and you don't know the sort of old woman you have to deal with. I wish you'd come over and see Bertha yourself, you'd find out the truth then. To tell you one of old Peggie's lies. You know she's always said that the Herons did not pay their rent, and that they only gave her five shillings at a time. Well, I've seen all their receipts, and the whole story is a cruel fabrication. Just come over and speak to Bertha, you'll soon see who's telling you the truth, if you can't believe me on my bare statement, as I should have thought you could have done." "What, me speak to that trollop!" cried Laura.

"Stay, Laura," said Rupert, with some assumption of dignity, "I can't have you or anybody speaking of her like that."

"Well I never! Goodness gracious! And highty-tighty!" cried Laura, her voice rising huskily. "*You* can't hev! Who are you? And what's she got to do with you?"

"If you must know," replied Rupert firmly, stung beyond prudence by his anger, "Miss Heron has done me the honour to promise to be my wife."

"What?" screamed Laura, "you mean to say that you are going to *marry* her?" She filled herself another glass and drank. "Then all I can say is that you're no brother of mine!"

"Oh Laura, Laura!" said Rupert, "you wouldn't speak like that if you were yourself. It's that confounded whisky talking! Do, dear—do, for God's sake, try to do without it."

Thus was the great subject crudely and awkwardly broached. All the introduction with which he had intended to lead up to it was lost. As soon as he had spoken he saw his mistake. He could not have chosen a worse moment for his attempt.

But the effect of his words was greater even than he had feared. Laura's face glowed crimson. Her eyes flamed with the passion of an enraged animal. She raised her unwieldy bulk with an effort. Then with a dramatic gesture she pointed to the door.

"Leave my house, sir," she said thickly. "This is my house, leave it."

Rupert rose, pale, but self-contained.

"Of course I'll go if you wish it," he said softly; "but, Laura, if I go now, I can never come back again; you see that, don't you?"

"Wait till you're axed," retorted Laura, with an air of triumphant vulgarity.

"One thing I must do before I go," said Rupert, "that is to beg you earnestly to take less stimulant. I've seen before that"

"Leave my house this minute!" screamed Laura again. "Never a farden o' my money shall you hev. That's the only thing you come down here arter. *I* know. I only wish I could get rid of you as trustee! I *hev* tried, but Mr. Strainer say ta can't be done. Sarah's allust been right about you. Leave my house, you"

At this juncture the door into the kitchen opened, and Sarah appeared. She had been eagerly listening at the keyhole, and did not want her name to be brought up for fear of inconvenient disclosures. "I've heerd ivery wud," she said. "If he doan't goo shall a send for the pleece?"

The revelation of the whole vile plot flashed upon Rupert. He stood an instant aghast. But the fear lest he should in any way lay himself open to the charge of submitting to humiliation for the sake of what Laura had to leave overcame his proper anxiety to deliver his sister from the two fiends which possessed her—Sarah and drink. He sacrificed what was, perhaps, his duty to his pride.

"Good-bye, Laura," he said. "Let me kiss you once, for the last time, for old sake's sake. I'll never enter your doors again unless you are in trouble and want me. Goodbye."

The earnestness and pathos of his voice momentarily shook the infuriated woman. A dazed expression passed over her face. Some recollection of her better self strove to assert itself. Before Sarah could interpose, Rupert kissed his sister. For a moment she clung to him. If he had stayed and fought out the matter with Sarah there and then he might possibly have saved much of the sorrow and crime that was to come. But once again his sensitive pride, together with a just indignation, prevailed. He released his clasp of Laura, turned, and left the house.

"Tha'ss caapital!" said Sarah to herself. "Now dee yew hev a little drop o' some'at," she suggested to Laura. "Yew neead it arter that warmin's impidence."

But Laura flung the stuff away, and falling heavily into her chair, she burst into the horrible laughter and sobbing of hysteria.

## XII A DEATH AND A MARRIAGE

AD and angry at heart, Rupert made his way back to

the little cottage which now more than ever was his home. His last link with the old life seemed broken, and all his future lay in his new love, and in his hope of success in his new profession. It was well for the darkness of his soul that a fresh tragedy confronted him immediately on his return.

He bent his steps to the Herons' back door, for he had left his key with Bertha. On entering the kitchen, sounds of lamentation from upstairs struck upon his hearing. Young Gilbert was alone in the room. The lad's face was flushed and eager with excitement.

"Bartha'll be glad yew've come hooam," he said. "Faa'er fared whoolly quare this mooarnin', an' lay abed. When I took him up his brekkust—blust! He di'n't knoo narthen. But he wuz a-snoortin' like billy-oh, an' as black in the faace as an ole ship. I hollers ta Bartha, an' she come a-runnin' up. But she cou'n't dew narthen, an'

'strew's Gord, I believe the old 's dead! Dee yew goo an' see."

Rupert hurried upstairs to the front room. Bertha was Norfolk sheep are a black-faced breed.

standing by the bedside weeping. But, shaken with sobs as she was, she ever chafed the breast of the old man, who was lying stretched upon his bed, still and cold. It was no time for love-making.

"Oh, Rupert," cried the girl, "I'm so glad you've come. Will you help me to rub father? He's so cold. And I can't wake him up."

Rupert laid his hand on the poor old heart. Then he turned and took his sweetheart in his arms. "My poor darling," he said, "come down with me. We can do nothing more for him."

She knew he spoke truly. But in the loneliness of her anguish she had tried to believe that her father was still alive. She let her lover lead her downstairs and into the parlour.

Bob was at work on the land. Jack had taken his gun to a distant level of marsh. There was no one left in the house but Bertha, Rupert, and young Gilbert, and the last seemed more pleased than anything else with the importance of the event.

"I tode ye he wuz dead!" he said blandly, when he saw his sister come down.

"Shut up, you young brute!" said Rupert savagely, to the boy's astonishment. He was quite unaware that he had been unfeeling.

When Bertha was partly soothed and quieted, Rupert left her and returned to the kitchen. It was clear that all the details and sordid technicalities would fall to him if he wished to save Bertha from seeing to them. He ascertained from Gilbert that a Chetbridge doctor had previously attended old Heron for an attack of apoplexy, and he sent off the boy to summon him.

The attack he had witnessed in the night had left its mark behind; and though he was right in attributing it to a surfeit, he had been unable to see the serious nature of it. The old man had been up to the "Grey Mare" the night before his death. Some fishermen had just come home after a successful trip, and set the beer flowing freely. The result was that old Heron had once again, and for the last time, overtaxed his constitution. He had fallen into a heavy sleep, and had succumbed to the plethora of excess without waking.

Dr. Abbott gave a certificate, and a humble funeral was arranged with Rupert's help.

There is little to tell of the days between the death and the funeral. The loutish boys went about their business in their wonted manner. Jack got rather more drunk than usual, and Bob and Gilbert fought over the distribution of the little property there was in true fraternal fashion. Any difficulty that might have arisen as to this was removed by the thoughtful action of the Noddyfields, who claimed for the half-year's rent due at Michaelmas, and for another half-year in lieu of notice. This effectually disposed of any family disputes concerning the division of the estate. The few household goods were advertised for sale. Jack and Gilbert decided to go on tramp. Bob took lodgings in the village. Jack and Bob both planned their lives without reference to their sister. Gilbert alone showed any anxiety as to her future, but on hearing that she was about to marry Rupert, he went off satisfied to the life he had always thought of in his dreams, but never rightly. To him the life of a tramp seemed to be one of living in comfort without work, and with the added charm of promiscuous poaching. Perhaps he was not more deceived in his ideas of life than most of us are who stand on the brink of it. He alone of the brothers promised his sister to let her hear from him from time to time, and asked her to write to him occasionally. He was not without affection, but he had been taught by his associates to consider love or consideration for anyone other than himself as weaknesses meriting coarse ridicule. He was about to try an experience of existence without affection or domestic care of any kind. That would rub his spectacles clean.

Bob and Jack evinced some disappointment on hearing of Bertha's engagement. It had been with a certain exultation that they had told her that she "'ould ha'e ta dew for harself now." And they were annoyed to think that her prospects were brighter than their own. They parted from her with language indicating a contempt for her future husband which roused her. And when they were gone she swore that she would have nothing more to do with any of her kin except Gilbert. She still had hopes of him when his imagination had been disillusioned.

Rupert overcame all her objections to a speedy marriage by the unanswerable argument that there was nothing else that could reasonably be done; and in the consciousness that this was so he exulted.

Poor Bertha was supple to his wishes. She had only him to look to now, and thanked God that she had him. He paid the pound or two necessary for a special licence, and before the day fixed for the sale at the old home Bertha was quietly married to him at the Chetbridge Registry Office. A brief honeymoon of three days was spent at the best hotel in Herringhaven, and the newly married pair were back at "The Castle" in time for Rupert to buy a few things at the sale which his wife especially prized. Some additions were made to the comforts of the cottage, and with very little left of his small capital, Rupert commenced life as a married man.

XIII HAPPINESS AND TROUBLE THE prudent would, no doubt, have thought the matrimonial venture somewhat precarious. Rupert had not yet entirely lost his old habits of extravagance. His marriage had given him an excuse, and during his short stay at Herringhaven he had lived in the style to which he had been accustomed in his younger days. Thus it happened that he had diminished his little capital considerably. A sum of *£10* or so, an income of about *£i* a week (and uncertain at that) from reviewing, with the vague possibilities of short story writing by an unknown man, cannot be said to form a satisfactory basis upon which to accept the responsibilities of a wife and a potential family. He and Bertha calculated that their household expenses could easily be kept within the *£1* a week, and the short stories could surely be depended on for rent and incidental expenses. The allowance for housekeeping would have seemed absurd to Rupert but a short six months ago; but he had learnt on how little it is possible to live in the country, where only necessaries are considered necessary, where new milk is a penny a pint and pork sixpence a pound. Fortunately, he said, he was fond of pork. His pain at the quarrel with his sister and Bertha's grief at the loss of her father soon became muted in the ecstasy of the first weeks of their married life. They found that mutual knowledge of each other increased their love—a rare matrimonial experience! Their social isolation from their neighbours was no source of sorrow to them. Bertha's natural gifts of intellect and disposition had full scope to grow to perfection. And day by day her husband congratulated himself on his good fortune. Nay! He did more! He found himself lifting up his heart in thanks to the Master of destiny!

In the very early days of his married life he was led to analyse the change that had come over his agnosticism. The sight of his wife kneeling at the bedside was in itself an illumination. She had the sense and delicacy not to ask him how it was that she never saw him doing likewise, and she had her reward. For one night, soon after their return to Frogsthorpe, he laid his hand on hers and knelt down beside her. He did not pray in the accepted meaning of the word, but he seemed to attain to a wordless communion with something higher than himself, and when he rose, he felt an exaltation of soul, a quiet gratitude for the good that he found in his simple life, that was new to his emotional experiences. Before they slept, he spoke on the subject of his belief and disbelief. "Somehow," he said, "there seems to be a kindly influence directing my life. Chance and coincidence may account for much, but a series of consistent chances and coincidences leading to this happiness of our married life can hardly be idiopathic. The popular conception of a deity is as ludicrous and repulsive to me as ever, but every day I seem to be guided by some mysterious intelligence, not myself, that "makes for righteousness." I cannot be presumptuous enough to pray; but I feel now that I can return thanks."

"Why do you call prayer presumptuous?" asked Bertha. "When I pray I only ask that you may be as happy as I am, dear, and that I may be able to make you so."

"That is hardly prayer in the ordinary meaning of the word," said Rupert. "Prayer is presumptuous when it dictates to a superior being what that superior being should do. Destiny is not to be called upon to answer a doorbell. What is, is. What will be, will be. The popular prayer sketches a series of events or a number of isolated occurrences, and requests that they may be placed on the agenda of fate, entirely careless whether they are incongruous with the general scheme of life, harmless to others, material to welfare, either personal or common, or not. George Meredith (by the way, you must read his books. You haven't, have you?)—George Meredith makes Sir Austin Feverel bid his son Richard tell a labourer who is puzzled at the theory of prayer (and no wonder) that 'he who rises from prayer a better man, his prayer is answered.' That is all very well if prayer is what I can alone conceive it to be, an endeavour towards communion with the Highest. But the average person prays for specific benefits to himself, even specified injuries to his enemies, and there can be nothing either elevating or reasonable in that. Even when prayers are for the welfare of others, there is the suggestion of action to a superior intelligence. It is as if a recruit gave Roberts tips for a campaign."

"But you do believe in God, don't you, dear?" said Bertha, with a woman's pertinacity.

Rupert fidgeted. He knew that his wife did not refer to a personage in golden robes sitting upon a throne before a glassy sea, but he was not sure how far she materialised the Deity, and he was the last person in the world to wish to shake anyone's substantial faith. "For," he thought to himself, "faith is beyond argument. The doctrine of Christ's divinity and his atonement cannot stand the simplest application of reason. It is beautiful, and only captiousness would object to its injustice. But faith has nothing to do with logic. It is beyond it. My ecstasy in hearing the slow movement in the octett, or in No. Nine, or at the Charfreitsburg music, is beyond argument. But it exists. The delight is inexplicable. But it is real. And so is faith, though I haven't got it any more than my old college dean had the musical element. Materialists would tell you that the musical fervour arose from the gratification of a cultivated sense. Well, but why should it so arise? Like all their explanations, it stops short of the vital point."

He thought for a moment, then he said in reply to Bertha's question, " I do not believe that man's intellect is the highest in existence. It may not be. I don't know. There are so many things that we don't know, and so few that we do. I do believe that any attempt to raise ourselves to higher things is good. And that there *are* higher things than man is sincerely to be hoped. It were a poor universe else. And, dear, lately I have seemed to be able to get in touch with some unseen power. And the purer the surroundings, the nearer to the simplicity of nature, the easier it is."

Bertha knew better than to press him further, and the subject dropped. But afterwards it became no uncommon thing for him to kneel with her, and the magnetism of each for the other thrilled them as they placed themselves at the threshold of the Unknown, and led them nearer to an understanding of it.

It was well for both of them that they were attaining to a simple trust in the decrees of destiny, for they were to be sorely tried.

The reeking mists of December were steaming up from the ooze and decaying vegetation of the dykes, and swathing all the low-lying land in a chill, dreary fog that hung inexorably still in the motionless atmosphere, when a foreboding of misfortune came to Rupert.

He had been accustomed to receive a cheque on the first Monday of every month from the weekly publication for which he reviewed. Now, for the first time since he obtained the work, this was not forthcoming. He wrote two letters asking for an explanation, but no answer was vouchsafed. Still the books continued to come weekly, and he did not like to appear too importunate. It was, however, impossible to confine the weekly expenses within the few shillings produced by the sale of the books to a second-hand shop. The little capital was dwindling to vanishing point. The acceptance of his first few short stories had been arranged through the introduction of Harry Lyndon. Subsequent work had, with horrible monotony, been coming back, accompanied by the sickening courtesy of printed or lithographed regrets and thanks. The tales which had been accepted were unprinted and, of course, unpaid for.

"Hang it all!" said Rupert, with a sense of indignation. "Some of 'em have been accepted six months. They *must* print 'em soon, and they will lead to other work, and then we shall be all right."

Poor fellow! He did not know that editors have a pleasing habit of keeping accepted work by an unknown man two or three years before allowing it to see the light of publication.

He wrote to his friend Harry, and for days he cultivated a feeling of ill-will against the postman, as the dapper little man swung round the corner with never a letter for "The Castle." He wrote again to his paper, again to Harry, and still the solemn silence continued, till even his optimistic heart grew sick in the midst of the happiness of his home. He did not like to trouble Bertha with his worries, but she noticed his depression and, ignorant of its cause, began to search for faults in herself to account for his unhappiness. He wrote harder and harder; spent pennies (that now began to swell enormously in importance) on stamps for delivery and return. Those sent for return were promptly put to the use for which they were intended. He had been at work on a novel, and now sent up some fifty or sixty thousand words of it to Harry Lyndon, in the hope that he might get some encouragement from his opinion. But neither opinion nor work came back. It spoke well for the vitality of his new theory, that there was a beneficent directing influence keeping guard over his life, that it was not shaken by despondency. Almost the only moments of peace he had were those spent with his wife kneeling at the bedside. The strain of anxiety had this effect upon him, that in his silent communion with the Highest an inarticulate appeal came involuntarily to form part of his thoughts.

A week before Christmas the weather changed, and there came a heavy fall of snow, which hid the marshes deep beneath a level expanse of white that shimmered under a cold, colourless sun, and soon blew up in powdery drifts as a biting wind-frost roared over the fen from the north-east. On Christmas Day, Bertha, in hurrying from the bakehouse to the living-room, slipped on the ice-covered "pamments," sprained her ankle badly, and bruised herself all down one side. Throughout the Christmas week, while all the marshmen were rolling home with the "fishin' chaps," shouting drunken obscenities of song in the night air, so that their foul howls steamed up a visible reek of filth, Rupert was sitting at his wife's bedside, comforting her, and assuring her that he was able to manage all right in the cottage by himself, and that she was not to worry. For her dread lest he should suffer discomfort pained her more than sprain or bruises.

The time was sad for both of them. The loss of her father recurred to the girl, as all such losses will at the season that usurps the title of festivity; and it was the first Christmas at which Rupert had neither sent nor received any token of goodwill to or from his sister. But the isolation and their consciousness of it only drew husband and wife closer together. Bertha had not known Rupert's love and care till she was dependent upon his attentions. Rupert did not know her sweet patience under suffering till these attentions became necessary. The sight of his wife lying in pain broke down all his economy. She was confined to her bed. Delicacies were obviously necessary according to his experience. (The dwellers on the marsh could have taught him differently.) His last few pounds

N did not go far in procuring them. His desperation, as much as his affection, urged him to obtain for her any comfort he could. He was, moreover, strangely borne up with the certainty that help would come to put them right again, even at the last minute. If the worst came to the worst, he must pawn or sell his piano. He broke into his last sovereign with little compunction. His trust in destiny had become blind and unreasonable, in spite of his appreciation of logical sequence.' Closer and closer his soul became knit with Bertha's, and now his anxiety for her, and his dread lest she should suffer pain and want, made his prayers articulate. In spite of himself, in the face of the "presumption" and unreasonableness of it, he found himself putting his hopes, his needs, into words. The morning after the first night he became conscious of doing this, an idea came to him for an article. He wrote a humorous sketch of a Christmas orgie at the "Grey Mare," and sent it up to the *Universe.* Two days after his stamped envelope came back, but its contents seemed meagre for his MS. He tore open the envelope, and a proof lay before him.

What logic could stand against this coincidence? He did not own to himself that he attributed the acceptance of his sketch to his prayer. He called it a strange freak of chance, and then pulled himself up lest his guardian angel should consider this ingratitude. His brain was in a turmoil with the strife between the undefinable influence that was leading him to mysticism, and the hard rules of pure reason which had seemed to him the sole guide for human thought, belief, and conduct ever since his intellect had attained independence.

The proof was returned to the office of the *Universe,* and three days afterwards he received a cheque. His was a buoyant nature, and secretive only of trouble. He took the cheque up to his wife, and then, with caresses and endearments, he told her all the cause of his worry and past depression. "But we're all right now, thank God!" he cried. "If they'll only take one a fortnight, one a month, we can get along. Thank God, we're all right now!"

In his heart he fully believed that he would soon be practically on the staff, and that success and prosperity were no longer in doubt. As for Bertha, her delight was beyond bounds at learning that her husband's sadness had not been caused by any fault of hers, or any diminution of his love for her.

"Why didn't you tell me what was troubling you?" she asked fondly. "And why did you get me all those things? If I have you, dear, I am happy. I am not used to delicacies."

The ecstasy of relief was so great that it almost made amends for the pain they had suffered. "Sweet is pleasure after pain."

Blended with all the exuberance of revived hope was a deep humility. He did not attribute his success to the merit of his work, but to destiny. Fatalism is generally a cruel creed. But in him it was tempered by a belief in the kindness of fate. Against every principle he owned he was building up a scheme of existence from a personal experience. He could not have justified it by a single syllogism. He had only to cast his eyes round the village, on the ignorance, prejudice, selfishness, animalism, vice, filth, and hypocrisy of the country people; he had but to remember his sister and Celibate Sarah, and the Noddyfields, to refute his optimism. But his association with Bertha and his spiritual experiences were making a new man of him. He was no longer bound by hard and fast rules of evidence. His soul was leaping free from materialism; and, right or wrong, he was the better and happier man for it.

When Bertha was able to get about again "*Schoene Frettde*" once more held sway in the little cottage, and the life of the young couple was brighter and fuller than ever before in the glow of still-increasing mutual esteem and knowledge.

THE HUMOURS OF FATE, WHEREBY OPTIMISM MEETS WITH A CHECK IT seemed as if the great firm of the Fates were determined to submit Rupert's trust (recently manufactured at their establishment) to a series of severe tests in order to prove its ability to stand wear and tear. For no sooner had his hopes received the fillip from the *Universe* than disappointment after disappointment fell upon him. The old stories of Job and Dr. Faustus were reproduced in his experiences with all their injustice. The spirit of mischief appeared to be given a free hand to do what it could to make him curse his Maker and the day on which he was made.

It was only to be expected that the absurd hopes which he had built upon the acceptance of his sketch should be disappointed. He had happened to hit the subject and the moment for once, and he never did it again. Article after article went up, only to be returned. But in addition to the natural frustration of his hopes he had to bear what may be termed abnormal ill fortune. For the books for review ceased to come down. And in reply to his urgent inquiries, he was at last informed that certain debenture holders had taken possession of the paper for which he worked, had ousted all the old staff, and that he would not only lose the reviewing for the future, but that there was no money to pay for the work already done.

His letter to Harry Lyndon explaining his position brought down a reply, enclosing two postal orders for one pound each, and the remark, " Beatus ille qui nihil expectat, quia id adipiscetur." Lyndon praised the novel as far as he had seen it, but cheerfully gave it as his opinion that Rupert would be lucky if he found a publisher for it within two years. One short story, which had been accepted, was returned to him without any other explanation than that a newly appointed editor had found it in his drawer.

In the folly of his heart Rupert wrote to another editor who had accepted two of his stories, begging him to print them. Of course he received no reply.

The bare necessities of life compelled him to take some of his things to a Herringhaven pawnbroker. His dress suit, his watch, and some silver were parted with in this way without their loss being greatly felt. But it came to it that his gun had to go, and this deprived the small household of many a meal of wild-fowl with which they had been accustomed to eke out the scanty allowance of butcher's meat they could afford. Rupert tried to make a little money with his camera. But he had taken nearly all the village people for amusement during the first weeks of his residence, and he found that though they were glad enough to get their "likenesses took" for nothing, it was a very different thing when they were expected to pay for them. A fortune cannot be made out of selling one print from a negative for sixpence, and it was impossible to charge more in Frogsthorpe or its neighbourhood. Many a time he walked ten or twelve miles through blinding snow to get a shilling or eighteenpence if he was lucky. And at last the camera had to follow the gun.

It was clear that things could not go on as they were doing. It was incumbent upon Rupert to find paying work of some kind.

"If my brains can't keep us," he said one night to his wife, "my hands must. I'd work on the land if the pay was better; but twelve shillings a week is not enough, and I could do nothing to increase it."

"It would break my heart to see you do it," said Bertha. "Even now I sometimes think you must curse the day on which you first saw me. If it weren't for me you would not be tied down so, and would soon be able to make your way again."

"If it weren't for you, dearest," rejoined Rupert, "I should be a lonely, selfish brute, without a soul in the world to care whether I lived or died. Come what may, you have brought sweetness into my life and made a better man of me. It is for you to regret. With your beauty and charm, you might have married a rich man and lived in comfort."

But this Bertha would by no means allow. And the little, tender dispute ended in caresses.

Although his home and home life were effectually cut off from the rest of the village, Rupert still associated with the marshmen; and in spite of his experience with Edith, he still looked for beer and copy at the "Grey Mare," although since stress of circumstances had emptied his pockets, it was the latter rather than the former that took him there.

A few days after he had spoken to Bertha of his determination to get something to do, he found Neetch Jinnis, the fisherman, in the "Grey Mare" kitchen measuring sovereigns out of a half-pint pot by way of ostentatious display of the value of his harvest from the herring fishing. Rupert was a yachtsman and a good sailor, and it immediately occurred to him that he ought to be able to get a berth on a fishing-boat, and so tide over his present difficulties until such time as editors should have a better appreciation of merit. His book was finished. He would send it to his agent, John Perkins, and leave him to do what he could with it, while he went to sea to earn the bread and cheese of daily life.

The great herring fishery was over; but he learnt from Neetch Jinnis that the boats would soon be going to the West Coast mackerel fishing. "An' I'll tell ye what," said Neetch, "I've took a fancy tew ye. For though yew be a gennleman, as anybardy can see, yew bain't tew proud ta drink along of a pore man. I bain't a-gooin' ta the West, an' if ye like I can git ye a barth abooard o' my booat. She'll sail from Herrin'haven in about ten days."

The comparison in his favour between himself and the "pore man " gave Rupert a flavour of bitter humour. But as he was not desirous that his business should be known to all the village—(he little suspected that his poverty was the subject of frequent discussion at the "Grey Mare" "settin'-ins," and that Neetch had been grinning to himself when he spoke)—he gave the external excuse of "copy" to account for his desire to go on a fishing cruise. It seemed to him that there was nothing better to be done. The parting with Bertha would be painful, but for her own sake it must be faced. His life had been insured for two or three years, so that if he were lost at sea, she would be provided for.

He broke the news to her that evening.

"I've found something to do," he said, taking her in his arms.

"What is it?" she asked. "Something unpleasant, I know by the tone of your voice."

"It won't be pleasant for either of us," he replied, "but try and think, dearest, that it will only be for a little while, and soon we shall be together again with better prospects and greater happiness than ever. I'm going to sea."

However sensible a true woman may be, when love and advantage, even when love and actual necessity of life come into conflict, her heart overpowers her brain. Bertha was a true woman. At first she pleaded with vehement passion against the idea of separation. But her love was not selfish. When she saw that the agony of her opposition only pained Rupert, she gave way and nursed her sorrow secretly.

It was a sad and bitter trial for both of them, but Rupert bore it for his wife's sake, and she assumed acquiescence for his. Each tried to cheer the other with hopes of better times to come, and with solemn assurances of love that was founded on a rock.

The days passed quickly in preparation. Rupert sold his piano for *£20* so as to leave a nest-egg at home. He went over to Herringhaven with Neetch, and got the berth without difficulty, for there is less competition in the spring fishing than in the autumn.

The eve of his departure came, and found all in readiness. "I'll write from every port," said Rupert, "and you will write too. I shall be able to draw some money soon with any luck, and will send you all I can. Dear heart, bear up, and think that every day brings us nearer to each other. Open all my letters, and let me know if there is anything from Perkins about the book. I've told him to take his instructions from you, and act as if the book were yours. I've left a power of attorney to enable you to do anything with it, but you will, of course, wait to hear from me before accepting or refusing any offer that may come, if we are lucky enough to get one. Only twelve or sixteen weeks, dear, and then we shall be set up again."

"I wish you hadn't to go," sobbed Bertha. "I know it's silly, but I have such a horrible presentiment of misfortune."

"Now, my darling, don't let your nerves make you fancy things," said Rupert. "I like the sea, and if it were not for the parting from you, I should quite enjoy the trip. But you'll be lonely here with no one to speak to."

"No, I shan't," answered Bertha, with an attempt at cheerfulness. "I shall always be doing something for you—knitting your stockings or making something for my boy. I don't want any of the horrid people about here to speak to. I shall always have the memory of you and the hope of your return to keep me company. And then there's old Sock. He's better company than most people. Aren't you, boy?" ("Grumph!" said Sock.) "But you *will* write, dear, as often as you can, won't you?"

"I'll tell you what," said Rupert, with a touch of Norfolk phrasing, "we know where young Gilbert is. Why not write and ask him to come and stay with you till my return? He'll be some company for you, and when he is with you, away from the other boys, I believe he'll behave himself well enough."

"I'm sure he will," cried Bertha. "It's kind of you to think of it. It did cross my mind this morning, but I was afraid that you wouldn't like the idea."

Rupert protested that he would like anything that fell in with her wishes, and the matter was settled.

There was little time in the morning for more than leavetaking, and Rupert had the sense to curtail this as much as possible without appearing unfeeling. "For," as he said to himself, "if a tooth has to come out, one wrench is preferable to a number of tugs."

The last kiss was given and taken, the last farewell spoken. Before midday the *John and Susan* was in the Roads standing south with a full westerly breeze, and under three-quarter steam. Like most of the modern boats she was a steamer, and a fine sea boat. She would soon be through the Channel, round Land's End, and making for Newlyn or St. Ives.

When Bertha had had her cry out, she wrote to Gilbert. He had soon tired of the tramping life, and had found temporary work at Aylsham, to the west of the county. But the boy was only a child in experience, and the difference between even such a home as Bertha had been able to keep together in her father's lifetime and his fare amid strangers ("wheer they cut yar bread an' butter for tea, 'stead o' gi'en ye the looaf," as he subsequently complained) made him think with regret of the many brutalities he had been guilty of towards his sister when she was doing her best for him.

He was delighted to get her letter, and lost no time in returning to Frogsthorpe. The third day after Rupert's departure saw him established as Bertha's companion and male protector—a position she impressed upon him with the hope that the dignity of it might make him behave with decency and responsibility—a hope that was fulfilled with humorous exactness.

i

"THE GUID MON'S AWA"' THE first few weeks of Rupert's absence passed with a dull lack of incident to those waiting at "The Castle" for his return. His letters were regular, and brought both money and good tidings. His boat had been exceptionally lucky in shooting her nets, and the sums he was able to draw and remit home were ample to keep the little cottage going without infringing on the twenty pounds odd he had left at home. Gilbert could get work on the land whenever he wished to; but for the most part his sister was glad to have him at home or to send him with his old muzzleloader and old Sock on shooting excursions over the marshes. She did not wish him to associate with his former mates, for the less he saw of them, the greater chance she would have of winning him to some refinement of thought, speech, and manner. On his part, he felt that his return to Frogsthorpe would be considered in the village as a weakness and a failure. And his shyness made him prefer to avoid those who might be disposed to jeer at him as being under petticoat government. He had at heart a sincere affection for Bertha, and did not wish to do anything to displease her now that he was no longer corrupted by the example of his elder brothers. He was an imitative youngster, and all his life had been more under the domination of his sister than either Jack or Bob had ever been. His foul language and brutality of bearing were rapidly becoming modified now that he was solely under her influence. Still there were one or two points on which his reformation was slow. It was difficult to overcome his dislike to soap and water.

At length Bertha said to him, "How can you like to be so dirty, Gilbert? I don't believe you've washed yourself for a week."

"Well, wha'ss the good on't?" replied Gilbert. "Look a' Tom Cracker! He's a fine chap, bain't he? Well, he hudly iver wash hisself. That doan't dew ye noo good, he say. That oony gi'e ye coold!"

"But aren't you ashamed to be seen going about like that?" asked his sister.

"Whaffor?" inquired the youth. "I bain't noo muckier than iverybardy. I allust wash my hands arter I've been muckin' out the pigs or cows. Old Sock, he doan't wash hisself, dew ye, bor?"

The old dog wagged his tail, and made his questioner look silly by at once proceeding to diligently lick his paws. Then he jumped up and gave a great lick down the right side of Gilbert's face. The space where his tongue had traversed shone rosy and clear in the midst of soot and grime.

Bertha laughed. "Now look at yourself in the glass," she said.

"Wha blaame the dorg!" said Gilbert, grinning; "now I shall *ha'e* ta wash!"

He went to the bakehouse sink for the purpose. When he returned, the fore part of his face was rosy, framed in a rim of black that extended round his face in a line running just in front of his ears.

Meanwhile Bertha had been thinking.

"Look here, Gil," she said, "why do you clean your gun if cleanliness is of no use?"

"That oan't shewt so sharp when ta be foul," said Gilbert, not seeing as yet whither this inquiry tended.

"Well, *you* can't do what you want to do so well when *you* are foul," said Bertha triumphantly. "Why don't you treat yourself as you do your gun?"

"But a wash that all oover," objected Gilbert, alarmed at the possibilities in ablution that lay before him. "I hain't washed myself all oover since yew bathed me t'ree yare agoo."

"At any rate, you see that you ought to do so now," replied Bertha. "Let me get you some water hot, and then you can have a good bath to-night."

The analogy on which she based her argument might appear of doubtful force to a logician, but it just appealed to Gilbert's understanding.

"Blust!" he said, reviewing her words to himself. "I niver thote o' that. If washin's good for guns that must be good for folk; but I'm blarmed if I'm a-gooin' ta *tie* myself."

After this Bertha began to take a pride in her brother, and he soon began to take a pride in himself. He was still only developed in mind and character about as much as a London boy of ten years old. The vice and beastliness which he had known amongst the villagers before his father's death had seemed to him natural and proper in that, as far as he could see, they were universal. Now that his shyness prevented him from mixing with his former companions, he fell easily into the new ways and looked down on the old ones with the contempt and intolerance of a proselyte. From Rupert's library Bertha picked out books of adventure and heroism, and by reading them aloud to Gilbert stirred up a desire in him to read them for himself. Self-education (the only kind that is of lasting profit) had commenced. A novel sense of honour and fairness was springing up in the lad, and this alone was sufficient to differentiate him from the rest of his coevals in the village. By the time that he was called upon to prove that he was capable of acting as protector to his sister he was ripe and ready for the task.

Neetch Jinnis, who, the reader may remember, has been described as the Don Juan of the village, had always cast envious eyes on Bertha. He had not been disinterested in getting Rupert out of the way. His experience had taught him that the few rustic girls that had any regard for virtue during their maidenhood lost it after their marriage, and that a grass widow was only too eager to supply the place of her absent husband with a substitute or substitutes. He had utterly failed to understand Bertha's character. The rebuffs he had met with had given a keener edge to his desires. Such a thing as real purity in a woman was inconceivable to him. He had been delighted to further Rupert's wish to go to sea. He had little doubt that he would get his reward. Young Gilbert's return did not in the least disconcert him. Such a thing as a brother at all careful of his sister's honour was an incredible eccentricity in Frogsthorpe. He believed that propitiatory offerings of "bare an' bocca" would win him an ally within the gates. All the company that was wont to assemble at the "Grey Mare" would have hailed his success with joy. Bertha was considered to be "consayted" and full of "mucka pride." Her fall had been prophesied in the early days of her acquaintance with Rupert, and her marriage was a bitter disappointment to her neighbours. Even Mrs. Pontifex, who might have been expected to evince jealousy, was eager to further the fisherman's projects, but Neetch felt a strong reluctance to open the campaign. Bertha rarely went outside her garden gate, and in order to commence operations it would be necessary to call at her cottage, a proceeding which the recollection of some inexplicable influence which emanated from her appeared terrific to the timidity of the man, who recognised the existence in her of something he did not understand. hiccoughed. "Hare ye be, Gil. Dee yew run out wi' yar bocca. Yew can goo up ta Pont's an' git a pint, an' tell 'em I'll pay foor't. Me an' yar sister want ta be alooan. Doan't us, me dare? T'ree bain't company, tew be. What are yew arter, yew young!"

Towards the end of February it became the fashion at the evening "settin'-ins" at the " Grey Mare" to banter the fisherman on his lack of enterprise.

"I rackon he's afeerd," said Edith. "D'ye rackon she'll tell mother on ye?"

"Wha lor, bor," said Mrs. Pont, "that doan't sigerfy ta me. A chaange fare good for all on us."

"I'll tell ye what," said Pontifex, "dee yew let my wife alooan for bit. Claybrooke's away. Why doan't yew goo an' chare up the pore wench? I'll look arter Milly, oan't I, me dare?"

"Wha goo along wi' ye, dew," said the worthy lady. "They allust say as a pooached pheasant eat better'n one shot on yar owan land!"

"He! he! he!" chuckled old Deep-un. "Tha'ss a fack, mawther; tha'ss a fack. If she fare timid, Neetch bor, yew want ta dew a bit o' decoyin', same as they dew a-gittin' o the fowl into the nets at Duckin'ham Mere. Star up har cur'osity, bor; star up har cur'osity, an' she'll foller till she's i' the pooke o' the net."

Netch said little, but he drank much. At last he leapt to his feet. "Blust I" he said. "Gi'e's a pint o' stout in a bottle, Milly; I'll take it down tew'r; an' gi'e's a halfounce o' bocca for young Gil."

"He! he! he!" chuckled old Deep-un again. "A bit o' meat for the yud dorg. Yew're a-dewin', bor; yew're a-dewin'!"

Neetch staggered off into the night down to Noddyfield corner. When he got to the little block of cottages he saw Bertha and Gilbert through the blindless window, sitting over the fire in the bright light of a duplex lamp that was the wonder and admiration of the whole village. Bertha's fingers were busy with knitting-needles. The boy's head was bowed over *Tales from the Annals of the British Navy,* and his lips moved to the words as he read them. There was a quiet charm about the scene which would have restrained a sober man and sent him back with better thoughts. But Neetch was drunk. He gazed greedily at the delicate beauty of the woman. "Christ!" he muttered, "she's whoolly pratty!"

Pulling himself together, and with leaping blood, he strode up the pathway to the door. He knocked heavily. "See who it is, Gil," said Bertha. "I don't know who it can be at this time of night. The baker's been, and he's the only person to come so late."

Gilbert rose and opened the door.

"Good evenin'," said Neetch; "I've brote ye a pint o' stout an' a bit o' bocca for Gil. Should a come in?"

"Do you want to see me, Mr. Jinnis?" said Bertha, surprised. She remembered his uncouth advances in former days, and had no desire to renew acquaintance with the man.

"'Strew's Gord, I allust want ta see yar pratty face," said Neetch, too full of Dutch courage to retain any caution. He thrust the door open and stepped in. "Hev a drop o' stout," he said, "that'll dew ye good. Tha'ss new brooached."

He leered and held out the bottle. Bertha started to her feet, and her face paled to the lips. There was no one within hearing but Gilbert and the Noddyfields, and she feared that the latter would never come to her assistance. She knew the violence that might be expected from a marsh Dane, mad with drink and lust, and her defender had not yet come to man's full strength.

Gilbert grasped the situation instantly. His mind was full of Broke of the *Shannon*, of old Benbow, Nelson, and Collingwood. The boy's ordeal of manliness was before him, and nobly did he sustain it.

He prepared for action, but waited for his sister's orders.

"Thank you," she said, "but I don't drink stout. Besides, you must see that I can't ask you to come in during my husband's absence."

She hoped that the man might be induced to go away without a struggle. But he heard the jeers of the "Grey Mare" kitchen which would greet him on his return if he failed in his attempt. He lurched forward, till he was brought up by Gilbert.

"Wha tha'ss the wery time as yew want ta ax me in," he

He felt his legs seized by the boy, who tackled him low, and held on, beginning to force him back.

"Oh, pray go, Mr. Jinnis," said Bertha.

"Now doan't ye be se timid," he said. "Come yew hare, my pratty bowty, an' gi'e's a kiss. Make this young leave goo."

"Shall a chuck him out?" asked Gilbert, with his head low, and his legs braced back and strained with taut sinews.

"Chuck me out? Blust!" roared the man. "Leggoo! leggoo! I tell ye!"

"Mind he doesn't hurt you, Gil," said Bertha anxiously.

"Leggoo! leggoo! Blust! I'll soon make ye," screamed Neetch. The drunken ruffian raised the bottle of stout in his hand.

Bertha rushed forward, but was too late to prevent the blow from crashing down on her brother's neck. Fortunately the bottle missed his head, but it broke, and the glass cut him cruelly. Blood and stout streamed on the floor.

Then commenced a gallant struggle. The shock and pain only raised the lad's courage to a higher pitch. With a heave and a push he thrust his assailant down, but fell with him, and the two writhed on the brick floor, fighting for life like a pair of animals, without regard to foul blows or foul clutches. Both groaned in agony, and it was evident that the lad would soon be overcome by the superior strength and ferocity of his opponent. Bertha saw him weakening, and watched Neetch grinding his teeth as he increased the power of his grip. She seized the old muzzleloader, hanging in slings to the main baulk, and was about to bring it down with all her force on the fisherman's head, when old Noddy's rolling voice was heard.

"Wha'ss a-dewin' hare? Wha'ss a-dewin' hare? Be anybardy asultin' o' yew, Bartha? Lemme git my hands on tew him."

The blind man felt his way forward with his stick, and then flung himself into the combat. With marvellous instinct he grasped the right one of the two, and soon had him half throttled. Bertha withdrew Gilbert from the grip of the enemy, and with some difficulty got him, half unconscious, into a chair. Neetch gurgled and gasped. "Don't kill him, Mr. Noddyfield," said Bertha. "He's getting black in the face."

"I oan't kill the!" said old Noddy. "Wheer's my stick?"

He turned the man over on his face, and then laid into him with his stick till the pain of the blows brought him back to his senses and made him howl with anguish. Then old Noddy lifted him up in his mighty arms and hurled him forth into the night.

He gathered himself up, and, completely sobered, went off up the road swearing vengeance.

During the whole of the disturbance old Sock, who had been asleep on some straw in the bakehouse, had been roaring to get out. Bertha determined as she heard him always to have him in the living-room with her for the future. It was as well for Neetch that he had been debarred from joining in the fray on this occasion.

"Oh, how can I thank you, Mr. Noddyfield?" said Bertha. "I never hoped for help from you!"

Indeed, since Rupert's quarrel with Laura and his marriage all associations between the Noddyfields and their tenants had been completely suspended. Whenever old Peggie caught Rupert's eye upon her she hid herself, squatting or running to the cover of her home like a little black rabbit. Had she been at home it is unlikely that Noddy would have gone to the rescue. But she was making one of her periodical visits to the Limes, and it was fortunate for Bertha that she was.

"Yew doan't want ta say narthen at all!" said old Noddy, with heavy courtesy. "But what wuz't all about?"

Bertha told him how the struggle had commenced while she bathed her brother's wounds and dressed them. The boy had come round, and was little the worse for the encounter. The glow of a good action well done thrilled him; he was eager to speak.

"I whoolly give him somethin'!" he said. "But, lor! di'n't he holler when yew cut intew'm!"

"Gi'e's yar hand, booy," said old Noddy. "Yew fare the right sooart, an' tha'ss a fack!"

"That a will!" answered the lad. "He'd a done for me if yew ha'n't ha' come. I'll niver say a wud agin ye ag'in," he added guilelessly.

"Ha! ha! ha!" laughed old Noddy. "'Tis the missus as can't dew wi' yew. Say noo moor. Say noo moor. Yew doan't want ta let har knoo narthen on't. Neetch oan't say narthen for fear of hevin' the grin put on tew'm. Soo if yew doan't puff, noobardy oan't knoo."

"We are not likely to speak to Mrs. Noddyfield," said Bertha, with a touch of hauteur; "but it makes it all the kinder of you. I'm sure my husband will wish to thank you when he knows of it. And I shall never forget it. *Never!*"

"When be the maaster a-comin' hooam?" asked Noddy. "I hope he won't be more than a month now," said Bertha.

"Well, me dare," suggested old Noddy, "yew'll ha'e ta let me look arter ye when the missus is away. I'll sune send that warmin' a-packin' if he come any moor of his narnsense. Good night tew ye. If yew want me ag'in yew want ta holler. Dee yew dew it. Fare ye well."

He walked off, upright and straight. Darkness made no difference to him. It was from the ease with which he found his way in the dark that his blindness was most noticeable.

It would be pleasant to attribute his action to that rustic courtesy that is so popular in fiction. But the real facts of the matter were that he, too, had heard of Bertha's beauty, and in the early days of her residence at Frogsthorpe had acquainted himself with her features by passing his hands over them—a privilege he claimed as an old man "who allust like ta knoo what my ten'ts fare like." The old rascal's appearance on the scene was the result of both jealousy and craft. He thought that his conduct would put him on a good footing with her. And in this he was right.

When Bertha knelt at her bedside that night his name was on her lips, in context with a prayer for a blessing on him, and thanks for her escape by virtue of his succour.

As for young Gilbert, she could not make enough of him. And indeed the boy had come to his manhood with a noble courage. The one brave effort, and the sensations it gave him, did much to make him appreciate the moral splendour of unselfish valour. He returned to his heroes with redoubled eagerness, and longed to grow up in the likeness of their great shades.

"MEN MUST WORK AND WOMEN MUST WEEP" TO people that dwell in civilised places, police-court proceedings would seem the natural result of the fight at "The Castle"; but in Frogsthorpe there is little desire to have recourse to the law. The marshes have a law, or a lawlessness, of their own, as well as a system of morality which may be codified as follows.

"Fais ce que tu voudras." But go to church or chapel regularly, and humbug the parson and doctor.

Self-preservation is the first principle of mankind. The second is self-indulgence.

Never say an ill word to the face of anyone "from whom advantage may befall." Nor a good one behind his back.

A man who does a kindness without expecting a return is an idiot. Take advantage of him, and laugh at his simplicity in his absence.

A sick person is best dead. Speed the desired consummation.

Anything new to the village is evil. Away with it.

"Furriners " are all fools. Rob them.

The best place in the world is our village. The best and wisest people we that dwell therein.

Neetch was left undisturbed by legal process. To account for his condition he told a beautiful story of being overcome by liquor on going into the open air, wandering on to the marsh, falling on the bottle and smashing it, and being trodden on by stock.

No one believed him; but the real facts did not leak out. In spite of the chaff he was subjected to, he left Bertha alone for the time.

The days passed for her in happy anticipation of her husband's homecoming, until a strange chance brought other work for her to do that was to be of vital importance to most of the characters mentioned in these pages.

The whole village required to drown its astonishment in much stimulant when it became known that old Granny the witch was to move from her hovel into the house between "The Castle" and Ozier Cottage, which had stood vacant since the flitting of the Heron family. In the second week in March the old hag was established in her new dwelling, with the pots and pans, boilers and gallipots, powders, broths, and syrupy concoctions appertaining to her craft, and the few sticks of furniture she could call her own.

The means by which she had persuaded Peggie to let her have possession of the house, and the arguments used by Peggie to obtain her husband's consent, were mysteries to be discussed with bated breath and with wonderment at this last exhibition of her powers.

My readers may be able to make a shrewd guess at the method employed to coerce Peggie. As for Philip, the feel of gold (procured by Sarah) satisfied him without arousing inconvenient curiosity as to its source.

For some reason or other, possibly owing to the break up of old habit, possibly because the new premises lay lower to the marsh, the change proved an ill one for the witch. She had hardly been in her new quarters a week when she was stricken down with ague and malarial fever. Remedies galore she possessed, but they were of little use to her while she could not rise from her bed to get at them. With the extinction of the fire she had kindled in her bedroom the old woman feared the extinction of her life, and she could not drag her old bones downstairs in search of fuel. One whole morning a hoarse cackle was heard intermittently issuing from her room.

"He'p! He'p! He'p! Hi! Hi! He'p! He'p! He'p!" croaked out.

Peggie listened terrified, but neither she nor any of her kind had the courage to render assistance.

"I rackon the daavil ha' come for his owan at last!" she said in awestruck tones.

"Lar him take har then," replied the old man, "an' the suner the better."

There was no knot of villagers waiting outside to listen to and laugh at her cries, as there would have been in the case of any other suffering woman. Everyone hurried past the corner and spread the news that the devil had come for his own at last. Probably there was only one person in all Frogsthorpe who disbelieved in witchcraft. Fortunately for the reputed witch, the one exception lived next door to her.

Bertha was long reluctant to offer her services. It was not from any fear of witchcraft that she hesitated, but she doubted whether Rupert would approve of her having any communication with so notorious an evil liver and evil doer. But as noon approached she could bear the piteous cries no longer. Calming Gilbert's fears, she went round to the old back door that was so familiar to her, and which the crone (secure in the knowledge of the dread in which she was held) never condescended to lock, and ascended the staircase upon which she had with beating heart once heard Rupert's footsteps.

She found Granny lying moaning on her sorry bed. Her fire was at the point of extinction, and the witch's eyes were fixed wildly upon it.

"Bless ye, bless ye," the old hag groaned. "Doan't let the fire die, an' I'll dew yar will so long as I live. I sweer it by the black man's book and by the evil sign of his clooven hoof.

"When the witch's fire die
The ind o' the witch's life be nigh."

Bertha hurried down, and presently returned with sticks and coal, which she fanned to a blaze. As the fire burnt up, old Granny laid her head back on her filthy pillow and grinned. "Yew'll niver regret it, me dare," she croaked. "Yew're the oony one wi' the pluck of a louse. Look in the cupboard downsteers, an' yew'll find a black bottle and a green bottle in the right-hand coarner. Bring 'em up, an' a cup an' a soorcepan. "

The things were fetched. Granny poured out a mixture, and Bertha set it on the fire to boil.

This was the commencement of days and nights of nursing. The remedies were slow in their effects upon the worn frame and impoverished blood; but the improvement was regular and plainly discernible. After the first morning the witch spoke little, save to give directions as to the preparation of her own medicines. She would lie silent, and watch the graceful girl, busying herself in attendance, with an expression of wonder. For as long as she could remember she had been an object of horror and fear to her associates. Now here was one who showed neither one nor the other, but only a kindly solicitude. Once or twice she had uttered weird rhymes in the presence of her nurse; but Bertha paid little attention to them, and only advised her to keep quiet and not to worry about anything. It was astounding!

When she was able to get up and sit on her old settle, crouched over the fire, she asked Bertha to give her her hand.

"Oh, nonsense!" said the girl.

This would have infuriated Granny in the old days, but a change had come over her, at least so far as her manner to Bertha was concerned.

"Dew it ta please an ole 'oman's fancies, me dare," she said. "I oan't hu't ye. "

Bertha held out her left hand in answer, smiling at what she considered an absurd ceremony. Granny peered at the lines of it. She bade the girl give her a drink out of a stone bottle that had to be fetched from downstairs. She gasped a little, and alarmed Bertha, who ran to her assistance, but was repulsed. Then, from the witch's throat, issued the voice which Peggie and Sarah had formerly heard.

"Tidin's is comin' ta gi'e ye pain.
For false can hu't as well as true.
But yew'll foold yar love in yar arms again,
An' the plots o' yar foes shall tarn askew.
Hoold fast ta yar trust wi' might an' main,
An' yar hoop an' yar trust shall come true for yew."

"Well, that's a comfort," said Bertha, laughing, quite undismayed at the horrible forced clucking tones, which she considered as part and parcel of an exhibition of humbug.

"Doan't yew mock at what I tell ye," said Granny, speaking very seriously in her natural voice, and touching Bertha's hand. "But when the bad news come, heart up, my pratty, an' doan't trust it. Trust yar luck, an' trust ole Granny, for yew're the fust livin' soul as iver said a kind wud or did a kind act ta me since I wuz a gal. Yew've a kind heart an' a lovin', sech as I hain't knowed for yares. I'm a-gooin' ta ax ye ta dew a some'at, as I doubt yew'll tarn ag'in. Will ye gi'e me a kiss? Yew've heerd o' the witch's kiss, noo doubt, as givin' power tew the evil eye, but ta won't dew ye noo harm ta kiss me. I'll sweer ta won't."

"Of course I will," answered Bertha, who had an affection for anything she had tended; more after the male than the female disposition. "I'm not afraid of any evil eye."

She bent down and kissed the withered, wrinkled cheek, clean now from her own ministrations.

A spasm shook the old woman as she felt the sweet, pure lips touch her.

"Theer. Goo, me dare, an' thanky," she muttered. "I little thote I should iver be sorry I'd lost the power ta bless. But theer's them as hain't; theer's them as hain't; an' I'll dew what I can for ye. Let them other s look out! 'em!"

"Oh don't, Granny," said Bertha. "Don't curse anybody."

"Hush, me dare; hush," said Granny. "Yew doan't unnerstand. The black man must hev his owan, *an' I'll see he dew."*

Her voice had sunk to a low murmur, and her gaze grew fixed and hard. Presently her eyes closed, and when she sank to sleep Bertha left the room.

The witch's words made little impression upon Bertha at the time, but she was to have them vividly recalled to her very shortly.

The equinoctial gales burst from the south-west with more than their usual force. Every day the papers were filled with tales of shipwreck, of disaster to fishing fleets, loss of nets, loss of lives, total disappearance of craft and crew. But daily papers are not seen in Frogsthorpe. There news comes slowly filtered through indiscriminate hearsay. It was not till a fortnight had passed without a letter from Rupert that Bertha began to grow anxious. Her attendance on old Granny cut both her and her brother more than ever off from the village folk. She was classed as a proselyte to the evil powers of the old woman, and it was rumoured that Granny, being about to die, had been bound by the devil to enlist a new recruit to take her place on earth, and that Bertha had taken the black man's wages.

The loss of the *John and Susan* was known in the village some hours before Gilbert brought back the news from over the marshes, whither he had been in search of hornpies' eggs.

The blow fell with cruel force. The very morning the tidings reached Bertha a letter had come from John Perkins, Rupert's agent, announcing that the book had been accepted for publication by a first-class firm of publishers, who were prepared to pay 25 down on account of royalties on publication. She was actually writing to her husband with the good news when Gilbert came in with the bad.

At first the poor girl sat stunned to silence. Then wail after wail burst from her, and the voice of her lamentation vibrated through the cottage. In the midst of her sobbing outcry and Gilbert's attempts at consolation, a halting, rickety step was heard on the "pamments" outside. Old Granny was about again, and had heard the outburst of sorrow. She limped in and thrust the boy aside. She laid her fingers on Bertha's temples, and instantly the paroxysm of grief was subdued. Then the witch fixed her eyes on the girl.

"Come," she said, "trust ole Granny. Ta bain't true. Yew'll foold yar love in yar arms again. Look a' me."

Bertha had lost all control over herself. Her eyes were drawn to the witch's.

Soon a haze drifted before her sight. Then the mist passed away, and she saw Rupert swimming in a rough sea, and a boat, urged on by strong and eager hands, approaching him. She saw him lifted from the broken water and carried to a large barque, lying to, head to wind, with her square sails backed and her mizzen flapping. She saw him leap on deck and fall to his knees with hands uplifted in thanksgiving. Then the mist again crossed her vision; and when it passed, she saw her little room again, with Granny and Gilbert standing beside her.

XVII AT "THE LIMES" LAURA continued in hysterical convulsions for so long «f after Rupert left her that Sarah began to be alarmed lest she might die or become insane before altering her will. At length applications of cold water and rough speech (for Sarah's nature led her to apply the right treatment) had their effect. The maniacal laughter ceased, and the sobs grew fainter and fainter till they died away into a low moaning.

"Wha come! Wha come! Tha'ss right," said Sarah. "Yew *hev* had the high strikes, an' tha'ss a fack! Yew gi'e me right a tarn. That warmin' of a booy! Impident toad! Ta say as yew drink! I'm shore noobardy carn't say as yew take moor 'an yew want. Will ye hev a little drop now? Yew hulled away the last in yar spassums."

Laura's attack had driven away from her recollection all the softer feelings which Rupert's farewell words had aroused. She came to herself with a heavy, dull sense of injury and insult suffered at his hands. She took the glass which Sarah handed her, and drained its contents. It pulled her round.

"Did you ever, Sarah!" she cried. "I never was so insulted in my life! Never a farden o' my money shall he hev. Write to Mr. Strainer at once, and tell him that we're going to call upon him on Tuesday. There's a 'scursion up to Odinton o' Tuesday, one-and-six return, an' we'll both go. I mean to alter my will."

"Hadn't yew best think it oover for a bit?" said the wily Sarah, who knew that to suggest delay was to ensure expedition.

"Not a minute!" said Laura. "To tell me I drink too much! A nice thing! And him going to marry a common wench after all he've been through! And how kind I have been to him! Did you ever, Sarah! I'm sure I don't know what he'd have done if it had not been for me!''

"Aah, that yew hev!" said Sarah. "I tode ye he wuz a warmin'!"

"But, Sarah! Did you ever!" repeated Laura. "Write to Mr. Strainer at once!"

"That's foortnit," said Sarah, "as yew ha' got other brothers ta leave yar brass tew. Though they did all try ta take adwantige o' me when I wuz a gal, an' used ta put the grin on tew ye, an' call ye addle-hidded, dotty, sorft, balmy, an' strike a light! They bain't noo wuss 'an that Ruput! Afoor the pore ole guvnor lost the use of his tongue he say, 'Seerah,' he say, 'I hain't left yew narthen in my will, but Miss Laura'll look arter ye. She'll look arter ye,' he say. An' I say, ''Strew's Gord, sir, I'll niver leave har sa long as she live.' An' I niver hev! Hev I? But *I* think ye ote ta leave yar brass ta yar brothers. Blood *is* blood. Tha'ss what *I* think. An' pore ole marmy she say when she lay a-dyin', 'Seerah,' she say, 'I trust ye, for I know as yew're a good heart. Yew look arter Miss Laura, an' I'll ax Mr. Claybrooke ta make it soo as she can make it right for yew,' she say. 'For whativer she'd dew without yew theer's noo tellin'. But yew'll niver leave har. Prarmuss as yew'll niver leave har.' An' I say, ''Strew's Gord, I niver will.' An' I niver hev! Hev I? But / think yew ote ta leave yar brass ta yar brothers, an' niver mind about me, though I *hev* looked arter ye as I prarmussed tew for the love I beer ye. For though none o' them booys niver keered a farden whether ye lived or died, or whether you went inta the wuckhus or not, yet blood *is* blood."

Spurred by the urgency of the occasion, Sarah found an unwonted flow of eloquence at her command. All the time she was speaking she watched her mistress out of her little pig eyes with the expression of a weasel on guard at a rabbit-hole. She knew her patient's constitution too well to err in her treatment of her.

"I shall leave my money as I please," said Laura. "I shall show my brothers just as much consideration as they have showed me, and no more. I know who's my best friend, and that's who I shall leave my money to. I shall leave every penny to you. Kiss me, Sarah."

The soft flesh and the hard plumped together.

"Noo, doan't yew dew noo sech thing," said Sarah, glowing with an inward exultation that made it difficult for her to command her expression. "I'm shore I shan't goo wi' ye if ye dew."

Sarah always made a point of reading Lloyd's weekly newspaper. She had thus obtained an indistinct idea of the result of proof of undue influence. She understood how much safer her position would be if Laura went up to Howard and Strainer's and gave her testamentary instructions by herself. She wrote the letter making the appointment for Laura, but adhered to her determination not to be present at it.

During the few days intervening between the Friday and Tuesday she played upon her victim with the skill of her master the devil himself. She studied the alcoholic thermometer carefully, and just kept Laura at the indignation point without getting her over the maudlin line. All day she recalled past injuries and insults, real or imaginary, which the male scions of the Claybrooke family had been guilty of years ago, always taking care to say, "Blood is blood, though that dew seem as if yar brothers di'n't pay much regard tew't. But tha'ss noo rayson why yew shou'n't. An' as for me, I shall fare right hu't if yew leave me all that brass."

It was with the consciousness of merit rewarded that she heard, on Laura's return from Odinton, that Strainer had taken instructions that everything was to be left to "her dear friend and companion, Sarah Chindaffy." That the will had been drafted, engrossed, executed, and attested then and there. If Laura were to die forthwith, she, Sarah, would be her sole executrix and legatee.

Nothing now remained between Sarah and the prize for which she had so long been diligently and patiently working but her employer's life, and that was at her mercy whenever she chose to take it. But she was not without discretion. She knew well enough the odious suspicion that might arise should Laura die too soon after making the will. She thought she could afford to wait. The game was in her hands, and the duration of it could not affect the issue.

Peggie kept the two old maids well posted in the passage of events at Frogsthorpe. The news of old Heron's death and the rapidly succeeding marriage were related with an affectation of sympathy and amazement at the shock to her family pride which Laura was called upon to bear, that raised a fury of passion and resentment in the poor muddled brain of the infatuated woman.

"I'd niver ha' believed it," said Peggie, whining and throwing up her eyes, "as a Mr. Claybrooke could ha' demeaned hisself soo! I fare somethin' wexed for yew, miss, an' tha'ss a fack! An' them tew a-livin' se cloose! Wha if they hev any baabes yew'll be theer aunt. Nice dewin's! Whativer would yar pore mother ha' thote on it!"

"Aah, pore thing!" chimed in Sarah. "I'm shore it's a mussy as she niver lived ta see it."

"He's no brother o' mine," said Laura. "I told him so the last time he was here. Di'n't I, Sarah? I told him what I thought of him. He won't come here no more."

"Doan't yew be tew sartin o' that," said Sarah. "He've got the cheek o' the daavil, he hev. He'll try ta come round ye ag'in. Yew mark my wuds if he doan't. I'll bet a sixpence on't. An' arter all, blood *is* blood, an' theer's noo gittin' oover it. An' Peggie say as the whool willage is a-laughin' at him!"

"I won't see him if he do come," said Laura. "Remember that, Sarah. If he ever come I'm not at home."

Laura bridled as she spoke.

"Ooh, I shou'n't like ta tell yar owan brother that," simpered Sarah.

"I insist upon it," cried Laura; "and I expect you to do as I wish. I've just left you my all, and I shall look to you to deserve it by not thwarting me."

With well-disguised complacency and well-simulated reluctance, Sarah promised to do as she was told.

But she was never to have the pleasure of keeping her promise. Days and weeks passed in the diurnal humdrum of the lives of provincial old maids, in alternate attentions to the poultry run and the whisky bottle. Every week Peggie went over with a report, and every week the two sisters had a discussion as to how long the crisis should be delayed.

Then came the tidings of Rupert's suspected poverty; then of his going to sea. A slight anxiety was caused to the conspirators by Granny's illness and Bertha's ministrations. But this was speedily allayed by the news of the loss of the *John and Susan* with all hands.

But the effect upon Laura of the reported death of her brother came as an unwelcome surprise to the two women, who had been playing and relying upon her lower nature till they were unable to comprehend that this did not really predominate, but had been artificially forced to appear to do so.

The suddenness and solemnity of the tragedy burst through all the panoply of selfishness that spite and cruelty had forged, and struck straight to the sister's heart. She remembered Rupert as a bright, lovable boy. She recalled his victories at school in the classroom and the playfield. She thought how her mother had loved him, how her father had not only loved him, but felt a pride in him. She saw him as he was on his return home after rowing in his college boat in his first "Mays," radiant with health and spirits, the clear white of his eyes hard and transparent as porcelain. She saw him sculling on the Thorwater at the bottom of the old garden, his muscles standing out in magnificent rolling curves. She remembered the proud toss of his head, his humour, his joyousness, the tenderness he had ever shown her. In spite of herself, she reviewed all his dealings with her, and knew that not in one single instance had he treated her unkindly or unfairly. She knew, none better, that she was a slave to a horrible vice, and she had turned him from her home at the moment when he was trying to reclaim her. She could see it all now, and he was dead. She could never ask for his forgiveness; never tell him that she had wronged him; never hear his voice; never feel his lips again.

A mighty wave of infinite sorrow and regret swept over her. The news was told her by Sarah, crudely, roughly, with an affectation of sympathy that was grotesquely assumed to her awakened insight. It seemed as if the mere word of his fate had cleared her vision from all the haze that had dimmed it so long. The strength of a great repentance was in her. She turned her back on her companion, and with never a word went to her room, and locked herself ia Then she threw herself on the couch at the foot of the bed, and burst into those harsh, guttural sobs that are wrung from the bitterness of irretrievable disaster.

"Rupert, Rupert," she moaned. "It was / who sent you to your death. I have enough, and to spare. Why could you not ask me to help you? No! God forgive me. I had made it impossible to one like you. Me! Your sister! Your own sister what loved you sent you to die!"

"Wha Loord ha' mussy upon us!" whispered Sarah at the keyhole. "Whativer bug's i' the bed now?"

"Miss Laura, Miss Laura," she cried aloud, "oan't ye hev a drop o' some'at?"

"It was you that made me do it, Sarah," Laura replied from inside, her voice rising to a scream. "You made me do it! Oh, why did you? You loved him once, or pretended to!"

"Theer! theer! pore dare!" said Sarah. "Now dee yew hev a drop o' some'at, an' let ole Seerah comfoort of ye. Doan't ye let the neighbours hare ye hollerin'."

"No, it was you. You and me!" cried Laura. "What can we ever do, Sarah? He's dead! Do you know that? He's dead! We can never, either of us, do anything to make up for it."

"Wha Lor'!" muttered Sarah, "she've gorn clane craazy! Tha'ss a good job as har will's made. Now dee yew let me in," she said aloud, "theer's a dare! Come ta yar old Seerah's arms, pore thing; dee yew, now. Doan't let the neighbours hare ye hollerin'." "Damn the neighbours," screamed Laura, with an insane recollection of Rupert's vivid language. "Go away, for God's sake," she sobbed. "I'm bad enough, God knows, but you made me worse. Go away, Sarah, you must leave me to myself. And mother loved him so! Go away!" she screamed again, and there was such an earnestness in her voice that Sarah was cowed, and crept downstairs, her boots creaking hideously on the hard oilcloth as she stepped from stair to stair with a clumsy attempt at silence that made the noise worse.

Thrice more did she try to coax her way into the closed room, but without avail.

That night, for the first time for over twenty years, the women slept separately under the same roof. The spirit of justice was roused from its normal lethargy, and when that happens strange portents may be looked for. It is a rare and notable awakening. Noorna ben Noorka, daughter of Feshnavat the Vizier, might have said that it foretold the mastery of an event.

XVIII SARAH AGAIN VISITS FROGSTHORPE BERTHA, already sufficiently unpopular with the villagers, still further shocked their susceptibilities by resolutely refusing to don weeds, or to mourn her husband as dead. In spite of her former disbelief in old Granny's powers, the vision she had seen when under the witch's influence had impressed her with its truth. Hope, and a belief in the goodness of God, fought against her acceptance of the news of her husband's death. Increasing intimacy with old Granny (who never failed to encourage her with quaint doggrel and with words of graver import) gave her a confidence which stood her in good stead during the trial of her strength to which she was subjected. However proof against superstition a woman may be, when her soul's prayer is supported by omens, dreams, or what is commonly called "the supernatural," she will in her heart cling to the encouragement she does not understand, even at the cost of a feeling of shame at her weakness. "Yew'll see, me dare," old Granny said. "I tode ye yew shou'n't niver regret it. I'm oold, an' I'm wicked. But I can dew ye a good tarn, an' yar husband tew. But the time bain't ripe. Yew must wait till yew 'foold yar love in yar arms again,' an' then yew'll see what yew'll see. The black man 'ull git his owan right enow. Hech! hech! hech! Doan't yew pay noo regard ta the trollopin' wenches o' these parts. They darsen't hu't ye so long as they knoo old Sally's yar friend."

The development of the intimacy between young and old created, as has been said, some disturbance in the tender bosoms of Sarah and Peggie. The latter would dearly have liked to evict her dreaded tenant, but she dared not. She carried the news to the Limes that Bertha would not wear mourning for Rupert, and, as the result of the report, the conspirators found themselves confronted with a new difficulty.

"I'm right wexed ta tell ye, Miss Laura," said Peggie, "for it fare like disrespeck, not ta call it ondacency tew yar name, but I think as yew ote ta knoo on't. That wench Bartha doan't weer noo weeads for yar pore brother what's drownded, an' she doan't set by harself a-blarrin' as is a widder's right an' duty. But she's for iver a-mardlin' along o' that wicked ole witch Granny Young as pussuaded me ta let har hev my house. She've sode harself ta the daavil I dew believe, an' she say as she knoo as he bain't drownded."

"Well I never!" said Laura, on whom the first effect of the news of her brother's death was lasting. "I must see her. She may know of something we don't. I can't believe that any woman who married Rupert would not have learnt to love him, and if she knew she had lost him it would break her heart."

"What did ye want ta tell har that foor?" hissed Sarah viciously into her sister's ear. "Yew'll spile the whool brew if ye bain't keerful." "Yew cou'n't niver demean yarself by a-gooin' ta see sech as har, for shore, me dare," she said to Laura. "What narnsense! O' coorse he's drownded!"

"I shall do as I like, Sarah," was the reply. "You've never liked him lately. If it hadn't been for you Oh dear! Oh dear! If it hadn't been for *my* wicked folly he might never have gone to sea."

"But I ha' heerd har say as she's whoolly glad ta be rid on him," said Peggie, with charming inconsistency.

"Oh, have you?" flamed out Laura, too confused to see through the weakness of the lie. "Did you ever, Sarah! Well, she may starve before I ever do anything for her. I'll never go near her. No! I'm wrong. I'll go over and have it out with her. I'll make her ashamed of herself, sure as I'm Miss Claybrooke. She can never have cared for him. And it was through his bringing up her name as we quarrelled. I owe her one for that. "

Laura, in her sorrow and repentance, had vowed that she would do her brother's memory honour by breaking herself of her besetting vice. A hard task for a man; an almost impossible task for a woman. To Sarah's dismay, she steadily refused the constant nipping suggested to her, and only had recourse to stimulant when the craving was more than she could bear. The shock had given her a firmness of purpose and a power of resisting the cruel temptation that never ceased to assail her, that was new to her character. Neurosis occasionally gives temporary strength, and her abnormal condition gave her abnormal powers. Time alone could show whether the new habits could obtain sufficient hold upon her to enable her to hold her own in the struggle which must ensue when she was no longer "beside herself" with passionate remorse. At this time she more nearly approached to being the woman she might have been apart from Sarah's influence than she had ever done at any previous period of her life. For the first time she was thinking for herself, and her strange independence alarmed both the women who were looking forward to her death. An interview with Bertha was the last thing to be desired from their point of view.

"I'll tell ye what, me dare," said Sarah, "if ye must goo, why ye must. But lemme goo an' see har fust. She's more like ta tell me how she feel about Rupert than she is yew, if she niver keered for him, for yew may be sartin as the pore feller tode har as theer worn't noo love lost atween us at the last. Though 'twuz oony t'rew thinkin' for yew as tarned me ag'in him. P'rhaps I wuz mistook arter all, pore feller," she added hurriedly, taking warning from a light of anger in Laura's eyes.

"We were all of us wrong," said Laura tearfully. "However we can have been so mistook I can't make out. We must ha' been blind. But I s'pose it was to be. Well, you may go, and mind you tell me esactly what she say."

Accordingly on the following morning Sarah appeared at Frogsthorpe. She called on Peggie first.

"Wha'ss come oover har I doan't knoo," she said, speaking of Laura. "If she keep on like this we shall ha' ta use ole Granny's powders afoor long. D'ye think it 'ud dew ta hev a h'arin' wi' the ole witch?"

"Ta tell ye the truth, I darsen't," replied Peggie. "She's that took up along o' Bartha, she might goo ag'in us now. We shall ha' ta make use o' what we ha' got, an' dew the best we can."

"But Bartha hain't got noo call ta be friendly along o' Laura," objected Sarah.

"Noo," assented her sister. "But I doubt she oan't goo so far agn har as we want, an' ole Granny fare whoolly wropt up in har now."

"Granny oan't puff, d'ye think?" asked Sarah anxiously.

"Not for har owan sake she oan't," said Peggie; "but I wouldn't ax noo moor on har."

"I spooz he *be* drownded right enow, drat him," said Sarah.

"Wha he *must* be," replied Peggie confidently. "Goo' Lor'! If he wuz ta come back now, wheer should *we* be?"

"Aah, yew're right theer," groaned Sarah. "But theer! Ta must be narnsense. O' coorse he's drownded. The booat went down like a stoon, an' oony har jolly-booat washed ashoor, bartom uppards. Well, I'll be a-gooin'. I'll gi'e Bartha a dewin', yew may lay yar life."

Sarah was rather taken aback at finding old Granny sitting with Bertha. She hesitated, but plucked up heart, and entered "The Castle" in response to the invitation that answered her knock.

Old Granny chuckled.

"I ha' come ta hev a talk along o' yew, Mrs. Claybrooke," said Sarah. "Miss Laura ha' heered as yew hain't gone inta moornin' for har brother, an' she say as if it's 'cos yew're tew pore she'll pay foor't."

Bertha flushed hotly. "Please thank Miss Claybrooke from me," she said, "and tell her that I want nothing from her."

"Then why doan't ye put on yar weeads like a dacent widder?" asked Sarah. "Noobardy'd knoo as yew'd looast yar maan by the look of ye."

"Perhaps I have not," answered the girl.

Old Granny chuckled again.

"Wha, yew doan't mean ta tell me as yew've heerd from him?" asked Sarah, with a rising intonation.

"No. I mean to tell you nothing."

"Well, if he bain't dead, then he's false," said Sarah, warming to the task. "He allust wuz a bad un. Him an' his brothers tew. All t'ree wanted ta taake adwantige 0' me in his pore mother's lifetime, an' he had a try arter she wuz gorn. But blessed be Gord, I niver give way tew a man yit! I'll keeap my wartew till I die."

"Aah!" said Granny, still chuckling, "wheere *dee* yew keeap it, hey?"

"That 'ull larn ye what he wuz," said Sarah, thinking it better to ignore Granny's gibes, "an' the gals he ha' took up with. Scoors an' scoors"

"Did you come here to tell me these lies?" cried Bertha indignantly.

"Aah, pore thing!" said Sarah. "Noo doubt that's hud for yew ta believe it on him," she simpered. "If he worn't drownded I'd tell ye"

"I want to hear nothing from you, thank you," Bertha interrupted.

"But I *dew* want ta hare some'at," Sarah retorted. "Wha'ss the meanin' o' yar saayin' as he bain't dead? If yew believe he's true, how is't he doan't write tew ye nor narthen?"

"I didn't say he had not done so," said Bertha calmly.

"Wha yis yew did," cried Sarah, "when I axed ye afoor."

"Not I," said Bertha. "I only said I meant to tell you nothing."

"Then tha'ss oony 'cos yew hain't got narthen ta tell," said Sarah triumphantly.

"Very well," said Bertha, "then you can't blame me for telling you nothing. "

"Hain't *yew* got a wud ta saay?" said Sarah to old Granny.

"Aah, that I hev," chuckled the old witch. "D'ye mind when yew an' Peggie come ta see me?"

"That'll dew! That'll dew!" interrupted Sarah nervously. "That hain't got narthen ta dew wi't."

"Yew doan't want ta be afeerd. Hech! hech! hech! All I want ta say is—

"The meshes o' faate<br>
Are booth small an' great;<br>
An' the fish may git<br>
T'rew the nettin' yit.

Tha'ss all; an' dee yew mind it."

"Wha wha'ss the meanin' o' that?" said Sarah. "Hare! Come yew outside a minnut. I ha' got a-some'at foor ye."

"Noo, noo, a thank ye. I'm wery comferable wheer I be," laughed Granny.

"But I'll tell ye this much moor, silly b Seerah—

"When ye goo ta set a snare, See the noose run tight an' true;
Or when ye goo ta take yar hare,
Yew'll find the gin ha' let har t'rough.
If ye set the black man's trap, take care
That the catch doan't slip an' the teeth cotch yew."

"Oh," said Sarah, "I can't unnerstan' yar riggermaroly!" Then turning to Bertha, she said, "Then I'm ta tell Miss Claybrooke as yew oan't shoo respeck ta yar pore maan's mim'ry."

"You can tell her precisely what you please," said Bertha. "And now will you please go?"

"Yew dare ta tarn me out?" screamed Sarah.

"I treat you as your mistress treated Rupert," answered Bertha. "But I have some cause. She had none. You can tell her that."

"Wha yew impident trollop," cried Sarah in a fury; "I'll make my sister tarn *yew* out! Out o' house an' hooam! 'Strew's Gord, I will! I'll"

"That'll dew, Seerah," chuckled old Granny. "Out yew goo, or I'll gi'e ye a touch o' the aager as'll make ye chatter wuss 'an iver.

"By the clooven hoof o' the black man's fut,
By the sooty trail o' the black man's scut
Hech! hech! hech! She ha' gorn!"

"Oh, Granny, is he really safe? Shall I really have him safe home with me once more?" said Bertha, rising and going up to the grinning old witch with pleading hands and eyes.

"Theer! Theer!" Old Granny consoled her and comforted her. "I hain't desaaved ye. Yew trust ole Granny, an' yew an' yar maan 'ull thank har togither. Doan't ye pay noo regard ta Seerah. Trust ole Granny."

"I will, I will," said Bertha; "and oh! I will trust in my God, in His goodness. "

"Well," said old Granny, "I rackon as this is the fust time as Him an' me wuz iver maates! But soo be it. Soo be it!" Q

A RELAPSE, AND WHAT CAME OF IT

ARAH unwittingly did the best thing possible to
further her plans by leaving Laura alone by herself for a day. The fact that in fighting down her weakness she was opposing Sarah's constant advice to "hev a drop o' some'at" helped the poor woman in her struggle. Contrasted with her former subservience to her companion's will, her new independence of thought and action had the zest of contrariety. There was a certain enjoyment in regarding every suggestion with a spirit of opposition, and the mere love of perverseness was a factor in deciding the point at issue between the desire to resist and craving to succumb. But with Sarah away, the incentive to resist was absent. She found herself lonely and despondent. Her constitution cried urgently for its accustomed stimulant, and the physical depression of the heart's action was (in the absence of the counter-irritation afforded by the thwarting of Sarah) necessarily accompanied by a corresponding mental depression. In spite of herself, she went to the cupboard, drew forth a whisky bottle, and poured out a liberal dose. It made her feel better.

"Poor Rupert would not wish me to make myself ill," she argued. "I must leave it off more gradually."

A second dose followed the first, a third the second. By the time that Sarah returned Laura was, as Sarah said with complacency, "herself again." Sarah thought now that she would only have to ply her mistress with drink, to see that she never became properly sober, in order to prevent any recurrence of the moods which had begun to wear so threatening an aspect. She described her visit to Bertha in a way that sent Laura into a frenzy of drunken indignation, a grotesque extravaganza of affronted dignity. All thought of any meeting between Rupert's sister and wife was abandoned.

The old dull tragedy of the Limes was renewed for one night with the original cast.

Bertha knew nothing of the change which had come over her sister-in-law on hearing of Rupert's death. Old Granny's craft could not tell her that. Even if she had been aware of it, she would never have applied for help in a quarter where her husband had been so flouted and insulted. But it was becoming clear that she would be sadly in need of help from some source or other unless Rupert came home without delay. The half-year's rent due at Lady Day would have to be paid promptly, for Peggie and Noddy always insisted that their tenants should pay their rents "on the day," and there was no chance of any consideration being shown her in this respect. The money she had in hand was wasting daily, and after she had satisfied the requirements of the Noddyfields and paid a half-year's rates there would be little left. She had spent more than she could afford during Granny's illness, for the old woman had been fanciful with her food, and had no money, or, if she had, did not disclose the fact. It was true that there were a good many articles about the house which might be sold or pawned (for Bertha had redeemed the things formerly pledged by Rupert out of the *£20* he had left behind him and the remittances he had sent home from time to time), but she was loath to avail herself of this resource. It seemed to her a dishonesty to her husband, whom she firmly believed to be alive. Nothing could be obtained on account of the book till it was published. Rupert's reported death had complicated matters. For death revokes a power of attorney, and it was by virtue of a power alone that she could deal with the publishers. She resolutely refused to take steps to prove the will, so she could obtain nothing from the life insurance people.

Gilbert had tried to get regular work as soon as his sister hinted that hard times might be coming. But the enlightened public of the marshlands boycotted him together with his sister and the witch. "They're all on 'em soold ta the daavil!" the people said. "Let *him* keep 'em! We doan't want none o' that sooart about our land!"

There was another anxiety coming upon Bertha, which would at another time have been a source of joy and pride, but in which she could not now take any delight till she had her husband safe home again. For in spite of her brave show and trust her heart sank at times in the absence of any word or token that her trust was justified. Sarah had been as good as her word, and Peggie did her best to turn Bertha out of house and home at Lady Day, but she was too sensible and too tenacious of what was due to her and her husband to allow herself to be overridden; and a wholesome fear of Granny, even more than the law invoked by Bertha, prevented the malicious old landlady from proceeding to extremities or overt acts of persecution of any kind. She gave Bertha notice to quit at Michaelmas, and Granny chuckled as she did so. "Hech! hech! hech!" the witch cackled. "Yew ha' give har nootuss, hev ye? Now I'll tell ye some'at.

"When yew cuss, yew'll find yew're cussed.
Dew yar huddest, dew yar wust.
The way that's foor ye take ye must,
And the time 'ull come when yew'll lick the dust."

But Granny's rhymes and Bertha's steadfastness could not keep the pot boiling. A night came when the last sixpence was changed for bread. When there seemed nothing to do but to give up the struggle, sell up the home, and depart to some new land where employment could be found and wages earned to keep body and soul together.

"Doan't ye fret, Bartha, doan't ye fret," said young Gilbert, trying to control the tremor of his under lip and to speak in manly tones of encouragement. "We'll leave wud at the poost orfice wheer we're a-gooin' tew for yar maan when he come hooam, an' he'll foller wheeriver ye be."

Gilbert had quite given up all hopes of Rupert's surviving, but he could have cut his tongue out rather than let his sister know it.

"But whatever are we to do in the meantime?" asked Bertha. "It is so hard that no one will let either of us earn our bread. But I won't despair. I *won't I* I have trusted in God, and he will not forsake me at the last. Let's go to bed, dear, and pray that some help may come in the morning. Oh, if only my darling would come home! I can't bear to sell his things and leave the home he brought me to. Pray God help will come in the morning."

And help *did* come. Mysterious but effectual help.

Gilbert was always up first to light the fire. Since Bertha had known that she bore the burden of the daughters of Eve she had allowed him to take her up a cup of tea in her bedroom. As a rule he made little noise before going up to her, but on the morning following Bertha's appeal for help his voice was raised in excited calls as soon as he got downstairs.

"Bartha! Bartha!" he called. "Hare be a couple o' pound on the bricks ag'in the dooar! Well, tha'ss a rum un! Tha'ss a rum un!" The boy's excitement was responsible for the slip of the tongue. He flushed hotly. "A beg y' pardon," he said, as if his sister were actually present.

Bertha slipped on a dressing-gown (a relic of the honeymoon) and hurried downstairs. Gilbert had allowed the coins to lie untouched. They were about a foot apart, between the door and the table, glinting in the light of the sticks crackling in the fireplace.

"Thank God!" cried Bertha. "I can't think who put them there, but I know through whom they come. Oh, thank God, we shan't have to leave yet! Rupert may be home any day. What would he say to this? It is even more wonderful than the cheque that saved us before. But who can have put them there? Did you see a scrap of paper with them, or anything?" she asked Gilbert.

"Noo! I niver see narthen!" the boy replied. "Tha'ss jest how they lay when I come down."

The reader may be able to make a guess at the anonymous donor, but neither Bertha nor Gilbert had any idea that old Granny was worth two pounds, far less that she would part with it. The old woman herself evinced the greatest surprise, a thing suspicious in itself, for surprise was foreign to her. As a matter of fact, she *was* surprised at herself—at the pleasure she found in doing a generous action—in repaying a kindness—at the affection she was learning to feel for Bertha. It was necessary for her to think of her old enemies to feel herself again. Then, indeed, her voice croaked, her eyes glared, and her limbs shook with venomous passion.

Granny had found the power of loving, but it had not displaced her power of hating, only supplemented it. She was becoming human in her old age, but with abilities generally considered superhuman. She had been a power in the land as a witch. She would exercise a regal sway as a woman. Her life took a dramatic interest. She no longer acted in a one-part play. She brought to her friends the aid of an inexorable will—a potent ally. She had not lost her sense of humour. She chuckled as she thought of Sarah's disgust did she know where the money went which she provided and her sister disbursed in order to accomplish Rupert's ruin. With her anonymous and timely succour the tide seemed to turn. Gilbert got some work on the railway, and earned enough to keep the fear of starvation from the door. There were bread and milk, potatoes, and dumplings enough for all, and even a scrap of meat (pig's fry or bullock's liver) or a few eggs now and then. Whatever there was Granny had her share. When in the presence of Bertha the old woman was hardly recognisable as the terrible witch. But others who saw her found little change in her manner, speech, or looks, save that the filth and squalor had disappeared. Her language was as fierce, her voice as raucous, her behaviour as truculent as ever to them.

May came, and still there was no word of Rupert. Bertha and Granny alone preserved their trust in his return. Interest concerning his fate had all but died out, save at the Castle, and one other place, the Limes.

There had been sorrow and distress at the Castle, but at the Limes there had been the bitterness of repentance for an irremediable wrong done. And now terror and the foul sin of remorseless cruelty—the murderous desire for a death — threw their black cloak over the commonplace, humdrum little provincial villa, and invested it with the romance of crime.

When Laura had slept off the effects of her drinking bout, she felt such a disgust at herself that it enabled her to resist Sarah's endeavours to induce her to swallow a hair of the dog that had bitten her. She forced herself to rise; and liberal applications of cold water, followed by breakfast and a smart walk in a stinging easterly wind, cleared her mental vision, and renewed her spirit of insurrection against Sarah's rule, a tyranny which she was beginning to understand in spite of its subtle concealment.

"I've been blind so long!" she said piteously to herself. "But am I to blame? She always pretended to be working in my interests. All my life she've been about me, and taken trouble and responsibility off me because I was too lazy to look after myself. I've been thinking a lot of Miss Claybrooke, but precious little use to anybody have Miss Claybrooke been! But there must be a change now. I'm not a babe. I must think for myself. I must try to find out what she really is. That won't do to let her suspect as I hev my doubts at last. Oh, if Rupert was only alive to help me! Now there's only God! I'm all alone! I've got no one to turn to but Sarah, she've took care of that. I should have liked to see Bertha. She's Rupert's wife. But after what Sarah told me I don't see how I can. Is Sarah telling the truth? Oh God, help me! I'm as helpless as a child! And, oh God, help me to get the better of this horrible habit of mine."

For some days her determination to test Sarah's honesty of purpose bore no fruit. Her manner and conduct were unchanged, save that she was more reticent than before, and held firm against the seductions of alcohol. She made no further mention of visiting Bertha. Sarah thought all danger was over, and that the only regrettable circumstance was the improvement in health which followed on Laura's abstention from drink. But this she knew she could counteract when the time came. She had not paid through the nose for old Granny's nostrums for nothing.

It was again through Peggie's shortsightedness that a critical stage in the sordid drama was reached. She had not broken off all communication with old Granny, and it was from the witch that she heard that Bertha bade fair to perpetuate the race of Claybrooke by giving birth to a child of Rupert's. Filled with the news (which seemed to her of vital importance, though she could not explain why), she hurried over to the Limes and blurted it out before her more cautious sister could stop her.

"A tode ye what I wuz afeerd on, Miss Laura," she cried, turning her little pig eyes up to the ceiling. "That Bartha's... an' it 'ull be able ta speak o' yew as its aunt."

"What's that?" said Laura eagerly. "Well I never! Is a child of my brother's likely to be born? Oh, I must go over and see the woman now! Surely, surely, she will think differently now. Surely we shall be able to make friends over the child. Rupert's child. And she'll let me know the meaning of her curious behaviour in not wearing mourning."

She rose, walked to the window, and looked out on to the cemetery opposite with mingled feelings of pleasure and regret.

"Now yew ha' done't, y'ole fule," whispered Sarah furiously in her sister's ear, "an' it 'ull take me all my time ta ondew it."

"Hode yar n'ise," whispered Peggie. "Yew think yew're the oony one as hev got any sense. Yew leave it ta me."

"Yew chatterin' innercent," hissed Sarah. But Peggie continued aloud, "Well, Miss Laura, that'll be Bartha's baabe right enow. But whether that'll be yar pore brother's or noo, I'm shore I can't tell ye. He! he! he!"

The little old woman crumpled her lips up, winked, and sniggered.

"That I shall find out," said Laura. "I mean to go over and have a hearing about it; and if I am satisfied, Sarah, you must write to Strainer again. You won't mind if I only leave the income of what I have to leave to you and leave the money to Rupert's child after your death. I ought to see, too, that Bertha has enough to bring the child up properly; so she'll have to have some of the income, too."

Laura saw a way of killing two birds with one stone—she could test Sarah's vaunted disinterestedness and at the same time fulfil what she considered a duty to her dead brother.

"Lor', me dare," said Sarah, "o' coorse I doan't mind. Hain't I allust kep' on a-tellin' on ye as blood be blood, an' a-beggin' on ye not ta leave all that brass ta me? 'Tain't for the brass I sarves ye, but for the love I beers ye. But how yew're a-gooin' ta find out I'm shore I can't say. 'Tis a wise child as knoo its owan father. That must be wonnerful aunt as knoo har owan newy."

"Then I shall go over to-morrow," said Laura. "You may expect me by the 10.30, Peggie. Ask Mr. Reed to have his pony trap at Willowby Station to meet me."

"I'll mind it," said Peggie. "An' I hoop yew'll stop an' hev a bit o' dinner along o' me an' my husban'. We're pore folk, as yew knoo, but yar fewd'll be whoolsome."

"Thank you," replied Laura, "I shall be glad to. But you must excuse me now. I must go and look arter my little chickens."

"Theer!" said Sarah when Laura had left the room. "Now yew see what yew ha' done! Theer's oony one thing foor't. We can't affoord ta wait noo longer! I shall ha'e ta use the fust of ole Granny's powders ta-night!"

"But is it saafe?" asked Peggy dubiously. "D'ye think as she'd reely alter har will?"

"I darsen't trust her," said Sarah. "I dooan't knoo what ha' come oover har laately since she heerd o' Ruput's death, drat him! She oan't drink, an' she fare ta be allust a-thinkin' an' she doan't talk like she used tew."

"Will the powder stop har from comin' oover ta-morrer?" asked Peggie.

"From what ole Granny saay," replied Sarah, "that'll make har silly sleeapy. I'll keep har like that for a bit, an' then if she doan't change har mind I shall ha' ta use t'other soort. Granny say as theer's noo fare on it's bein' found out."

"Right yew be, then," said Peggie; "but for booth our sakes be keerful."

"Tha'ss what yew ote tew ha' thote on afoor yew come blabbin' out about Bartha," retorted Sarah. "Keerful yar granny! Hare! Yew'd best be a-gooin'. I shall put it in har coockoo ta-night."

Come, Rupert! If you be alive, hasten home! There is a chance of saving your sister yet. But delay is dangerous. The evil compass her about, and she is within sight of the Valley of the Shadow of Death.

An' I doubt they oan't tell me so long as I'm thick along o' yew. I doan't fare as if I could cast my eye so far o' late. Things ha' growed thick as used ta be clear. I doubt my gift is a-gooin'. I hain't been true ta the black maan, an' tha'ss a fack! An' I rackon he'll let me knoo on't."

"Never mind the black man," said Bertha, smiling; "you are better without his help."

"Aah! But yew doant knoo, my innercent pratty," answered Granny. "Tha'ss ill tryin' ta cheeat the daavil."

"Then shame him instead," replied Bertha.

"Aah! That 'ud take a bit o' dewin'," grinned the witch. "But dee yew holler an' tell me ta goo an' be damned to me. Holler soo as ole Peggy can hare."

"No, I won't act a lie," said Bertha. "I'll keep away from you, and I won't contradict you if you say we've quarrelled; but my Rupert wouldn't like me to be false in any way."

"Dary me!" grinned old Granny. "Love dew maake yew whoolly pertickler! That doan't some folk! Howsomedever, that doan't sigerfy. I'll dew the hollerin'. Fare ye well."

Granny opened the door, and at once became transfigured. "Yew dust saay that tame!" she screeched. "111 pay ye, yew impident trollop! I'll cast the ban o' the black maan on ye if iver yew come nare me ag'in. Yew think 'cos yew're young and pratty as yew're his faav'rite. I'll lar n ye! I'll larn ye!"

The old woman went her way screaming down the path into the loke and round to her own back door. All her terrible fluency of anathema was vociferously exercised as she drew near Peggie's scullery window. She stopped an instant on her threshold, and raised her quivering hands while she stormed and blasphemed at the girl.

"Phillup, Phillup," whispered Peggie. "Hark at har! She's whoolly a-mobbin' o' that Bartha. I'm right pleased. I'll goo round in a minnut an' ax har wha'ss up."

"Yew'll dew as yew like," said old Noddy, "naturallie. But what yew want wi' th'ole is past my tellin'."

"Har rint's paid, bain't it? Wery well, then," said Peggie. "Tha'ss all yew want ta knoo."

Presently Peggie's thick, dumpy legs trotted round to Granny's door.

"Are ye theer?" she asked, and entered on being answered by a croak from inside.

Adopting the precedent created by the Ancient Mariner, Granny held her with her eye.

Whatever other mystic powers the witch might have lost, the magnetism of her gaze had not deserted her.

Peggie sat down, and, without waiting to make the inquiries she had intended, she launched forth into a garrulous relation of the *status quo* at the Limes. "An' she's a-gooin' ta put one o' them powders inta har coockoo tanight," she concluded.

"Aah!" said Granny. "Dee yew tell har as she'd best not use t'others till I ha' seed har. Sartinly not without lettin' me know. They're ockud stuff an' want a bit o' management. I'll lam ye how ta use 'em when the time come."

"Thanky," said Peggie.

Then did Granny pour forth her fictitious injuries at the hands of Bertha. According to her account (implicitly credited by her hearer), Bertha had endeavoured to supplant her in the black man's graces, by means of the allurements of her youth and beauty.

"But the maaster bain't like some o' his sarvants," said Granny. "He's oold hisself, as oold as time, an' he doan't forgit ole friends for an insinivatin' young baggage like har. Not him! Hech! hech! hech! I'll larn har some'at afoor I ha' done with har. Tryin' ta push me out what interduced har. Noo! noo! The maaster like his owan.

"The black man favour the black man's kind,
An' Peggie an' Seerah be booth tew his mind.

Soo yew're all right. Yew doan't want ta be afeerd o' narthen. I'll help ye, but yew must ax me afoor them other powders be used. I'll help ye, but yew'll ha'e ta ax Seerah for another smell o' goold. We oold uns love goold, the daavil an' me.

"Black an' red. Red an' black.
Red for the quick, an' black for the dead.
The shadder o' faate in the low sun's track.
The gush o' blood in the murk night's rack.
The blaaze o' the flaame on the black man's back.
The colours of hell be black an' red.

Hech! hech! hech! Now dee yew be a-gooin'. I've wark ta dew, wark ta dew."

At the Limes Sarah had effected her purpose, and when she prepared Laura's nightly cup of cocoa (which had now taken the place of grog), she stirred in a dark powder that looked like the crushed seed of some plant. It was the seed of henbane, or hyoscyamus.

The next morning Laura felt too drowsy and lethargic to get up.

"I can't think what's the matter with me, Sarah," she said. "My liver must be out of order. It's never been right since I had that jaundice. If I'm not better tomorrow I shall get you to go for Mr. Marigold."

Throughout the day she lay sleeping or half awake. Her dreams were vivid and painful. Over and over again she dreamt of her last parting with Rupert. And then she seemed to see him drowning and to hear him curse her as the cause of his death. Towards evening the narcotic lost some of its force. She wished to get up and go downstairs to see her fowls, but was dissuaded by Sarah, who again administered the hyoscyamus in the cup of cocoa.

In the morning Laura woke with difficulty, and felt worse than on the previous day. She requested that the doctor should be sent for, and Sarah readily acquiesced. But like the youth in the Parable, she said "I go" and went not.

During the day Laura was too drowsy to concern herself greatly whether Mr. Marigold came or not, but, as before, she woke up slightly in the evening, again expressed a wish to get up, and was again dissuaded.

"I wish Mr. Marigold would come," she said. "I can hardly keep awake during the day, and I have such horrible dreams. What did he say, Sarah? Did you see him?"

"Noo, me dare," replied Sarah, with truth. "I see the young maan in the dispensuary," she added, launching into fiction, "an' he said as he'd be shore an' tell him."

"He must have forgotten it," said Laura. "If I'm no better to-morrow you must see him yourself and ask him to come."

Another dose of hyoscyamus made her torpor more difficult to shake off than ever. Sarah was ordered to seek the doctor and ask him to come without delay. The day passed without his appearance. Laura roused herself in the evening, and, without ringing for Sarah, dressed herself wearily and went to the door. It was locked from the outside. She rang violently, and, overcome by the little exertion she had undergone, lay down on the couch at the foot of her bed.

"Well I never!" she said to herself. "Why ever hev she locked me in! What is this illness of mine? What is the matter with me?"

She tried to think, but the drug was already affecting her brain. She could not concentrate her thoughts.

Sarah's heavy footsteps were heard clumping up the

R stairs. The door was unlocked noiselessly, and she entered, expecting to see her mistress in bed. She started nervously when she saw her up and dressed. Then she said—

"D'ye want me, me dare? D'ye think yew fare wise a-gittin' up?"

"Why did you lock me in, Sarah?" asked Laura. "And how is it that Mr. Marigold has not come?"

"I foorgot ta tell ye at dinner-time, me dare," said Sarah. "An' ye seemed soo sleeapy that it di'n't seeam wuth while a-waakin' on ye up. Mr. Marigold ha' got the gout, an' can't leave the house. An' I di'n't knoo if yew'd like young Hare ta see ye."

Hare was the junior member of the firm of Marigold and Hare, and Laura would never consent to consult him, as Sarah very well knew.

"No, I won't see young Hare," said Laura. "You know I never will, Sarah. But if I'm not better to-morrow you must get a cab at the ' King's Head,' and I'll go and see Mr. Marigold at his surgery. But why did you lock the door?"

"I've been down the garden a-seein' arter the fowls," explained Sarah, rather weakly for a woman of her inventive powers. "An' I thote it ud be better ta lock ye in saafe."

"Well I never! What a funny girl you are!" said Laura to the grey-haired woman. "I think I'll come down for a bit."

She rose as she spoke, but a horrible dizziness seized her, and she had to sink back on the couch again.

"Oh dear!" she sighed. "I feel very queer. I can hardly see. Did you ever! Sarah, I hope I'm not going to be right ill!"

"Wha noo, me dare," said Sarah, "but d'ye think yew'd better come down?"

"I don't think I can," answered Laura. "Help me to undress again. I feel better in bed, though I do have such horrible dreams."

Sarah administered the drug again that night, and when her mistress had sunk into a heavy stupor she went downstairs, mixed herself a strong glass of whisky and hot water, and sat down to consider.

The situation was getting critical. Laura would insist on a cab being sent for on the following day, and it would be impossible to put her off longer. It was too dangerous to wait for the insanity which Granny had told the sisters would be the ultimate result of the hyoscyamus if its administration were persisted in. The crisis would evidently be reached within the next twenty-four hours. She had heard from Peggy that Granny had quarrelled with Bertha and was again an ally, but that she wished to be consulted before the other lot of powders were resorted to. She had sent over a couple of pounds to buy the witch's co-operation.

She had no special desire to murder her mistress if her end could be attained by other means; but she had not the slightest repugnance to doing so if her victim proved intractable.

Like most cruel women, Sarah gained courage from the presence of an ally. She was confident that Laura would not wake till morning, so she slipped upstairs, locked the door of Laura's room, put on her bonnet and her boots, and started off to the town to find "Bartie."

She found him sitting on the edge of his bed in tears. "Ooh aunt, dare aunt," he cried, "I'll niver goo back to wark noo moor. Oh hoo! Ooh!" and the semi-idiot fairly burst out blubbering.

"Wha wha'ss the matter, my bewty booy?" asked Sarah solicitously. "Whew've been interfarin' along o' yew?"

"It's the men," sobbed Bertie. "They wanted me to pay foor some bare foor'm, an' 'cos I 'ouldn't they tarned me uppards an' spilt all my brass out o' my parkuts.

Ooh, hoo! An' then they smacked me half-way up. I'll tell my mother I will."

"Theer, theer!" said Sarah soothingly. "Kiss yar ole aunt. Theer's my dare booy. I'll goo an' see the maaster tamorrer. He'll give 'em a dewin'. Oony the tother day he toold me as yew had as good a hand at a corfin as any man in St. Meery's. Yew tell me theer naames. I'll see the maaster myself."

"Ooh noo, aunt," sobbed Bertie. "I darsen't let ye. They toold me if I puffed they'd take my breeches off an' larrup me till my noose bled. They di'n't steal narthen, but 'tain't the fust time as they ha' stood me on my hid, ta run the water out, they say, 'cos I doan't drink. Doan't yew say narthen ta noobardy."

"A nasty lot of peevish warmin's a' parsecutin' my pore booy," said Sarah. "Well, I oan't say narthen this time, but if they dew't ag'in dee yew let me knoo on't, an' 111 sarve 'em out somehow soo's they oan't knoo whew ta be." ("I'll see ole Granny ag'in," she whispered to herself.) "Now look yew hare, Bartie. Dee yew feel well enow ta goo oover ta Frogsthorpe on yar bicycle ta-morrer moarnin'?"

"Yes, aunt," said the boy, beginning to subdue his sobs.

"Then goo an' tell yar ma as I want ta see har, an' she want ta come oover hare by the fust train she can catch."

"Yis, aunt. Yew want ta see ma, an' yew'll be oover by the fust train yew can catch."

"Wha drat the fule," said Sarah. "Noo wonner they stand him on his head an' spank him, the aggerawatin' warmin'! Twanty yare oold an' all, an' six fut!"

"Ooh, aunt," said Bertie, beginning to weep again. "Doan't yew set a-mobbin' on me, or 'strew's Gord I'll drownd myself."

Sarah had repented of her harsh words before her godson had finished speaking. He was the only thing in the world that she really loved. It was as much for his sake as her own that she had made up her mind to stick at nothing to get Laura's money. She put her arms round him and said, "Wha theer, I di'n't mean narthen. Yew ote ta knoo yar ole aunt love ye true. Gi'e me a kiss. "

"Then yew shou'n't git a-mobbin' on me," wept Bertie plaintively. He raised his mouth and slobbered his aunt.

"Theer's my dare booy," said Sarah. "I oan't gi'e noo message. I'll write it. " As on a previously recorded occasion, Sarah drew forth an old envelope and a pencil, and scrawled a few words to her sister. Then she again kissed her nephew and bade him good night. "Be a good booy, oan't ye?" she said fondly.

"Yes, aunt," replied the dutiful youth. "I hoop I shan't dream o' them warmin's. I git soo frighted when I fare ta dream."

Sarah reassured him, and trotted off back to the Limes.

The next day Laura did not open her eyes till past ten o'clock. A terrible languor possessed her. She could hardly raise her head from the pillow. She was quite incapable of coherent thought. She rang for Sarah, and ordered her to go and see if Mr. Marigold was still unable to visit her, and if so to proceed to the "King's Head," and to return in a cab which was to wait to convey the invalid to the doctor's surgery.

Peggie was not yet come, so to gain time Sarah said she would start as soon as she had brought up her mistress's breakfast.

By the time this was done (after some intentional delay attributed to the fact that "the kittle wouldn't bile noohow, the fire fared ta hev the daavil in't"), Peggie had arrived. Sarah put on her walking things and went upstairs to exhibit herself thus apparelled. Then she went down, stepped noisily across the hall, opened and slammed the front door, and stole quietly back to the kitchen, there to wait till impatience should cause Laura to ring again.

Peggie was nervous. Her limbs shook and her eyes winked incessantly.

"I wish I'd brought ole Granny," she said; "I wish I'd brought ole Granny."

"Wha hode yar n'ise, dew," said Sarah impatiently. "Yew an' me ote ta be a match for that pore thing upsteers; whew've lost what little sense she had wi' them powders. Aah, they're caapital! They whoolly muddle har. If oony the others fare as good, that'll be *all* right. Hev ole Granny tode ye how ta use 'em yit?"

"Not yit," answered Peggie, winking and jerking as if possessed by the imps of St. Vitus. "But p'raps we shan't ha'e ta use 'em. I hoops not."

"We oan't if she dew as I tell har," said Sarah, "though I doubt they'd be the safest way. Yew want ta git ole Granny ta tell ye about 'em ta-night if things goo wrong. I ha' got Laura's keys, an' I'll gi'e ye some moor brass ta taake hooam wi' ye for the ole witch."

Laura lay upstairs, alternately dozing and waking to a sense of heaviness and helpless lethargy. As the hours drew on she became vaguely uneasy, and with an effort recollected the cause, namely, that by this time Sarah should have returned with a message to say that the doctor was coming, or with a cab. Her room was over the kitchen, and every now and again she fancied she could hear a subdued hum of voices. But everything was so indistinct in her confused mind that she could not be certain that this was not another of the delusions which whirled fantastically through her semi-consciousness.

At length her attention was fixed by a shrill crow from her poultry run. She recognised the crow. "That's old Nod," she said drowsily. The cock crowed again, and this time roused his owner to action. She sat up in bed and looked at the clock. It was close on one. Nearly two hours since Sarah had left her ostensibly to go to Mr. Marigold's. She rang smartly, and then sank back upon her pillows, overcome by the dizziness which oppressed her as soon as she raised herself.

The bell hung in the kitchen, and its sharp vibrations struck the hearing of Peggie and Sarah with a shock of terror. The hour had sounded, and for an instant even Sarah wished that it had not. But her stronger nature asserted itself.

"Wha come along dew," she said to Peggie, who was gasping, winking, and shaking all at once, and whose face was like a quivering white jelly.

"Taake that theer Bible. She ha' oony got a Preer-book up in har rewm. An' pull yarself togither. Hare! Hev a drop o' this."

A stiff dose of raw whisky brought the colour back to Peggie's face and gave her heart.

"Come on, bor," she said, wiping her mouth on the front of her skirt. "Le'ss git it oover."

Sarah primed herself in like manner, and the two accomplices proceeded upstairs.

Laura saw the door open, and the entrance of the two women, with listless astonishment. Sarah withdrew the key from outside, inserted it within the room, and turned it in the lock. She advanced grimly to one side of the bed, and motioned to Peggie to range herself on the other.

"Well I never!" said Laura faintly. "Whatever do this mean, Sarah? Have you seen Mr. Marigold? Is he coming?

How is it that Peggie is here? I did not expect her. Why did you lock me in again?"

"Good moarnin', Miss Laura, an' how are yew?" said Peggie, fatuous with the internal struggle between natural cowardice and Dutch courage.

"Hode yar n'ise," said Sarah furiously.

"Answer me at once, Sarah," said Laura, a faint flush tinging her cheeks, which had lost their blowsy red of late. "What is the meaning of this?"

"I'll answer ye, doan't yew make noo mistake," replied Sarah coarsely, throwing off the pretence of civility and appearing in her true colours. "Hev I seed Mr. Marigoold? Noo, I hain't seed Mr. Marigoold, an' I hain't been a-nigh him, an' bain't a-gooin' neither. Be he a-comin'? Not as I knoos on, an' if he dew come I'll sune send him off with a flea in his ear. How is it Peggie's hare? 'Cos I axed har ta come oover an' hev a h'arin' along o' me an' yew. Why did I lock the dooar? 'Cos I wished tew, an' 'cos I doan't mean as yew should leave the rewm ontil yew dew as yew're told. "

"Good God!" grasped Laura. "Is *this* real? Or is it another of my fancies?"

"Come, noo narnsense," said Sarah, shaking her. "Waake up. Yew'll find 'tis reel enow."

"Are you mad, Sarah," asked Laura, now thoroughly roused by the indignities put upon her. "Whatever are you talking about? Do you know what you're doing?"

"Look a hare," said Sarah. "Yew've brote it on yarself. Oover thutty yare hev I been pestered wi' yew. Did ye think as I waited on ye for love an' the little I iver got out o' ye, though maybe that's moor an' yew knoos on? Noo! I allust meant ta hev yar brass! An' hev it I will. If yew'd ha' kep yar prarmuss an' let yar will aloan, yew'd ha' been comferable enow till ye died. But yew say as yew're a gooin' ta leave it ta that Rupert's brat if he hev one, an' that I oan't put up with. Now hare I ha' got ye. Yew fare tew weak ta help yarself, or even ta holler wery loud. An' out o' this rewm yew doan't goo afoor yew ha' took yar Bible ooath yew oan't niver tell noobardy what I ha' said tee ye this moarnin', an' niver alter yar will from what 'tis now. How long yew'd live shet up in this rewm, o' coorse I can't say. But they dew say as confinement be bad for fleshy folk like yew. Soo hare lie yar ch'ice. Libutty an' life, or shet up in this rewm ontil death rob me on ye! He! he! An' I've a sooart of an idee as that mightn't be long. Wheer's the Bible, Peggie?"

"Hare ta be," replied Peggie, who had plucked up courage on seeing the pitiful state of stupefaction into which Laura had fallen.

The poor woman was aghast with indignation and amazement. A torrent of suspicion poured through her mind, and justified itself by innumerable memories that now took substance and became intelligible facts. She— Miss Claybrooke—to be insulted in her own room—by her own dependant whom she regarded as a humble and admiring domestic, even when most swayed by her will. All the vile plot against her brother flashed clear before her. All her own perverse blindness and infatuation.

"Oh Rupert, Rupert," she moaned; "if I had only known! If I had only known!"

"Tha'ss noo use yar hollerin' for Rupert," said Sarah. "He's fewd for the s'rimps long afoor now. Gi'e me the Bible, Peg.... Hare. Take an' kiss this hare an' say sa help ye Gord yew'll dew as I tell ye. Yew'll ha'e ta say the wuds arter me as I speak 'em."

Laura was not without courage. Until lately her life had for years been spent without any sense of responsibility. She had relied on Sarah for everything. She had shifted every decision, every duty, from her own shoulders. Her periodical attacks of the Miss Claybrooke mood had been mere temporary assertions of a dignity ridiculous in its unreality. Her occasional obstinacy had been merely another way of asserting a fictitious self. She had never understood that this was so until now. But now she knew things as they were, and a new sense of identity came with the knowledge. Ill as she was, stupefied with the repeated doses of the drug she had swallowed, her courage rose "like a lark on a May morning." She had found a proper pride at last. No more burlesque dignity! Humble herself to this thing? To this woman she and her family had raised from poverty and squalor to comfort? Wrong Rupert (whom she had so deeply wronged already) through his child at the dictation of this vile hypocrite—this villainous impostor and her despicable sister? Never! She would die first! She would make a fight for life and liberty if only this horrible stupor would pass—if only she could gather her faculties together again. But if she failed, then she would die for honour arid justice! Danger and insult transformed her. Her recent abstemiousness, no doubt, helped in the change. She could not vent her thoughts in speech; she was too weak for that. But she could signify her determination and hold to it with a prayer that she might be supported in her ordeal.

"Now then!" said Sarah, "be yew a-gooin' ta dew what yew're toold, or bain't ye?"

"No! Never!" Laura gasped in accents pitifully incongruous with the tenour of her speech. "I'd sooner die! Submit to you, you devil? Never!"

"Wery well, then," said Sarah. "Then yew'll stop hare till ye dew die. An' yew can't make noo new will, nor yit destroy the one yew hev made, 'cos Mr. Strainer ha' got it."

The completeness of Sarah's schemes struck Laura with horror. Should she pretend to swear, and break her oath as soon as she was at liberty? No! She could not submit to the humiliation. She could not abase herself by acting a lie or defiling the sanctity of an oath! She would trust to chance—to God—to succour her—to foil the machinations that beset her.

"You've had my answer," she said. "Now go!" "I shall goo when I like," screamed Sarah, furious at her failure. She seized Laura and shook her savagely. "*Now* will ye dew't?" she cried.

"No! No! No! Oh Rupert!" moaned Laura. "Oh God, help me!"

Sarah raised her coarse red hand and struck her victim full in the mouth.

"*Now* will ye?" she cried again.

"Doan't. Ooh doan't!" begged Peggie, who was shaking the whole room with the tremulous jerking of her limbs. "Ooh doan't, Seerah! Leave har now. She may change har mind. Doan't hit har. Oh doan't! That'll Show A BRUISE IF SHE DIE!"

"Hode yar ni'se," said Sarah. "I strook har oopenhanded. That oan't shoo.... Be yew a-gooin' ta answer me?" she continued to the figure in the bed.

But the blow had proved too much for Laura's feebleness. With a muffled moan as it fell, she had relapsed into unconsciousness.

"Christ!" screamed Peggie. "Yew ha' kilt har!"

"Noo! moor's the pity!" said Sarah. "She's a-breathin'. Le'ss goo. P'raps yew're right. We doan't want noo bruises on har body. But as sewn as I see that that doan't show— well, it 'ull be a case of 'ax my Granny.' He! he! he!"

With a last curse at the victim of her cruelty she turned, unlocked the door, and took the key. Peggie followed her out, and the door was again locked from the outside.

"Come an' hev a drop o' some'at," said Sarah. "That ha' gi'e me right a tarn!"

And they went.

A STRUGGLE FOR FREEDOM DURING the rest of the day Laura lay with closed eyes, scarcely waking once to the realities of existence. Sarah took up food, but it was left untouched. The time came for Peggie to return to Frogsthorpe without any alteration in the position of affairs.

"Now mind yew ax ole Granny about them powders ta-night," said Sarah, taking leave of her sister. "An' yew'd best come oover ag'in ta-morrer an' tell me what she say, an' how the land lay. Theer, now I've made a rhyme. Some un's a-gooin' ta gi'e me a prasant! P'raps it 'ull be Laura. He! he! he!"

"I'll ax har," replied Peggie. "An' I'll be oover by the same train ta-morrer. Dary me, ta think o' yew aloan shet up in the house with har up theer! That whoolly gi'e me the creeps. Bain't ye afeerd?"

"Afeerd? What on?" asked Sarah. "I must git another powder down o' har ta-night somehow, tha'ss all I'm afeerd about. Dee yew be a-gooin'. P'raps she'll change har mind afoor ta-morrer. But, anyhow, tha'ss best ta be riddy."

Peggie found old Granny busy over her fire with her pots, saucepans, and boilers. The witch looked up at her visitor's entrance. "Well, how dee yew git on?" she asked.

"Seerah want ta knoo how ta use them other powders," said Peggie.

Now the second lot of powders were made from the fruit of the deadly nightshade, mixed with its root, powdered and dried. Granny had no intention now of permitting their use.

"She morn't use 'em yit," she answered. "The mewn's oony in har fust quarter, and she must wait till it be waxin' ta the full. That'll be in about ten days' time."

"Well, I spooz we can wait till then," said Peggie doubtfully. "But Laura fare some cantankerous! Tha'ss lucky t'other stuff keep har soo sleepy."

"Aah," grunted Granny. "Ha'e ye brote any moor brass?"

Peggie handed over what Sarah had given her for the witch. "Thanky," said Granny, "an' good night."

As soon as the young moon had made an early retirement suitable to its tender age, and the marshes were left to their purple darkness under the stars which multiplied themselves a millionfold in the gloss of the dykes and winked at their cleverness in doing so, old Granny went clicketing down the loke across the big marsh to where the great black mill stands, which drains the whole of the Frogsthorpe level through the conduit of the mill dyke. The waters were low, and the mill stood swart and still in the hard clear starlight.

There is a willow that stretches athwart the widest part of the pool, where the fat roach lie waiting for the larvae of countless insects that still fall from the tremulous white glow of the leaves to the black depths beneath. Hither hobbled old Granny, and here through the night she sat out on the leaning trunk, over the water, till her incantations were complete, her mysteries of divination ended.

The whisper of the wind before the dawn was stirring the willow leaves, and the pure fresh scent, the harbinger of sunrise, was upon the marshes ere her work was done. She slid back to the bank, chuckling with glee.

"Tew days an' tew nights," she croaked. "Tew days an' tew nights, an' he'll be hooam ag'in. Noobardy mustn't knoo but Bartha. Noobardy!"

In the morning, when Peggie had departed on her way to the Limes, Granny crept round to the window at the back of Bertha's bakehouse. Blind old Noddy could not see her, and the window was invisible from the loke. The girl was busy washing at the seething copper. She looked up on hearing a faint scratch at the window.

"Sst! me dare," whispered the old woman. "Tew days an' tew nights, an' yew'll foold yar love in yar arms again. "

Bertha could not repress a cry; but the witch checked her with a gesture. "Not a wud ta noobardy," she hissed. "Yew may git a letter afoor. If ye dew, doan't let noobardy knoo, or yew'll spile everything. As sune as he come, bring him round ta me at once."

She slunk off again noiselessly to her cottage.

Bertha could not but believe. "Oh, thank God!" she cried. "I shall have him with me at the time of my anguish. 'He, remembering His mercy, hath holpen His servant.' Oh, thank God!"

For a few minutes irrational emotion (for surely trust in such antiquated folly as witchcraft is irrational and gratitude to God an eccentricity) mastered her. Tears of joy and thankfulness rained down her cheeks.

"But I mustn't let anybody see me like this," she said, with a happy shake of laughter. "Granny says it's to be a secret, and it shall be. Oh! I'm to see him in three days! And the book's waiting for him, and success prophesied! No more pain! No more grief! Oh, my dear, my dear!"

When Laura woke to full consciousness of what had happened, her room was dark, and there was no sound about the house. She lay for a long time thinking and trying to evolve some scheme for frustrating her enemies. She was more determined than ever not to give way one jot. "If only I could get my strength back," she thought. "Surely I could make someone hear next door. But I can't understand this feeling. Does Sarah put anything in my food? I can't starve. That would make me weaker than ever. But if I feel worse again tomorrow I'll only eat the simplest things and drink nothing but water. *That* can hide no deviltry."

As she was deliberating, Sarah opened the door and entered with a light and a supper tray.

"Hare be yar fewd," she said; "I shan't starve ye yit."

Laura swallowed down the indignation that struggled for expression. She lay still and silent.

"Well," continued Sarah, "ha'e ye changed yar mind yit?"

"I must have time to think," answered Laura. She realised now that her life was in danger.

"Yew'll hev a planty o' that," chuckled Sarah. "Theer's noobardy as I knoos on whew's likely ta ax arter ye. Yar time's yar owan—in rayson."

"Leave the tray, then," said Laura.

"Is theer anything moor ye want?" asked Sarah. "Yew knoo 'tis allust a pleasure tew me ta sarve ye, doan't ye? He! he! he! Should a bring ye up a bottle o' whisky?"

"Go, please," said Laura. "I'll try to make up my mind by the morning."

"Ooh, doan't hurry yarself," replied Sarah. "Theer's a planty o' cash in the box for t'ree weeks yit. Goo' night. Pleasant dreams tew ye. He! he! he!"

"Now I shall see if I get more drowsy after supper," thought Laura. "If I do I shall know something has been put in the cocoa. The chicken and bread can't hide anything."

After supper she got a book and read, in order to watch her sensations. She soon felt the lethargy and heaviness stealing upon her again. Before it quite overcame her, she murmured, "Now I know."

The next day passed for her in dull stupor, varied by an occasional visit from Sarah or Peggie. She could not rouse herself to speak, and, persuaded by Peggie, Sarah forbore to take violent measures to "bring har ta rayson," as she called it.

But by night-time she felt that the effects of the drug were dying. "Now," she said to herself, "I'll drink nothing but water to-night, and then to-morrow I may be myself again."

Since she commenced her fight against Sarah, her speech had lost the trace of dialect that it acquired under Sarah's guidance. She spoke more as she had spoken in her youth, before she became so subject to Sarah's thraldom. Her whole nature seemed to have changed since her eyes were opened to her servitude.

"If I am better," she continued, "I'll make a bid for freedom somehow." s

When Sarah brought up the supper tray Laura asked for some fresh water, giving it as an excuse that she had suffered from thirst on the previous night, and found what was in the room flat and unpleasant. This was brought her, and Sarah left her for the night, after inquiring if she had yet changed her mind and being answered in the negative.

Laura ate as much as she could, and felt better. The cocoa she threw out of the window among some tall laurels which stood beneath on one side. It would not be seen from below. She went to sleep without any return of the dreaded heaviness, and felt confirmed in her suspicions. "To-morrow," she said, "I may be able to do something to get free. I will pray that God may help me. Oh, He will if He will forgive me all my folly and wickedness to Rupert. Oh God! If you will save me I will try to make amends as best I can. I will help and cherish his wife and child. Oh God, help me to do something to right the wrong before I die."

The old belief in offering up a sacrifice to propitiate the deity will never die. Men and women who would ridicule the idea of offering a five-pound note to Mr. Andrew Carnegie as a prelude to asking him a favour see nothing inconsistent in promising destiny to do what destiny alone can permit or forbid. The apotheosis of bribery and corruption is constant and unending so long as human beings shall find a place in the universe. Not one in a million can conscientiously say, "Not as I will, but as Thou wilt."

There were once two shipwrecked sailors on a raft. No land was near, no sail in sight. Their food and water had given out, and there seemed no prospect before them but death. Then said Jack, " Oh Lord! If ye will but let me get safe ashore I'll sell my house, and all my gold and jewels, and all my ships, and give all away to the poor." "Why, Jack!" said his mate Bill, "you ain't got no 'ouse, nor no jules, nor no ships!" "Shut up, ye fool," replied Jack. "*Tm a-kiddiri on him J"*

The humour of the story is saved from blasphemy by its terrible truth to nature. Poor Laura may be pardoned for being guilty of an absurdity which many, far more able than she to gauge its wicked folly, commit every day of their lives. Most religious profession is based on selfishness. "There must be a heaven to reward me and a hell to requite mine enemy," is the thought of thousands of nominal Christians.

"And the poor Pope was sure it must be so,
Else wherefore did the people kiss his toe?"

Laura woke on the following morning to hear the second cock crow. She felt that clearness had been restored to her brain, strength to her body. A healthy hunger made itself felt. The events of the past few days seemed like a bad dream. But no! There was the supper tray. She had slept alone. The door was locked.

She determined to feign a stupor when Sarah brought up her breakfast. Then, possibly, she might be left alone in the house during the day. That would be her chance.

When Sarah came up as usual, and asked if she had made up her mind, she showed no sign of intelligence, but lay silent, looking up vacantly at her questioner.

Sarah was getting impatient. She had not expected so long a resistance. She was tired of it, and annoyed at the delay which Granny said would be necessary before the other drug could be used to put her in possession of her heart's desire. Laura's expression exasperated her. She shook her roughly. "D'ye hare? ". she said. "Ha'e ye made up yar mind?"

"Give me till to-morrow," was the faint reply. "Only till to-morrow."

"Well, dee yew dew't by then," said Sarah, "or 'twill be the wuss for ye. Hare! Take yar brekkust."

She slammed the tray down on to the bed and left the room.

Laura ate heartily. She was hungry, and wished to strengthen herself for the trial. She listened eagerly to hear if Sarah went out of the front door. Just before eleven she heard the welcome slam.

"Now," she thought, "now for it!"

She dressed herself hastily, hesitated a moment, then flung open the window and screamed for help.

"Help! help!" she cried. "Mrs. Peck! Anyone! Help! help! Quick, for God's sake! Oh, make haste'. Help! help! help!"

She heard the front door furiously flung open and the rush of footsteps up the stairs. She screamed with redoubled energy, and fancied she could hear voices in the nextdoor garden, but before she realised her fatal error in not specifying the nature of the help she craved she was seized from behind and flung violently on the bed. A pillow was immediately thrust over her mouth. She struggled with the violence of despair, but she was in the hands of Sarah and Peggie, and Sarah was strong, and Peggie's muscles had been hardened by washing and garden work. She was helpless in their hands.

Sarah had started out to meet Peggie, but her time was wrong, and her sister met her almost at the gate. They were nearly back to the house when they heard Laura's screams, and rushed with terrified haste to stop them. Muffled as Laura was by the pillow she did not hear Mrs. Peck's voice downstairs calling out, "What's the matter? What's the matter?"

"Hare, Peg," said Sarah, "set yew right on har, an' hoold har down. Doan't let har git the piller off, for Gord's sake. I must goo down an' see the ole from next dooar."

She hurried downstairs, and found the neighbour in the hall.

"What *is* the matter, Miss Chindaffy?" said Mrs. Peck. "I *hev* been frightened! I heard Miss Claybrooke crying for help, and I thought you were out, so I came in."

"An' wery kind on ye tew," simpered Sarah. "I *wuz* out, an' pore Miss Laura had a accident. She hain't been wery well, an' she jes' now fell an' cut harself drefful, an' cou'n't stop the blood. But I jest got back in time. She's all right now a thanky. I'll tell har yew come in. She'll thank yew harself in a day or tew. "

"Well, I'm glad it's no worse," said Mrs. Peck. "It gave me quite a turn! Good morning, Miss Chindaffy."

"Good moarnin', an' thanky," replied Sarah. "Meddlesome ole!" she said as she hurried upstairs again.

Peggie was still blandly sitting on Laura, who had ceased to struggle. Sarah shut the window and then went to the bed. "Take off the piller," she said, "but pop it on ag'in if she holler."

Laura lay panting. She had hardly been able to breathe. Tears of mortification and despair were rolling down her cheeks. The pillow was wet where it had touched her eyes.

"Now, then," said Sarah, "wha'ss the meanin' o' this? Yew fare wery strong an' lively all on a sudden; but I'll mind as yew doan't git another chance."

Laura said nothing. She felt that all appeals for mercy would be futile. In any case she would have disdained to make them.

"Hand oover that theer Bible, Peg," said Sarah. "Now, then! Kiss the book an' sweer yew oan't try noo moor o' yar tricks till I come back. I'm jest a-gooin' down wi' Peggie for a minnut. I oan't leave ye by yar prashus self for long, my bewty. Yew may lay yar life! I'll prarmuss ye. Come. Sweer."

Exhausted by her struggle, disheartened at her failure, and ignorant of her neighbour's call, Laura took the oath demanded. The two sisters thereupon left the room and locked the door behind them.

"Look hare, Peg," said Sarah, when they had got down into the kitchen and were busy with the whisky bottle, "this oan't dew! I bain't a-gooin' ta wait noo longer. Yew must goo oover at oncet an' ax ole Granny for some'at as oan't ha'e ta wait for noo mewn. A pack o' narnsense. An' come back ag'in an' tell me what she say. Hare, take this ten shillun. Yew'd better git a trap ta take ye back ta Willowby Station arter yew ha' seed har."

During Peggie's absence Sarah stood guard over the prisoner, only leaving her for food, and exacting a repetition of the oath whenever she left the room.

Laura spoke little throughout the day. She was distraught with fear lest Sarah should succeed in her aim. Her anxiety was not so much on her own account as for the sake of Rupert's wife and child.

Towards evening her clearer insight enabled her to comprehend that an oath obtained under duress might be broken without fault. She was about to consent to swear to leave her will unaltered, and to grant an amnesty for the injuries she had suffered, when Peggie returned. Then it was too late. For word was brought that Sarah was to have the lethal draught ready by eight o'clock on the following evening, when Granny would herself come to the Limes and make it effective in spite of the moon.

When Laura suggested that she would yield and give the pledge demanded, she was met with a grin and a refusal.

"Tew late, me dare," said Sarah. "Mrs. Peck knoo as yew've been ill an' fell down an' hu't yarself. I doubt that'll tarn out moor sarious than I thote at fust. But chare yew up! I bain't a-gooin' ta leave ye noo moor. An' if ye *dew* goo hoam yew'll hev the comfut of knooin' as yew've done yar duty ta yar lovin' Seerah. He! he!"

Throughout the night one or other of the weird sisters kept watch. The time of waiting was short, but it would not do to run any risks.

Laura slept little, but lay quiet, racked with dread of what the morrow might bring forth. She had no fear of *immediate* death, in spite of the hint thrown out by Sarah. She did not know the assistance on which her persecutors rested their hopes, or she might have felt less secure. But neither had she any hope of leaving her room till she was driven mad, or had succumbed to the arts which she knew would be practised upon her, unless some unforeseen help should come from outside.

XXII GRANNY'S WORDS PROVE SOOTH

IT was hard work for Bertha to keep her joyous secret from Gilbert. The boy had been so faithful to her, he had shown such splendid promise of noble manhood, that it seemed unfair to her to leave him in the dark. But she had given her promise, and was staunch. For the first time since Rupert's departure her voice was heard about the cottage singing with a fervour of happiness that could not be concealed.

"Why, Bartha," said Gilbert, "whativer ha' come oover ye? I'm right pleased ta see ye so jolly. Hev ye heerd anything?"

"I've heard that I've got a good brother," she said gaily, kissing him. "Aren't you glad that I feel happier? Oh, Gilbert, how lovely the spring is!"

When the second day dawned, her eager longing for happiness and joyous expectation of it became leavened with anxiety. What if Granny should, after all, be mistaken? Could it be true that she would have her love safe back again so soon? Why did he not write if he were so near? Long before post time she was watching the turn of the road. Surely if Rupert was coming home to-morrow she would hear from him this morning. She saw Peggie start on her first trip to the Limes, and wondered impatiently why she was always going out.

"I suppose I shall see everyone but the postman," she said, with unusual petulance.

But just before ten o'clock the dapper little figure in the peaked cap swung round the comer into the loke and made straight for the Castle. Bertha ran out to meet him, her heart in her mouth. Was it from him?

She despised the little postman for the careless way in which he handed her the letter, wished her good morning, and was off again.

"Oh, thank God!" she cried, with a sense of infinite relief, of overwhelming joy. The envelope was addressed in his handwriting. She hurried indoors and tore the letter open.

"My dearest" (it ran),—" You will have got my letter telling you of my narrow escape and rescue. We had a slow passage out. Bad winds and heavy. And for reasons which I will tell you when I have you in my arms (and what an age it seems since you were there), I had to make the whole trip. Thank God, I'm back again in England at last, and longing for my darling's kisses. But that I've been doing ever since I left you. I must have a day in town to see Perkins and an editor or two, but I shall catch the nine train down the day after tomorrow, and you may expect me home about two. Don't come to meet me, my own. I could not bear to have my welcome on the platform. I want one very different from what that would have to be. All news when we meet.—With fondest love, I am always your own, Rupert."

"What letter does he mean?" asked Bertha. "I've had no letter. But never mind that. Never mind anything now. He's safe! He's coming home! How pleased he'll be about his book! And how pleased he'll be to hear that

I "She stopped and blushed. "Thank God! Oh, thank God!' Oh Lord of hosts, blessed is the man who trusteth in Thee. ' 'I will give thanks unto the name of the Lord, for it is good. For He hath delivered me out of all my troubles.' Sock! Sock! Dear old Sock! Your master's coming home. Your master!"

The old dog pricked his ears and leapt eagerly to the door.

"No, not yet," said Bertha, embracing his grey muzzle. "But soon. Very soon. Home to you and me. But I must go and tell Granny."

With eyes plaintive with disappointment, Sock looked after her disappearing figure, and with a sigh settled himself down again on the hearthrug.

Laughing and crying in an ecstasy of happiness, Bertha ran round to the old witch, oblivious of the pretence that they had quarrelled.

"You're right! You're right!" she cried exultingly. "Read this."

The old woman hobbled up and shut the door. "Sst," she said. "Tha'ss lucky as Peggie's away. But yew doan't want ole Noddy ta hare nuther. Dee yew read it tew me. I can't read writ hand."

With trembling lips and little bursts of delight Bertha read out the good news.

"Aah, tha'ss caapital!" chuckled Granny. "My sparruts toold me as he wuz a-comin'. But my sparruts, like myself, doan't allust tell the truth. Tew o'clock. Hey? Now if Peggie come back this moarnin', as I especks she will dew, I shall knoo for sartin what ta dew."

"Whatever do you mean?" asked Bertha.

"Niver yew mind that now," said Granny. "But doan't yew forgit ta bring him round ta me as sune as iver he come. Theer's wark ta dew, an' not a minnut ta speer. I tell ye it's life an' death. Yew shall knoo all ta-morrer."

"Mayn't I tell Gilbert to-night?" asked Bertha. "It seems a shame to keep it from him."

"Doan't yew tell noobardy," urged Granny, "or yew'll spile the whool brew. It's for yar maan's sake."

"All right, you old dear," said the joyous girl, kissing her. "Without you I should have broken my heart. I'll do anything you wish. Good-bye."

"Ole dare!" muttered Granny, when Bertha had gone.

"Ole dare! Ole is what folk moostly calls me. Ole dare! Blust! Tha'ss the fust time as anybardy iver called me that. Ole dare! An' she kissed me hearty as if she liked it. Ole dare! Well, tha'ss a rum un! Hech! hech! hech! Tha'ss a rum un!"

Bertha had not long returned to her cottage when old Noddy came round.

"Is anybardy at hooam?" boomed his ponderous voice.

Bertha, grateful for his former assistance, and at peace with all men by reason of her exceeding happiness, cheerily asked him in.

It was an idiosyncrasy of the blind man's that he always made love to his female tenants sooner or later, provided that they were young, and he had satisfied himself by manual research that they were fair to look upon. He had not always been blind, and he knew a pretty face when he felt one. His respect for Rupert's social position had hitherto restrained him from any attempt on Bertha, but now that there could be no question but that Rupert was dead, the old man's inclination began to turn towards the widow-apparent. He had heard Bertha's exultant entrance next door, and made it an excuse to call and ask for news.

"Good moarnin', me dare," he said. "I heerd the poost stop at yarn an' heerd ye goo round ta ole Granny's a-laughin'. I hoop as yew ha' heerd onespected good news o' yar maan."

"I'm afraid that's past hoping for, Mr. Noddyfield," answered Bertha, ashamed of the duplicity, but excusing it on the ground of Granny's behests.

"Aah! Pore Maaster Ruput!" said the old rascal. Edging a little closer he said, "Doan't a hansum young wench like yew fare looansum like, all alooan wi' noobardy but a slip of a brother?"

"I have been very lonely," replied Bertha, wondering what was coming and stepping back.

A leer stole over the old man's face. "Doan't ye think as I could consool ye, my pratty?" he said. "Come yew hare ta me."

"Whatever is the matter, Mr. Noddyfield?" cried Bertha, startled into a suspicion of the truth.

"Look yew hare," said Noddy. "Come yew hare an' gi'e th'ole man a kiss, an' we'll say noo moor about that ere nootuss ta quit."

"Oh, please go," said Bertha. "I'm sure you're not in earnest, but I don't like jokes of that sort."

"Tain't noo jook," said Noddy, "I mean it, 'strew's Gord I dew."

He lurched forward and endeavoured to catch the girl, but she eluded him and got the table between him and herself.

"I must ask you to go at once," she said firmly. "It is unworthy of your years and of your boasted religion to come here and insult an unprotected woman. Go at once, or I shall call for help."

"Call an' welcome," was the response. "Yew say as yew be unperritected, an' I rackon yew be. Now dee yew come hare, theer's a dare."

He groped out in front of her, and with a sudden movement pressed the table against the wall, penning in Bertha, who was not quick enough to slip out.

The noise of her efforts to free herself acted as a guide to her whereabouts to the blind man, and Noddy reached over the table and clutched her.

"Let me go, let me go," said she.

"Not afoor I've had a kiss," chuckled Noddy, stretching his head across the table and endeavouring to draw her to him.

"Sock, Sock," called Bertha.

With never a sound the old dog bounded up and seized Noddy by his right arm, held on, swung his weight, and strained his jaws together through coat sleeve, vest, and all.

With a yell of pain Noddy let go his hold and tried to clutch the dog.

"Drop it, Sock, and come to heel," said Bertha, smiling in spite of herself.

The well-trained bulldog "dropped it" and, avoiding a kick, ranged himself under the table against his mistress.

"Yew!" roared Noddy. "Yew shall paay foor't! Yew shall whoolly paay foor't. Di'n't I hull that Neetch out foor ye? Whew are yew a-settin' a dorg on to anybardy? I'll prarsecute ye! I'll tarn ye out o' hare ta oncet. I'll"

"If you don't go," said Bertha, "I shall set the dog on again."

"Goo? I'll goo! Blust, I'll goo!" said Noddy. "An' yew mind my wuds. Yew shall be out o' hare afoor a week's oover. Yew trarlopin'!"

Roaring out blasphemies and insults the baffled old rascal stamped home.

"She shall goo," he said to himself. "I oan't put up wi't! That a oan't! Settin' that brute on to me."

For hours he planned schemes of vengeance, till Peggie came home on her mission to see Granny. She hardly stayed five minutes, and then was gone again. Philip recommenced growling and swearing, and kept it up till it was time for him to go to chapel and preside at the weekday prayer-meeting.

Bertha panted with indignation for a time, but she was too full of her news to dwell long upon the insult offered her. "Disgusting old man!" she soliloquised. "All the tales about him must be true. I've never believed them before. Thank God, my Rupert will be here to protect me to-morrow. He'll give that old brute a talking to. Good boy, Sock," she said, patting the old dog, who was mightily pleased with himself. "That's the second brute you've attacked for my sake! And I believe this one was worse than the bull! Old Horror!"

Philip's attempt and repulse were useful. His anger decided him to go over to Chetbridge on the following day and consult a lawyer as to the possibility of turning Bertha out. This brought about his absence from home at a time when it was most desirable. Had he been at Ozier Cottage the next day, he might have sent a wire to the Limes to show his own importance, and so have prevented the completeness of the coup which old Granny was preparing.

It was fortunate for the concealment of the news that Gilbert came home too tired and hungry to be observant of aught beside food and bed; for Bertha's joy was irrepressible, and the old dog, reminiscent of the morning's words, was restless, and obviously expectant of a well-known footstep. But thanks to the boy's weariness, the evening passed off without any disclosures.

There was little sleep for Bertha that night. She was up at sunrise, and never had a May morning seemed so fair and bright to her before. She puzzled Gilbert by asking him to take a day off from his work and try to net a pike. Rupert liked pike.

"Well, tha'ss t'ree shillun out o' my week," he said; "an' a doan't knoo what ha' come oover ye! Still, if ye think as yew can speer the brass, I doan't mind a day's fishin', yew may be shore."

"Not a day's," said Bertha. "You must be home to dinner at half-past two. There may be a surprise for you."

"Aah! Yew fare tew many for me," grinned Gilbert. "Yew're up ta some'at, I 'specks. Howsomedever, fare ye well. I'll be back a little arter tew."

He trudged off down to marsh with his net and leapingpole, which was to do the double duty of getting him over the dykes and of frightening the fish into the net.

"Oh dear me," said Bertha a few hours later, "how slowly the time goes! Not twelve yet. I'll lay the table. Fancy! Laying the table for him again. My dear! My dear! And then I'll run down the loke and look over the marsh to watch for him."

Rupert got into Duckingham shortly after one, and escaped from the wondering congratulations of the railway servants.

"Didn't you know I was saved?" he asked in astonishment.

"Niver heerd a wud on't," answered the station-master.

"Do you mean to say that no news has come? Has no letter been received from me?"

"Not as I ha' heerd on," was the puzzled reply.

"Good God!" cried Rupert, and started off as quickly as he could.

"I hope to God she's all right!" he murmured. "Poor little darling! But how is it that none of my letters seem to have reached her? Surely she hasn't gone away! Surely she's living! Oh Lord, grant that I may find her safe and well!"

Rupert's ideas of prayer had evidently become modified, for this was not a mere ejaculation, but a heartfelt appeal to a Power whom he was learning to recognise and to reverence.

He met no one on the way to the marsh. He hesitated at the "Queen's Head," Dingleton, half inclined to go in and ask for news. But the idea that he might have to hear tidings which meant death to his happiness checked him. He felt that he could not face such a possibility in a public bar.

Along the line, over the stile, across the marsh he sped. His heart was thumping against his ribs with dread of what might meet him on the other side. He saw Gilbert far off on the level, apparently making his way homewards.

"He's here, at any rate," he gasped. "She can't be dead. Not that! Oh God! spare me that!"

But as the mouth of the loke opened out and its gate became clearly visible, who was it standing by the side? Who was it that waved to him, that flung open the gate, and ran with little eager footsteps to meet him at the ligger over the Fleet? And see! Old Sock was bounding at her side, mad with joy.

Oh "Love! matchless in fight!" Bitter and cruel as you can prove, what ecstasy is more supernal than when two true hearts meet again after separation and despair? What cynicism can put one spot on the bright aegis of your presence when you hallow such a meeting as this, between two lovers sorely tried, but triumphant in the strength and steadfastness of their faith?

Let us leave them uncontaminated by any sketch of mortal pen, for they have that which no hand can portray, the fervour of a passion which has been tested in the crucible of adversity and proved pure gold. And with it all a deep and humble thankfulness to God.

T XXIII THE END OF CELIBATE SARAH

S soon as the first transports were over, and husband,

x. wife, and dog shut up in their little cottage, Gilbert came home. He nonchalantly threw down his net and leaping-pole outside the door and entered.

"Wha bless my ole heart alive!" he cried. "Soo yew bain't drownded arter all!"

Explanations were hurried over, and then Bertha took Rupert round to old Granny's. The tale the old woman told him made him fume with anxiety and anger.

"We mustn't lose a minute," he said. "Those devils may have killed her by this time! As for you But you've acted for the best at last, and done me and mine a service which it will be hard for me to repay. It is no time for recriminations," he said to Granny.

"Tha'ss noo good yar gittin' ta the Limes afoor eight," said the witch. "Yew may leave it ta me. Yew want ta cotch 'em at it, doan't ye? Wery well. We'll all goo oover by the six train. That'll gi'e ye time ta git riddy an' see the p'leece. I'll goo up fust, an' yew jest behind. Arter they ha' let me in I'll make some 'scuse an' git 'em booth upsteers. Then I'll let yew in, an' yew'll cotch 'em prarper."

Laura (confined to her bed by Sarah's orders) had passed another day of misery and despair. Either Peggie or Sarah was constantly with her, so that she had no chance of making another dash for liberty. She had kept her decision to drink nothing but water, and her brain by this time was quite clear of the effects of the hyoscyamus. But the fever of anxiety was telling upon her. Her plump face had become haggard, and the silver streaks above her ears and forehead had spread. She thought she could see a new expression on the faces of her gaolers. They were more resolute, more implacable, and upon Peggie's she noticed a kind of speculative look, a look of curiosity and interest, which alarmed her even more than Sarah's sternness or hideous attempts at jocularity. Her brain, at no time strong, was weakening beneath the prolonged tension. The slightest thing brought on hysteria. There was no time to lose if either her life or her sanity were to be preserved.

Just before eight she heard a knock at the front door. Sarah was her attendant at the time, and when she too heard it she rose from where she sat and went to the washing-stand. Laura heard a clink of glass, but could not see what was being done, as the other kept her body between the bed and whatever vessel was being handled.

"What are you doing?" she asked.

"Oony a-gittin' riddy a some'at as ull dew ye good," chuckled Sarah, careless of concealment now that she could reckon on old Granny's mesmeric powers to compel Laura to swallow the potion.

"I'll drink nothing whatever but water," said Laura firmly. Then bursting into convulsive sobs, she cried, "Oh

God! Do you mean to kill me?"

Sarah returned no answer, but continued to stir something in a glass.

Presently Peggie came up and whispered to her sister, "Granny say as she must be aloan for a minnut. She ha' got a some'at ta dew as doan't want noo lookers on."

"Is it all right?" whispered Sarah.

"Right as ninepence," said Peggie.

"Sst! Wha'ss that?" said Sarah nervously.

"Oony somebardy in the rooad," Peggie answered.

"Sst!" said Sarah again. "I'll sweer theer's somebardy a-comin' upsteers quiet like."

"It's oony ole Granny, then," said Peggie. "Wha whew else can ta be?"

Even as she spoke the door was tried, found locked, and burst open by a stalwart shoulder.

"Blust! We're done!" screamed Sarah.

When the composite party, consisting of Rupert, Bertha, Gilbert, and old Granny, reached St. Mary's, they proceeded (in a close cab, lest any of the enemy might be about in the town) to the "King's Head." There three of them were left in a private room with tea to occupy their attention, while Rupert went out to seek legal and medical auxiliaries. The tale he unfolded at the police-station was so extraordinary that he was in some danger of being detained as a lunatic wandering at large. But on his requesting to see the divisional surgeon, and on his laying the case before that functionary, the superintendent consented to detail a constable to accompany the rescue party, together with the surgeon. Rupert returned to the "King's Head," and the plan for the confusion of Sarah was threshed out till it was time to make a move.

Shortly before half-past seven the whole party started out. They picked up the surgeon and constable on the way, and walked quietly up the Ipswich Road to the Limes. They opened the garden gate noiselessly and tiptoed up to the front door, taking care to keep upon the grass plat, which was intersected by a gravel path.

The evening was dark for the time of year, and there was a damp fog that increased the obscurity of the dusk. Close to the door was a thick clump of yews and hollies. All except Granny hid themselves in the shelter of this cover. Granny went straight to the door and knocked. Soon after she had been admitted and the door closed behind her, the remainder of the party stole from their concealment and assembled on the doorstep. The men had removed their boots and stood in stocking feet. Presently the fastenings of the door were softly undone. The men crept in and slunk upstairs, their feet making little noise on the stone hall or on the oilcloth covering of the stairs. Outside Laura's door they listened for an instant, and at Peggie's reply to Sarah's eager question, that the footsteps she heard could only be old Granny's, someone (I regret to say it was Gilbert) sniggered. Then, with a crash, the door was burst open. Bertha heard the noise, and joined Granny in the hall.

"Hold that woman," cried Rupert, pointing to Sarah.

But he spoke too late. As soon as the noise of the crash came she had made for the window, flung it open, and with a yell jumped clean through. She missed the laurels which she intended should break her fall, and fell sheer on to the hard brickwork of the yard.

Gilbert seized old Peggie with great glee. "Now I ha' got ye," he laughed. "Yew wicked ole!"

"Good arternune, Maaster Ruput," said Peggie, idiotic with terror. "An' how are yew?"

Rupert and the doctor hurried downstairs to see to Sarah, whose groans came up from the yard incessantly. They carried her into the drawing-room, and then Rupert left her in the surgeon's charge and returned to his sister's room, taking his wife and old Granny with him. They met Gilbert on the way down hauling Peggie along joyously. The constable followed grinning.

When the husband and wife and old Granny entered Laura's room, the poor woman was sitting up in her bed in a wild state of hysteria. The shock of the sudden rescue had been too much for her, and for the time she was quite beside herself.

"Laura, Laura!" cried Rupert. "Look! It's I! You are safe now. I said I should come if ever you were in trouble. Don't give way, old girl. It's all right now.

"Oh! Oh!" screamed Laura. "Rupert's drowned! You're his gho-o-o-ost! Oh!"

Rupert tried to soothe her. He tried to take her in his arms. But she was terrified at his approach.

She looked at him without ceasing her cries and convulsive outbursts of hysteria. Then her eyes wandered to Bertha and Granny. "More ghosts," she said inanely. "Well I never!"

"Let Granny try," said Bertha; "she can quiet her if anyone can."

The old witch hobbled forward. "Hi!" said she.

At the sharp, authoritative cry, Laura's eyes were drawn to the old woman's, and at once fixed by her scintillating gaze. Immediately her cries grew less, and the convulsive movements were checked. After a minute or two, during which Rupert watched the performance with astonishment, Granny advanced, laid her hands on Laura's temples, chafed gently, and said, "Now yew fare all right. Look about ye."

"Bertha dear, come here," said Rupert.

He took his wife by the hand and led her to his sister. Laura was now lying back pale and exhausted. But her eyes were intelligent, and all symptoms of neurosis had left her.

"Rupert," she said, "dear Rupert, will you forgive me? I wronged you, and now you've saved my life!"

"Hush, dear," said Rupert; "there's nothing to forgive. But it wasn't I that saved you. Here's the girl who did that. Won't you kiss my wife and your rescuer, Laura, and forget all the wicked lies you've been told about her?"

It is not in any woman's nature to feel great love for a brother's wife at a first introduction. Moreover, Laura's ridiculous notions of family pride had not quite deserted her. She was only too glad to welcome her brother and beg his forgiveness, and to love him for his care of her. But as for his wife, that was a different matter. Jealousy alone, born of a love resuscitated, would have made the position a bitter one.

But when she looked in that pure, sweet face, and saw in it pity tempered by a timid happiness, her better nature conquered. Taking Bertha's hand in hers, she said, "Kiss me, dear, and forgive me for all my injustice to you and Rupert."

And Bertha kissed her. And then and there began a friendship which has never lessened, but grown with the growth of time.

"Where's Granny?" said Rupert. "She must be forgiven too, for she has repented and made amends."

"Hare a be," said the witch, stepping forward; "but doan't ye mind me; oony mind my wuds—

"The meshes o' fate
Are booth small an' great,
An' the fish ha' got T'rew the twisted knot;
An' the black man's a-welcomin' one o' his kind,
For Seerah's the one whew is moost ta his mind.

Goo ye down for the sake o' the game yew ha' won t'rew ole Granny. Seerah oan't pass till ye goo, an' the less she keep my ole maaster a-waitin' the better."

Bertha understood the old woman better than did Rupert. "Go down, dear," she said. "I'll stay with your sister."

Stretched out on the couch in the drawing-room lay Celibate Sarah. Her leg was fractured in two places, but she felt no pain from it. She had no feeling below the waist. Her spine was fatally injured. At her request Peggie had been allowed to come to her side, and she was asking for Rupert when he entered the room. The surgeon, the constable, and Gilbert guarded the door and window. Peggie seemed dazed and incapable of comprehension. She stood winking, and every now and then she rubbed her hands together and moistened her lips with her tongue.

But the fire of concentrated hate shone clear and unquenched from the dying woman's eyes.

"Yew ha' come then?" she said to Rupert, "an' ye bain't drownded arter all. I wish ta Gord yew had a been."

"Why, Sarah?" said Rupert gently. "What harm have I ever done to you?"

"I allust hated ye," replied Sarah reflectively, "an' yew thote yew wuz a faav'rite o' mine oncet, I rackon."

"I thought you were fond of me," answered Rupert. "I was fond of you till I found out what you really were."

"He! he! he!" chuckled Sarah. "I allust hated the sight of ye. If yew'd been at hooam much arter yar ma died (an' I rackon yew doan't knoo what she died on, but I dew! He! he! he!), yew'd ha' been out o' my way afoor. I meant tew ha' married the ole guvnor, but he worn't fule enow. An' a nice game I led him arter he wuz strook helpless!"

"Good God," thought Rupert. "Now I understand what father meant at the last. "

"Celibit Sarah they called me," resumed Sarah. "Well, tworn't my fault if I wuz celibit. None o' yar brothers nor yar father'd iver look a' me, an' yew wuz tew young. I meant tew ha' had that brass. Me an' Bartie. D'ye think I'd ha' spent all my life lookin' arter that silly wench for narthen?"

She spoke excitedly, with feverish energy. The surgeon stepped forward to quiet her.

"Git out," she said, "I knoo as I'm a-dyin'. I should ha' won the game if that ole ha'n't ha' puffed! Damn her! Now yer can stand an' grin while I die. Damn yew tew, an' the whooll bilin' on ye!"

"Oh, don't talk like that, Sarah," cried Rupert. "You've only a little time. Can't you say you are sorry? I won't talk to you of repentance. I have no right to take that upon myself. But can't you say that you are sorry? Can't you go to your rest with one softer feeling in your heart?"

"Looard ha' marcy upon har, Christ ha' marcy upon har, Looard ha' marcy upon har, we beseeach Thee" said Peggie, suddenly breaking into speech.

"Hode yar n'ise, ye idjit," said Sarah savagely. "A pratty fule I should look a-sayin' I was sorra. I *am* sorra I'm be't, an' tha'ss a fack!"

Unable to stand the horror of the scene, Rupert left the room, and at the dying woman's request Peggie was removed into the kitchen by Gilbert and the constable. The surgeon alone remained.

Presently Sarah said, "Pore Bartie! He oan't git the brass arter all! An' he fare half a fule, though I've allust swoor he di'n't. Whativer'll become on him?"

She was silent for a minute or two. Then the light of the lamp grew prismatic in her eyes. A gush of tears burst from her.

"Send for Bartie," she said. "Lemme see him afoor I goo."

The half-witted lad was fetched, and led, terrified, to the death chamber.

"Leave us alooan," said Sarah.

"She's only got a few minutes more consciousness now, my boy," said the surgeon, speaking low. "I'll leave you alone with her."

"Bartie," whispered Sarah.

"Yis, aunt," said Bertie. "Wha'ss the marrer wi' ye?"

"Listen hare," continued Sarah. "Look in the righthand drawer o' my washhand-stand, an' yew'll see a packut o' powders. They doan't sigerfy ta me, but they may dew ta yar ma. Bu'n 'em, bu'n 'em. An' Bartie, kiss yar ole aunt. I ha' tried hud for ye, me dare, but I'm be't; I'm be't. But, Bartie, if yew could git oover Laura, yew might— arter If yew oan't git me my tea I must git it myself.
VVaake up. Waake up, Laura. Oh Gord, what is it? Surely ta can't be the guvnor!"
Sarah's voice rose to a scream of terror as the scene of over six years ago crossed her fading vision. At the last word her eyes closed.

Bertie stood gaping, unable to comprehend anything of what was passing before him.

Once more did Sarah's eyes open. She looked up at the boy fondly. A smile was on her lips. "Goo'-bye, Bartie," she said. "Kiss yar ole aunt. Yew'll be a good booy, oan't ye?"

"Yis, aunt," said Bertie, as he stooped

and kissed her. "Wha'ss the marrer wi' ye? Wheer are ye gooin' tew?"

He received no answer. Sarah never spoke again.

When he found sufficient presence of mind to do anything he shouted for help.

But no help was possible. Before midnight there was no more good or evil about the thing that lay upon the couch.

Celibate Sarah's course, for good or ill, was run.

EPILOGUE

Six months after. Rupert Claybrooke to Harry Lyndon.

"the Round House,

"Stalham,

"Norfolk.

"my Dear Harry,

"Very many thanks for your congratulations upon the success of my book. You always spoke well of it, but I do not think that even you expected it to get into a second edition so quickly. I am sure that I did not.

"I promised you when I last wrote to let you have a fuller account of my adventures, and what came of them. But I have been so busy settling down in this new place, and so anxious about my wife and child (you may have seen the notice in the *Times),* that I have had no opportunity of writing you a letter of such a length as will be necessary to make things at all plain to you.

"Thank God we are straight at last, and Bertha and the boy are as well and strong as I could wish.

"I had better tell a plain tale plainly, and commence with the evening on which the sou'-wester caught the *John and Susan.* The first rush of the gale was so terrific that it laid us on our beam ends, although we were steaming with no show of sail. Very soon after we had righted (for the waves rose with extraordinary rapidity) a huge sea took the masts, funnel, and deck hamper clean out of us, and spun them overboard. Within three minutes the stokehole was flooded and the fires extinguished. We were ten or twelve miles from land, and no other boat was near. The sea got higher and higher every minute, and more broken. I thought it was folly to try to get ashore in the jolly-boat, but was laughed at for my pains. However, I remained firm to my decision to stick to the steamer, and the others left me aboard of her, after commenting on my sense in no very flattering terms. Poor fellows! They had not got a couple of hundred yards when a sea curled and broke right over them, swamping them at once. As is usually the case with fishermen, none of them could swim, and I, of course, was powerless to help them. They went down like stones.

"The dangers of my own position soon distracted my thoughts from the fate of my mates. The *John and Susan* could neither sail nor steam, and she was rolling helpless in the trough of the sea, getting lower in the water minute by minute. The dusk was falling fast. Fortunately for me, the wind lulled a trifle, and though the sea remained high it was less broken. Before the second fury of the storm burst I saw a large barque driving down on my port quarter. Could I make her see me? And if I could, was it possible for her to come up into the wind and lie-to while she lowered a boat? And would the skipper take the trouble anyhow? It was an anxious time. But as I look back on it I seem to remember that I was sustained all through it by a certainty of rescue that was afforded me, but whence or how I had no time to consider at the moment. To be brief, I was seen, the ship luffed up head to wind, and a boat put off. I did not wait for the steamer to sink and suck me under, but tore off my boots and heavier clothing and took to swimming till I was picked up and carried aboard the barque. I found she was bound from Bristol to Halifax, N.S., and that the captain was glad to get another hand, for he had sailed short-handed, and lost four men overboard in the first burst of the storm. He would not hear of shipping me on a homeward-bound craft, but promised to see that I got a berth on the mail-steamer home from Halifax. He also agreed to hail any craft homeward-bound to enable me to send a letter. And,' said he, 'if I were you I should write under cover to your owners. The letter will stand a better chance of getting where it's bound for then.'

"As it happened, we were five clear days before we signalled a home-going ship. But I had no chance of getting my letter written in advance, for the gale blew up again soon after my rescue, and for long it was all we could do to save the ship, and to put her to rights when the terrible experience was over. At last a London-bound tramp took charge of a short note to my wife, which I scribbled in a hurry and slipped into an envelope addressed to her. I then enclosed the packet in a larger envelope which bore the owners' names.

"The letter was delivered at the office when only the manager was there. He opened it and saw the enclosure. A man named Jinnis was in the office at the time who hailed from Frogsthorpe, and the fool of a manager, to save a stamp I expect (with the usual provincial thrift), gave him the letter to deliver by hand. He does not appear to have worried his head by thinking from whom the letter might be.

"Now Jinnis had a spite against my wife. He seems to have guessed whom the letter was from, opened and destroyed it. He got the berth that he was seeking at the office, got drunk on the strength of it, fell in Herringhaven Harbour, and was drowned. Thus all record of my safety was lost as far as England was concerned.

"We had an awful passage out, and were more than three weeks overdue. Then I had to wait for a mail-boat home, so that I had been given up by all (with the exception of my wife and old Granny, the witch whom I have mentioned to you before) long before I reached the old country again.

"Since then I have been greatly occupied by a family affair, the particulars of which I do not feel at liberty to mention, and when this was settled came my removal to Stalham, which was closely followed by my wife's illness.

"My sister has taken a small house near here, and has engaged old Granny as housekeeper and companion. The quaint old woman does her work very well, and, under her care, I am glad to say that Laura has entirely recovered her health, which had become seriously affected during her residence at St. Mary's-on-the-Fen. She and Bertha are great friends, and Laura is more affectionate and brighter than I have seen her for years. She insisted on being the boy's godmother (for I have had him christened; it can't do any harm, and he can make up his mind on religious questions when he is old enough, as you and I have tried to do; I may say as I at last have done), and has 'made him her heir,' as she says with a funny air of pomposity which I doubt if she will ever see the humour of.

"You ask me if I have formed any opinion as to the spiritual experiences which I have hinted to you before, and although this letter is already unconscionably long, I am afraid that I must answer this question at some length.

"You know how cautious I have always been to weigh every scrap of evidence in connection with what are generally called 'supernatural' matters, but which might much more properly be named 'superhuman.' For to assert that a thing is supernatural is to say that it is non-existent. I must at once admit that were I to judge my own case from my previous standpoint, and were I to dismiss the personal equation entirely in arriving at a personal conclusion, my beliefs might be different to what they are. With this reservation (in making which I feel a traitor to what I now believe to be my better self) I think I can formulate my views without excessive demands on your patience.

"i. I believe that I have experienced the direction of invisible intelligences possessing powers generally attributed to 'spirits.' I believe that more than one such intelligence has interested itself about me; and that (although on occasions there would appear to have been some struggle between different influences, some being beneficent and the others the reverse) with the assistance of the human subject influenced the beneficent intelligences have more power than the malignant.

"You will no doubt refer me to Voltaire's *Le blanc et le noir,* and, except that I do not confine the intelligences at work to two, that story gives a fair idea of what I mean under this head.

"My reasons for this belief are based—

"*(a)* On a consistent series of events too extended and too complicated to be due to mere coincidence.

"(£) On direct responses to direct appeals to something higher than ourselves, which have been vouchsafed both to me and my wife.

"() On an undefinable nervous sensation, whereby I have seemed just to fall short of establishing direct communication between my waking senses and the intelligence, or intelligences, for the time being having charge of my fate.

"(This may be objected to as purely emotional, but it is real. And under certain conditions, on the marsh, at sea, or in any wild spot where nature and nature's ruler are not secondary to the modifications of man, I can rely, almost with certainty, on arousing the sensation. Subjectively I am so convinced of this that in time I hope to establish actual communication with those beings whom, for the sake of brevity, I shall for the future call'spirits.')

"2. I believe that these spirits are all ministers of a

Master Spirit, and that the Master Spirit corresponds to the 'unknown God' of all religions. That all religions arise from Him, and that their differences are attributable merely to the circumstances of time, place, and temperament. That, therefore, all differences of ritual are immaterial, so that 'the something not ourselves which makes for righteousness' be regarded.

"To quote a hackneyed phrase, 'The fear of the Lord is wisdom, and to depart from evil is understanding.' I have already given my ideas of what is meant by 'The Lord.' The more practical question remains, 'What is meant by evil?' And here I must fall back on my utilitarianism, and say that an evil action or line of conduct is one calculated to do more harm than good to the happiness of the majority of those whom it affects.

"3. I do not think that it is given to every man to be conscious of the influences about him. And where this is denied I can conceive no way in which the decrees of destiny can be varied, or the doctrine of free will be tenable. But in the case of those who are conscious of their spiritual guardians I believe that prayer and communion with the Unseen may be of effect. I believe that such prayers may be entertained by a beneficent guardian spirit, without the ridiculous notion of a 'receiver general' of supplications; and that while the expression 'prayer to God' is useful, as being reverent, and, perhaps, ultimately correct, yet the immediate effect of prayer is communion with one of God's servants. I mean by 'God' the Great Spirit, the Highest, the Eternal, the Universal Cause, the Origin of Existence. The difficulties which might appear to arise when the interests of the clients of two spirits conflict may be considered as left to the judgment of some higher spirit. For I can see no reason why the grades of spiritual life should not be infinite until unimaginable infinity is reached in the Highest.

"4. The question as to a future life I dare not touch. I am afraid that I cannot go beyond Ecclesiastes. I wish I could. I can only say, 'I don't know, and I have no instinctive belief.'

"I have been so particular because I know the interest you take in psychology and psychological tenets. If you can ever rise to the height of keeping your promise to pay me a visit, I hope I may be able to impart some of my feeling of reverent gratitude and trust in the Highest to you. But you must not suppose that I am suffering from the fanaticism of a proselyte. My beliefs are certainly good so far as I am concerned, in that they have tended to increase my happiness and the happiness of those about me.

"I am sure of one thing—that dwellers in cities stand less chance of getting into touch with the unseen than we who live on the wild fens and waters or those at sea. Come down and spend a night on Hickling Broad, and see for yourself.

"With many apologies for the length of this letter,

"I am, my dear Harry,
"Ever yours,
"Rupert Clavbrooke."

Some years have passed since Rupert wrote his confession of faith to Harry Lyndon; but he has seen no reason to modify it as yet, and has rather become confirmed in it by a continuance of the causes which led him first to formulate it. Few mortals are happier than he and his wife. His success has been assured and reassured, and he may lay claim to being a wealthy man. But he has altered the simplicity of his life but little. There are more plain comforts about his house on the borders of the broad, more simple delicacies, than at Frogsthorpe. He keeps good horses, and has a yacht and good shooting; but there is no attempt to "make a show " or to associate with those who live for ostentation. He and his wife do much good in a quiet way about their part of the county, and it need not be said that Bertha is always happy when about some work of charity. And she finds time for many such works without in the least neglecting her husband or her children. Any man may be thankful for such a wife, any children for such a mother.

Laura, established hard by, looks ten years younger than she did at the Limes. She is a veritable instance of a cure by hypnotic suggestion, for whenever her weakness came upon her (as it did occasionally for a few months after she had left St. Mary's-on-the-Fen), a minute's experience of old Granny's mesmeric gaze put her right, and in time she lost all desire for stimulant. The fresh marsh air was tonic enough for her. She grew firm in figure and wholesome in face, and, best of all, most sweet and tender at heart; so that her nephews and nieces (whom she idolises) are devoted to her, and their play and their prayers are only perfect when shared with " Aunt Laura. "

Peggie's nerves never recovered from the shock caused by her sister's defeat and death. She and Bertie are both in the Eastern Counties Lunatic Asylum. Old Noddy has taken "Polla Barley " for a housekeeper.

Young Gilbert, having expressed a wish to be apprenticed to a gunmaker, had his desire, and he now owns one of the best shops in Herringhaven. His brothers regard him with scorn as a renegade. There is no change in them.

But the most marvellous transformation of all is to be seen in old Granny. The old woman is still alive, but her face now wears a benevolent and refined expression; her eyes have retained their humour, but lost their malevolence. She still does great things with herbs and roots, but the fear of the black man (which was long upon her) is gradually dying out beneath the persuasion of Bertha and the consciousness of present well-doing.

What her powers were and whence derived, who shall say? Her type may be found to this day in many wild spots upon the marshes.

THE END PLYMOUTH

WILLIAM BRENDON AND SON, PRINTERS

ending."
*The Times:* "The style is full of poetry and carries one along like a flood."
*The Morning Post:* "A stirring tale from start to finish
... full of passion and colour."
*The Daily Express:* "Mr. Hewlett has... a rival in romance. A stronger plot than *The Forest Lovers,* and an equal charm of style."
Roy Devereux REPROBATE SILVER 6s.
*Morning Post:* "The book is strikingly original, and its outspokenness on some points is remarkable... Altogether this is a book to be read." *Daily Telegraph:* "Roy Devereux... is to be congratulated on a very clever and original piece of work." Herbert Flowerdew
THE WOMAN'S VIEW 6s.
*The Athenaum:* "This is a work of unusual merit."
*Pall Mall Gazette:* "A novel of great strength and magnificent dramatic truthfulness."
*The Week's Survey:* "Nothing we have met in recent fiction has so impressed us with a sense of the author's power as this story. It bears on every page the marks of a master hand."
FRENCH FICTION OF THE NINETEENTH CENTURY
Edited by A. R. Waller. With Preface to each volume by Arthur Symons. With Frontispieces. Crown 8vo. Cloth gilt. 3s. 6d. net per volume.
1. SALAMMBO
By Gustave Flaubert. Translated by J. W.
Matthews.
*The Star:* "Ought to be very popular. The translation is admirable."
*The Daily Chronicle:* "In its new form, *Salammbo* has the advantage of a competent translation, and that in itself is a rare assistance." 2. THE LATIN QUARTER
By Henry Murger. Translated by Ellen
Marriage and John Selwyn.
*The Athenteum:* "The translators have entered fully into
Murger's spirit, and have a good command of idiom."
*The World:* "A translation of considerable merit.... The
Introduction by Mr. Arthur Symonds is brilliantly written.
... The translators... deserve no little praise."
3. THE ABBE AUBAIN AND MOSAICS
By Prosper Merimee. Translated by Emily
Mary Waller.
*The Literary World:* "The short stories of Merimee, in
*The Abbe Aubain and Mosaics,* are wonderful bits of condensed drama.... His stories carefully wrought are yet highly impressionist in their effect, glowing with colour and rapid in movement."
*The Scotsman:* "Not one of these stories... will fail to delight any lover of artistic fiction."
Keble Howard LOVE AND A COTTAGE s. 6d.
With Eighty Illustrations by J. Hassall *Westminster Gatette:* "A delightful picture of matrimonial squabblings and reconciliations drawn with real humour. ..
The illustrations by Mr. Hassall are admirable. Altogether it is a very delightful little book."
*Daily News:* "A lively and amusing book."
Maurus Jokai
TOLD BY THE DEATHS
HEAD 6s.
Illustrated *Daily Telegraph:* "He has an extraordinary imagination,
a fund of the driest humour, and beneath his clever fooling there is a wealth of sentiment which occasionally rises to the top and surprises us by bringing the tears to our eyes."
*The Speaker:* "Maurus Jokai's *Told by the Death's Head* is invigorating and fascinating."
Albert Lee
THE BARONET IN
CORDUROY 6s.
*Dundee Advertiser:* "Mr. Lee has a graphic pen. The picturesque scenes he provides and the vivacious story he tells should win him many readers." *The Times:* "A pleasant novel... picturing the early eighteenth century."
Marie Connor Leighton IN GODS GOOD TIME 6s.
*Morning Post:* "... She displays extraordinary ingenuity in piling sensation on sensation, so that those who like plenty of incident will have no reason to complain."
Mrs. Fred. Maturin THE THIN RED LINE OF HEROES s. 6d.
*The Queen:* "A light little piece of frivolity that will beguile a railway journey quite pleasantly.... It is a brightly written little book."
W. B. Maxwell FABULOUS FANCIES 6s.
*The World:* There is considerably more than meets the eye in this collection of brilliantly written storyettes.... Those who can read between these satirical lines will find lessons far more wholesome than are to be derived from a year's average sermons, and withal abundant laughter, with its near relative, tears." *Glasgow Evening News:* "The book is composed of bright, even brilliant, short stories, which may be read with keen enjoyment.... In the brief space at one's disposal it is hard to convey the curious charm of the stories."
Leonard Merrick CONRAD IN QUEST OF HIS YOUTH 6s.
*The World:* " Mr. Merrick's latest book is an achievement." *British Weekly:* "This is a book on which the author and the reading public are to be congratulated.... The characters are all admirably drawn, while the situations are handled with skill and a dramatic sense." THE QUAINT COMPANIONS 6s. *Daily News:* Mr. Merrick may be congratulated on having written a very readable book."
*The Scotsman:* The story is able and interesting throughout, and should not fail to stir a poignant bitter-sweet feeling in anyone who can read it with intelligence."
G. B. McCutcheon CASTLE CRANEY-CROW 6s.
*The Scotsman:* The story will be found most racy and exciting reading." *The Times:* "An exciting story."
Andrew Merry PADDY-RISKY 6s.
*The Dundee Advertiser:* Mr. Merry knows the people of whom he writes, and his sketches are instinct with life. His delineation of Irish character is admirable."
Frank Norris THE OCTOPUS 6s.
*The Times:* "A remarkable book....

Colossally vigorous." *The Academy:* "It is a brave thing, and a decisive victory over all sentimentalism. It is alive. You cannot do what you like with it; you have got to read it." *The Daily Nevis:* "One's mind is full of it for days after its perusal." THE PIT 6s. *Spectator:* "A really striking novel." *The Athenceum:* "If proofwere needed, this book is in itself sufficing evidence of the fact that Frank Norris had more in him than literary promise. His literary methods were those of Zola... he had a fine feeling for the bigness of things, for the grandeur of nature, and for the absorbing interest of life, bare life, with its millions of intersecting and conflicting currents. His death is a loss which we sincerely regret." *The Scotsman:* "Pages... vivid as the cinematograph." Frank Norris—*continued* Leo Tolstoy *A* DEAL IN WHEAT: and other Stories 6s.

Illustrated *Manchester Guardian:* "Spirited, vivid sketches... a fine example of sensational realism."

A MAN'S WOMAN 6s.

*The World:* "Mr. Frank Norris has surpassed his

*Shanghaied* in *A Man's Woman."*

McTEAGUE: A Tale of San

Francisco 6s.

*The Speaker:* "Mr. Norris writes with conviction. It is a fascinating, engrossing tale, vibrating with power and quivering with life." SHANGHAIED s. 6d.

*The Daily Telegraph:* " Mr. Norris has written a delightful book in *Shanghaied.* It is fresh, breezy, original and full of interest." BLIX 38. 6d. *Black and White:* "If I were asked to name the most absolutely delightful book, the most youthful, the most joyous that 1 have read these years, I am afraid I should nave to throw discretion to the winds—and say unhesitatingly, unreservedly, *Blix 1"*

Elizabeth Stuart Phelps AVERY 3s. 6d.

With Frontispiece *Daily News:* "The book is masterly."

*Morning Leader:* "A story that the author may well be proud, of.... No one but a clever woman could have written it."

David Graham Phillips GOLDEN FLEECE 6s.

Illustrated *British Weekly:* "The intrigues and complications of the plot are cleverly managed, and the book is brisk and amusing." *Pall Mall Gazette:* "A series of entertaining sketches... cleverly and humorously described."

E. Livingston Prescott THE MOST SECRET TRIBUNAL 6s.

*Times:* "This is a well-written tale." *Scotsman:* "It is a strong study... of an endeavour to expiate a crime judged by the tribunal of the heart." KNIT BY FELONY 6s. *The Sheffield Daily Express:* "A wholesome, brightly written story... which is sure to win a welcome everywhere." *The Guardian:* "The story marches on smoothly and the interest grows rapidly. The characters are excellently drawn, each with a distinct individuality which is preserved throughout."

Illustrated *The Academy: "A* spirited romance of the eighteenth century."

*Morning Post: "Franceska* begins with such a swagger that you are led captive, or ever you are aware of it.

Even when you know it there is nothing but to rejoice in your captivity.... Told with care, power, and feeling,

and commands our admiration."

*Spectator: "Francezka* is a very clever book."

*The Dundee Advertiser:* "Mr. Shiel is a genius in his special branch of fiction." THE LORD OF THE SEA 6s.

*The Speaker:* "Mr. M. P. Shiel has surpassed himself in his latest novel... This is a whole battery of artillery, whose reverberations, if they do not deafen the world, will long rumble in the public ear." *The Daily Chronicle: "A* romancer of the first rank, with the romancer's gift of fire and spirit and transfiguring magic." CONTRABAND OF WAR 6s.

Illustrated *The Scotsman: "A* book which anyone with the slightest liking for excitement is bound to enjoy." THE YELLOW DANGER s. 6d.

Mr. L. F. Austin in *The Illustrated London News:* " I sat up half the night with *The Yellow Danger."* THE REVISED EDITION OF THE WORKS OF LEO TOLSTOY

Edited by Aylmer Maude Large Crown 8vo, cloth gilt, 6s. per vol.

Translations by Louise and Aylmer Maude

Vol. I. SEVASTOPOL and other

Military Tales

With Portrait, Map, Preface, and Transliteration

Scheme

Popular Edition, paper covers, 6d.

Vol. XX. PLAYS

With Illustrations, Preface, and List of Tolstoy's

Works

Vol. XXIV. RESURRECTION

With Preface, Appendix, and 33 splendid Illustrations by Pasternak.

Cheaper Edition, with Illustrations, 2s. 6d.; or without Illustrations, 2s. Popular Edition, paper covers, 6d.

"Your translations are very good, and I do not wish for better ones."—Leo Tolstoy. *Athenceum:* "Thoroughly competent and satisfactory, not to say authoritative." *Academy:* "Able, conscientious, and workmanly version of *Sevastopol." The Scotsman:* "Looks as if it were going to prove the standard edition." *Morning Post:* "Very well done. " *Morning Leader:* "Entirely satisfactory." *Black and White:* "The standard and definite English version of *Resurrection."* THE VICES OF THE VIRTUOUS s. 6d.

By the Author of "Lady Beatrix and the Forbidden Man" *Vanity Fair:* "The book is, moreover, ' smart' in dialogue and style—so pood, in fact, that it will worthily maintain the reputation that its author made with the story of Lady Beatrix."

Richard Whiteing No. 5 JOHN STREET 6s.

Cheap Edition, re-set, with preface. 3s. 6d.

*The Morning-Post:* "The book which is talked about most at the present time, and will be remembered."

*St. James's Gazette:* "No compliment could be too high for so remarkable a social study, with its keen satire, true feeling, and vigorous expressive style."

Barry Pain

THE ONE BEFORE is.

With eighty Illustrations by Tom Browne *The Daily News:* "Full of good things." *The Daily Telegraph:* "It deserves commendation for its ingenuity no less than for its fun." STORIES IN THE DARK is.

(Also an *edition de luxe,* printed on large paper, limited to 250 copies, each numbered and signed by the author. Crown 8vo, buckram, 5s. net ) *The Morning Post:* "Excellent short stories. ... There are very few people who can use a peculiar gift of humour both to divert their readers and to ' make their flesh creep,' but Mr. Pain has shown that he possesses this power." 14

Jane Austen NOVELS. Winchester Edition. Ten Volumes. Small demy 8vo. Printed on antique paper, bound in Irish linen with design in gold. The set, 50s. net; or, each novel separately, 5s. a volume, net SENSE AND SENSIBILITY

Vols. I. and II. With Portrait PRIDE AND PREJUDICE

Vols. III. and IV.

MANSFIELD PARK

Vols. V. and VI.

EMMA

Vols. VII. and VIII.

NORTHANGER ABBEY

Vol. IX.

PERSUASION

Vol. X.

15 POPULAR EDITIONS *Crown 8vo. Paper Covers, is. each*

A DUET. By Sir A. Conan Doyle THE FALL OF THE CURTAIN. Bv Harold Begbie

THE ISLAND. By Richard Whiteing

THE BLACK MASK. By E. W. Hornung

BAGSBY'S DAUGHTER. By Marie Van VORST THE BISHOP'S GAMBIT. By Thomas Cobb GOOD SOULS OF CIDERLAND. By Walter Raymond THE HOOLIGAN NIGHTS. By Clarence Rook THE IDLER OUT OF DOORS. By Walter Raymond THE KIDNAPPED MILLIONAIRES. By F. Upham Adams LINNET. By Grant Allen LOVE THE LAGGARD. By R. S. Warren Bell LAZARRE. By Mary Hartwell Catherwood MORGAN HAILSHAM. By F. C. Constable SELLCUTS' MANAGER. By Mrs. Ormiston Chant SCRUPLES. By Thomas Cobb

CPSIA information can be obtained at www.ICGtesting.com
Printed in the USA
BVOW07s1251240214

345830BV00012B/662/P